Walter Kumme

The Dark Wood

The Dark Wood

by

CHRISTINE WESTON

1946 · CHARLES SCRIBNER'S SONS · New York

AMERICAN BOOK—STRATFORD PRESS, INC., NEW YORK

For
John Walcott and Andy Dana

"Nessus had not yet reached the other side, when we moved into a wood, which by no path was marked.

Not green the foliage, but of color dusky; not smooth the branches, but gnarled and warped; apples none were there, but withered sticks with poison . . ."

The Inferno, Canto XIII.

The Dark Wood

1

IN APRIL the city stood upright and splendid; above it the airplanes circled, painting vaporous epigraphs across the sky, and to the gay boys who rode in them the city looked like a handful of needles thrusting upward between strands of water where liners crawled, and tugs, and corpulent ferries emitting toots.

"Oh boy!" thought the sky-writers. "Look at her down there, sweet and unscratched. What a target!" And some, remembering the cinder heaps of London, Rotterdam, Cassino and Berlin, and the wastes of Hiroshima, speculated on how many missions it would take to translate the wondrous city to a pile of blackened straws. Like children or like men in daydreams, the fliers took the lovely thing apart and smiled, seeing it stretched beneath them, seemingly eternal under the April sky.

On a humbler level other eyes appraised the twilight which travelled from cube to cube and from pyramid to pyramid. For a moment in this season space and mass had achieved a tenuous balance, then evening stepped forward, the fliers flew home to roost, women clustering like bees round shop windows swarmed reluctantly on their way. The great shaft of the R.C.A. building stretched and leaned backward towards the sun; the cathedral darkened, and Atlas, gritting his teeth, raised his head a trifle and shifted, a fraction, his load.

A taxi deposited three people at the entrance of a night club in the East Fifties, and as he shepherded his women companions towards the door Dick Sparrow said: "I hope you girls like this joint. It was recommended to me by Bill Symes."

"Are you trying to establish your usual alibi?" demanded his wife.

"Habit. My lawyer's training, you know."

They passed through the doors into a gale of music. "I reserved a table," said Dick. "Where's that captain? He's a pal of Symes." He turned to a dignified personage. "I'm Mr. Sparrow, and I have a table engaged for four people."

The stranger glared blankly, and Dick apologized. They moved on and Miriam Sparrow laughed. "That was a mistake your friend Symes would never have made! The old boy looked like a retired brigadier at least."

Bill countered: "Remember the time in the Biltmore when you asked an admiral the way to the ladies' room?"

"He looked like the doorman."

Dick lifted a chastened eyebrow at a real waiter, and they were guided deftly to their table. "There were to have been four of us," Dick explained as the man bustled round them with glasses and napkins. "The other gentleman let us down. What shall it be, girls?"

The waiter took their order and departed, and Dick looked at Stella Harmon.

"I'm sorry Symes couldn't come tonight. I wanted you to meet him before you take the plane tomorrow. He'll be on it as far as Lisbon."

"I've been composing a speech of thanks. It was really kind

of him to fix up about my seat. The airplane people had told me I might have to wait a month."

"Symes is always doing little things like that for his friends," said Dick.

"In grateful recognition of the numerous little things they do for him," Miriam remarked maliciously.

"Obviously he's not your type, my dear."

"But where does he get his influence?" asked Stella. "I mean this ability to find unknown women seats on transatlantic clippers, and all that?"

"He's in with the airlines. He's in, actually, with most of the worthwhile people. Isn't he, Dick?"

"That's one way of saying he's highly intelligent, and in his quiet way important. Imagine a guy hardly forty, as confidential adviser to the State Department."

Stella inquired what Mr. Symes did for the State Department, and Miriam answered:

"No one knows. It's something very confidential. Symes speaks several languages, and is an expert on what are called natural resources. You know, uranium and that sort of thing. His work takes him all over the world. He once showed me a snapshot of himself dressed in a bournous, gazing contemptuously at the Sphinx."

"But why should he bother his head about me?"

"Dick asked him to. He's one of Dick's clients, in an informal sort of way. You see, a man in Symes' position can't afford to take ordinary chances, so whenever he meditates doing anything of a personal and more or less dubious nature he looks to Dick for the green light."

Dick shook his head. "You're exaggerating, Miriam."

"But," said Stella, "how does it happen that he never figures in the newspapers? I hadn't so much as heard his name until you spoke of him the other day."

"Oh, he's the soul of modesty," Miriam explained. "In fact I think you might say he has a pathological dread of publicity."

"You're damned unfair," Dick accused her severely.

"I'm merely being intuitive."

Stella wanted to know whether Mr. Symes was married.

"Not so far as I know," said Miriam, with a visible increase of malice. "And if he contemplates marriage only Dick knows about it, and he won't tell. But I did run into Symes one day outside Saks, with that handsome what's-her-name, the woman who is always writing and making speeches on social uplift. Tell us, Dick. Does Symes want to marry Mrs. Uplift?"

"She happens to be married. I've never met her, but I recall some newspaper account about her husband. He'd been decorated, or cited, or something, in Germany."

The waiter brought their drinks. The dance ended and the dancers drifted back to their tables. "This is nice," said Stella. She lifted her glass. "You were sweet to give me a party."

Miriam looked at her earnestly. "You're really going to Italy? I wish you'd change your mind. We both wish it."

Dick said: "Or if you feel you must go, won't you wait till Miriam and I can go with you?"

"After you and Mr. Symes have gone to all the trouble to get me a seat on the clipper?"

"That's easily changed."

Stella appeared to ponder the suggestion. A slight frown

gave her face its only animation. She looks, Dick thought, like some lovely pieta, the gilt of youth, the color of the past, barely visible in the deracinated flesh. At thirty she is dedicated to grief. Pity held him silent, but it did not silence his wife. "Stella, there's still time to change your mind. Travelling is getting easier, and maybe we could all go later on. When could you get away, Dick?"

"In about three months." He remembered an earlier conversation with Miriam:

"I'm not particularly clever," Miriam had confided to him then, "I merely use my intuition. And I think it would be a mistake for Stella to go to Italy alone."

"What could possibly happen to her?"

"It's dangerous for sleepwalkers to be wakened too abruptly."

"Alec's dead. For her to visit his grave couldn't be worse than knowing he's dead."

Miriam had replied obstinately: "She shouldn't go alone."

This evening Dick felt his wife's compelling glance, and added his persuasions to hers: "Stella, my vacation is due in July. That would give us ample time to arrange about passports and reservations."

Miriam added urgently: "You know we wouldn't intrude! All it would mean is, Dick and I would be around in case you should need us." But while Miriam spoke she reflected: "It's no use, she's made up her mind and we can't make her change it now."

Stella shook her head. "You're both sweet to worry about me, but you know I must go."

"I hate the idea," said Miriam. "I dread it, for you."

"Don't, my dear. After all, what could happen to me? Let's not argue about it now."

Dick agreed quickly. "Let's not. I'm sure you know what you're doing."

The orchestra returned, drums and saxophones throbbed and pealed, and Miriam smiled at her companions. "Dance, you two."

He rose and drew Stella to her feet. They drifted away on the music and Miriam watched them with the curious pleasure she always derived from seeing her husband dance with other women. She realized that Dick had become increasingly aware of Stella as he had not seemed aware of her during Alec's lifetime. The realization complicated her own feelings towards her husband and her friend, but that's better, she assured herself, that's a lot better than to feel nothing, or to feel the wrong things. Now as she pursued Dick's back, barred by the pale column of Stella's arm, Miriam reflected on her friend's tragedy. She pictured Stella preparing for this evening's gaiety, drawing the black dress over her head, arranging the white lace scarf, pausing to tighten the pearl in her ear—gestures beloved by men. She thought of Stella in her silent room, glancing about her at its loneliness before she snapped out the light and crept into her cold bed. How natural and how comforting to see her dancing, enfolded in a man's arm, her body supple, a smile on her lips! Could it be that all the moments of Stella's life had marched inexorably towards this evening, prelude to her journey to Italy? What was to follow, what would happen when she had found her young husband's grave among the Italian olive trees? Would she go to pieces, or would she awaken from the trance in which she had existed since his death? I know I'm right, thought Miriam, singling out the dancers as they turned to the rhythm of drums. She's walking in her sleep, dancing in her sleep. It's Alec she's dancing with! It will always be Alec. And in this crowded room where Alec had never set foot, Miriam remembered him with piercing clarity. She shuddered and thrust the memory from her. The waiter brought her another drink, and the trumpeter sent a shrill blast over the heads of the dancers.

The sound quivered through Dick's nerves. "We shall miss you, Stella. Sure you're going to be all right?"

"Quite sure."

"If you should need us you won't hesitate to cable? Promise?"

"Promise!"

He held her closer. "Stella . . ."

"No, Dick. Really, it's no use."

He did not need to be reminded that it was no use, yet his pity blazed inevitably into something else nor was he one to question this response to pathos. Women might have questioned it, but he was a man, filled with confused remorse for what men's wars do to women. The waste of death was beyond dispute, but what was to be said, what done, about the waste of the living? Meeting Stella a few days after he had the news of Alec's death, he had taken her in his arms in a wordless embrace, all his brotherhood in tears for her and for Alec. Months later he embraced her again, murmuring: "Why not, Stella? I can't sleep, thinking about you." But she put him aside with a resolution that surprised him when he came to reflect on it afterwards. "It's no use, Dick. There's nothing left. There never will be anything else, for any one, ever." So far as Dick knew there had been nothing for any one else. For almost three years he watched her youth fall away piecemeal. Death, which had dealt swiftly with Alec, took its time with Stella, matching her vitality second by second, pulse by pulse.

They danced, and he said: "When you come back let's all go down to Jarley. You ought to do something about the house, anyway. Bad for a place to be left unoccupied for so long." He thought of the white house in its meadow above the sea, of sheep grazing under the firs; he saw Alec walking up the pasture with arms full of driftwood for autumn fires.

"Better rent the place to strangers if you don't want to live there yourself," he went on, steering her through the crowd. "Don't you agree, Stella?"

They had discussed this before; her face assumed the abstracted expression he had learned to associate with any mention of the house, or of the past.

"I suppose you're right. I'll think about it when I come back from Italy."

The dance ended and Dick led her back to the table, where Miriam sat examining her face in a little mirror. "I'm getting fat," she told them dismally. "I *am* fat, fat and middle-aged."

Dick patted her hand. "What about me?"

"You, my dear, have distinction. You may grow bald but you'll never be fat." She smiled. "Can you remember what any of us looked like ten years ago?"

They argued about it over their drinks. A spotlight, travelling over the darkened room, came to rest on Stella. Ten years ago she was twenty and wore her hair tied with a black ribbon.

She flushed easily, and seemed always on the brink of laughter. Ten years ago, thought Dick, I was forty-three, and God! I felt fine. Ten years ago, mused Miriam, following the beam of light on its journey round the room, ten years ago I was thirty-six, and there was peace on earth, and it was spring at Jarley, with ice still lingering along the beaches, and the first robins building in the balm o' Gilead tree by Alec's door.

It was after midnight when the Sparrows left Stella at her apartment, and after the taxi had borne them away she emerged from the dim entry and stood for some minutes on the sidewalk, gazing at the walls which towered, unsubstantial as honeycombs, towards the sky. The city breathed gustily, resisting sleep; late traffic purred on a subdued note, and from the distant river came the plaintive bellowing of a vessel. Like many lonely people Stella had a perverse longing for the open. She walked up the street to Madison Avenue, and an old terror came upon her, the terror which she had often experienced before she married Alec, and which returned after his death, the terror of being watched, of being stealthily followed. It took all her courage not to run, not to scream. Quickly she made her way back to her door, through it to the automatic elevator. The bronze grille closed behind her, the cage mounted to the floor where she lived. Opening her door, she reached for the light switch. It seemed to evade her hand, then darkness engulfed her, arms enclosed her in a rigid embrace, lips sought hers.

"Let me go!" shrieked her mind. "Let me go, let me go!"

She found the switch and light streamed into the room where

her suitcases stood packed and labelled for their journey. Petals from a vase of dead tulips had drifted on to the rug, a note from her maid stood on the mantel. Stella picked up the petals and carried them to the fireplace, casting them on the uncharred log. Then she read the note, which said briefly that Anna would be on hand to give her breakfast before she left for the airport.

I must go to bed, thought Stella. She put the note back on the mantel carefully, as if it were something precious which gave her hands something to do, and gave her mind a focus. I must go to bed. How kind of Anna. How kind people are—Dick and Miriam, Mr. Symes! When I come home this room will look just as it looks now, the books on the piano, the clock on the mantel, the paper frill under the birch log, the silence, the dark door of the bedroom. But Dick and Miriam will have sent fresh flowers, the clock will have been wound again, pigeons will be making love on the roof across the way. Everything will be just the same, when I come back. Oh my darling, she whispered, calling upon the presence she had just rebuffed.

2

THE THROBBING of motors seemed part of her own circulation as she sat, next morning, in the clipper that was to take her to Lisbon. She could hear, above the reverberation, the voices of the stewardess and the co-pilot conversing in the rear of the plane. The pilot was already in his cubbyhole forward. Except for the empty seat beside her the big ship was filled, and Stella learned that the delay in taking off was due to the nonappearance of her neighbor, evidently a person of importance, and, as she began to suspect, none other than the Sparrows' friend, Mr. William Symes. He had not been visible at the airport, though Dick, who with Miriam had come to see her off, searched everywhere for him. Stella hoped rather ungratefully that he would not show up at all, for she was in no mood for a conversation with strangers. It was with relief that she had said goodbye to the Sparrows, whose zealous concern had become oppressive. Now she longed for the moment of departure, for that curious wrenching apart of one's body from the earth, the suspension of flesh and nerves.

The motors throbbed, a breeze flung spears of water against the window, and she could see the airport with its runways glistening in the sun. People were strolling on the catwalks, watching planes arrive and take off. Regrouped by distance the city wore an antique and shadowy appearance under the cloudless sky. Stella felt withdrawn from its life, and from her friends; she felt aloof as that speck which she took for a bird, then recognized as a plane melting into the void.

There was a commotion in the rear and she turned to see the stewardess tuck a curl under her cap and assume an expression of welcome. Though Stella had never seen Mr. Symes she recognized him as he stepped aboard, hatless, carrying a brief-case and overcoat. In a minute he was beside her, smiling, diffident, smelling of talcum powder. "Mrs. Harmon? I am William Symes. How nice that we should be sitting together. I hope you don't mind? Miss, will you take my coat?"

The pretty stewardess took his coat, smiled, and was smiled upon in return. The co-pilot, on his way to join the chief pilot, also smiled. Every one seemed pleasantly affected by the arrival of this florid young man who had kept them waiting more than twenty minutes beyond the official hour of departure.

"Safety belt," Symes murmured, and bent forward to assist Stella. He fastened his own and leaned back. "Whew! I nearly missed the boat this time." And he explained that he had arrived in New York from Washington in the early hours of the morning, and had slept through the ringing of his alarm clock. "So I called the airport and told them to hold everything. Then I went out and waved a ten dollar bill at a taxicab, and by God, we made it!"

She perceived that the near-catastrophe amused him, that he was not a man to lose his head, or his dignity, over such misadventures. There were other planes for Lisbon, and whatever his mission, it would wait on his pleasure. While they talked Stella tried to recall the conversation of last night, but she had drunk a good deal and her mind had been preoccupied with thoughts of the journey. All she could remember now was that Dick Sparrow said he liked Symes, and that Miriam had implied she did not. Stella guessed that as a fellow traveller Symes would be tactfully unobtrusive. Later, not to embarrass him by a perfunctory show of gratitude, she would thank him for getting her accommodations on the plane and for using his influence—as Dick had intimated he had done—with the officials at the passport office. For the rest, she was not especially curious, merely relieved that he and not some one crude or garrulous was to be her companion on the hop to Lisbon.

The noise of the motors settled into a steady orchestration and the plane began to move; walls, water, the broken edges of the city slipped past, sank, flattened. Symes loosened his belt a little and crossed his legs. He thought: "She's not pretty and she seems dull. Sparrow should have tipped me off." He tried to remember what Sparrow had told him about Mrs. Harmon; it couldn't have been of any significance or he would have paid more attention. Now he felt disappointed in his companion, for he would have enjoyed impressing a pretty woman; it would have soothed him, and he needed soothing. The ordeal of the past twenty-four hours had left him in a state of acute irritation. Washington had been hot, and he loathed heat; the men he was supposed to meet had eluded him, the individual he was supposed to talk to had remained drunk and uncommunicative. The story Symes had just told Stella, like many of his stories, was only partly true. Circumlocution was second nature to him and he had become so adept in the art of concealing his personal life from others that there were occasions when he almost succeeded in concealing it from himself. The fact was he had spent the night with Regan Bycroft, and this morning they had quarrelled. The quarrel took time, and for Symes to have missed the plane might have resulted in consequences considerably more serious than he liked to think about. However, the reconciliation had been satisfactory, even charming; he had not missed the plane, and the irritation he felt was nothing more than a gradual subsidence of panic. The discovery that his travelling companion was neither good-looking nor apparently even interesting, prolonged the irritation, though no trace of it appeared in his manner.

"Look," he exclaimed, pointing. "Gorgeous, isn't it?" Gorgeous was a word he had learned to regard as vulgar, but it occasionally slipped out, probably from habit. Stella stared at the receding earth, at broad ribbons of water and the fading delicate bridges. Then the sea appeared, blue and immaculate, and between the sea and herself a few silvery gulls.

"I have often thought," said Symes, "that to die in the air would, artistically speaking, be preferable to dying anywhere else, and less painful too. Icarus, for instance, must have been dead long before he hit the ground—or was it the sea?"

As he spoke he remembered what Dick Sparrow had told him about Mrs. Harmon, that she was a widow going to Italy to visit the grave of her husband, killed in the war. Embarrassed, he decided to affect ignorance.

Stella said: "I don't see death as artistic! As far as I'm concerned it is the final ignominy."

He reminded her that the art of the world had been greatly concerned with the phenomenon of death; that artists had achieved a vision which often transcended the ignominy. She shrugged. "Why not depict it as being hideous, which it is?"

"As a lesson against war? Goya tried, didn't he? But whom did he persuade?"

"He persuades me," she replied, coldly, and Symes was made to feel that his reference to Goya, like his reference to Icarus, had been unfortunate. Irritation returned and he decided petulantly that had she been pretty the conversation could not have taken this depressing turn, and he would have been spared embarrassment. Stella broke the uneasy pause by turning to him with a strained smile: "I want to thank you, Mr. Symes. Dick Sparrow told me of the trouble you went to in order to get me the seat."

"It was no trouble, just a matter of a telephone call."

"It couldn't have been so simple!"

"Well, I admit there may have been a certain amount of wire-pulling. I happened to learn that the airline people had a seat saved for some one who wished to go to Lisbon on a trivial errand which could easily wait, so I persuaded them to switch him to another flight, that was all."

Stella felt a shock of guilt. "I hate to think that I caused some one so much inconvenience."

"Nothing to worry about, I give you my word."

She noticed for the first time the tough, irregular beauty of his face, where animation and brooding seemed continually at odds; it occurred to her that no one would ever actually guess what this man was thinking, or where his loyalties or his sympathies might reside. She wondered whether this suggestion of something perennially young and volatile was what inspired liking in men as sophisticated as Dick, though it antagonized women like herself and Miriam.

After a slight pause she said: "I know there are still all sorts of difficulties about foreign travel, and Dick told me that you helped iron those out for me, too. How can I thank you?"

Well, if she were not pretty she was grateful, and Symes relented.

"Just forget all about it, Mrs. Harmon!"

"That's not possible."

"Then promise me you won't mention it around." His manner was gay, but Stella's uneasiness persisted as she reflected on the plight of the stranger whose seat she had usurped. Symes studied her with renewed boredom. Not only was she plain, she was positively naïve, and he despised naïve people. He hoped she would not tell all her friends about his share in this business. He had exerted himself in her behalf purely out of friendship for Dick Sparrow, who happened to be indispensable to him in a legal capacity, but as any fool would understand, such gestures were always performed behind the scenes. Symes' instinct was to bribe and propitiate, an instinct which had psychological roots in an unhappy childhood. He had developed the instinct to a fine art, and it rarely failed him. When people gave him good advice he suffered from a sense of having been saved in the nick of time from some nameless catastrophe, and out of relief and subconscious guilt he was moved to reward his benefactor out of all proportion, as this morning he had rewarded his taxi driver with a tip so huge that the man departed wondering whether the whole thing were not a mistake. These extragavant gestures were usually followed by a revulsion of feeling, when Symes retreated into miserly asceticism and the brooding suspicion that something had been put over on him.

In the pause which now fell between himself and Stella he reflected on the last conversation he had had with Dick Sparrow. Dick had said: "There is no chance of Mrs. Bycroft getting a divorce until her husband is back from Europe, even if he were agreeable, and we have no reason to suppose he will be agreeable."

"But Dick, you understand that Regan and I don't want Bycroft to bring the suit. That's *out*. Regan feels that for Neddy's sake as well as for her own she should be allowed to get the divorce. I realize it's going to be tough, but after all she and Bycroft have been separated four years, practically, and the whole thing is on the skids anyway."

"That may be, but she can't do a thing till he comes home. My advice to you is to keep out of the picture as much as you possibly can."

Symes had seen the point. He knew that he could not expect to compete with his rival in the eyes of a hero-worshipping society, and he knew, too, that while justice might be a sentimental fool it was also an extremely obstinate one. Regan was not in love with her husband. She was in love with William Symes, but unless the husband were to prove accommodating he left her no alternative except the ugly one of putting herself in the wrong. From that prospect both lovers shrank in dismay. Regan was ambitious and self-conscious. During the war, and ever since its termination, she had been exceedingly active in civic affairs, and had gained considerable publicity, which she enjoyed. In fact, she revelled in admiration of all kinds, while nourishing a corresponding dread of criticism. Symes shared her feelings. For his part he was touchy on the score of his war record, for he had never been in uniform. Nevertheless he believed that he had served his country every bit as gloriously as the men who distinguished themselves in the field. Naturally, this was not something he could discuss with friends, and he had counted on Dick Sparrow's sympathy. In the course of the discussion he managed to intimate that even peace demanded sacrifices from a man in his somewhat anomalous position, and that sooner than provoke a scandal and cause threefold suffering he was prepared to renounce his love and step out of the picture entirely. "I can always get myself sent away somewhere—Brazil, Peru, the East. Anything, anything to avoid a mess."

Dick stared at him in surprise. "What about Regan? Would she stand for that?"

Symes shrugged with a wordless eloquence.

This conversation took place in a restaurant called Philippe's, on Third Avenue, where the floor and the waiters were dirty, but the food good and the atmosphere secluded.

In a moment of candor Symes had exclaimed: "God, Dick! What in hell would I do without you?" Dick laughed, but Symes continued earnestly: "I wish there was some little thing I could do to show my gratitude."

"I'll be sending you a bill." Then he remembered something and turned to his client. "On second thoughts, maybe there is something you can do for me." He went on to speak of Stella, of her wish to go to Italy, and of the difficulties and delays in obtaining passports and transportation. Symes replied eagerly that there certainly was something he could do, and that he would attend to the matter at once.

*　　*　　*　　*

Land had disappeared and the sea stretched tight and blue from horizon to horizon, a single vessel pinned to its surface. Stella felt the air move under the plane, like waves under a ship. A squall struck, darkening the cabin, then they were out in the sunlight again, raindrops glittering on the windows. Symes inquired whether she had friends in Rome or Florence, and she replied that she knew no one in Italy and that her visit was to be brief. He scribbled addresses on an envelope and gave it to her. "These are old friends of mine, and if you should feel like getting in touch with them I know they will be delighted to see you."

He was really kind and she felt that she was proving a disappointment. To retrieve herself somewhat in his eyes she asked him to tell her something about Italy. "You see, I've never been there. I've never been much of anywhere. It seems sad to think that we shall never see Europe as it used to be before the war."

While Symes deplored naïveté, he regarded humility as an attractive trait, especially in women. He was quite willing to talk about Italy. "A mess, like the rest of Europe. I doubt that you'll find the Italians very cordial. I'm told they dislike Americans almost as much as they do the English and the Russians. But then, every one in Europe dislikes every one else." He embarked on a long disquisition on the political and economic condition of Europe since the war ended, and of the general expectancy of a third conflict in the not too far future.

"I'm inclined to agree. Europe may be down and out, but Asia is not. And Asia is in our bailiwick—you've only to look at the map to see why."

The stewardess appeared with lunch on a chromium tray. Symes went on:

"To protect Alaska and the Pacific Islands we've got to hold Japan and the China coast. To protect Australia the British have got to hold India. And the Indians and the Chinese and the Japs don't want us. The Russians don't want us. They've got billions against our millions. Only, we're smarter." He spread butter on a roll and Stella noticed that his hands were well-kept, almost dainty for a man.

"Yes, sir," he repeated, nodding. "Yes, sir, we're smarter. They'd better not forget it."

Stella looked out of the window and saw the sea and the sky meet in a single radiant arc. What was it Alec had written her in one of his letters from Italy?

"Men do not die, they are killed."

3

THAT EVENING they flew above violet clouds between which they glimpsed the gold and level sea. People were talking Spanish in the seat behind Stella; beside her Symes slept, his dark head touching her shoulder. She gazed from the fabulous tides of sunset to the book which she had brought to read on the journey. It still smelled of Dockett's Book Store. She could see the dusty shelves stretching from floor to ceiling, the long tables stacked with volumes, and the figures which moved like characters in a Kafka novel. That had been in the fall of 1935. She had been working in Dockett's for a year, and there seemed no reason to hope that she would not be working there for the rest of her life, since she was penniless and Dockett's kept her in food and rent if it did little besides. She had a room in the basement of a house on West 4th Street, and got her meals at a drugstore. When she was not in her basement room or eating a sandwich at the drugstore she sat behind a desk at one end of Dockett's basement—she seemed doomed to live in basements—and waited on the few customers who drifted down the stairs in quest of bargains. Spectral silence invested Dockett's basement, the air smelled brittle and lifeless and only the mice moved with alacrity. There were occasions when Stella brooded over the life encased within all these books of ancient explorations, adventures, discoveries, glories. What had any of it to do with her, or indeed with the shabby dreamers who came to browse, sometimes to buy a volume? Her father had been a teacher and a scholar, but Stella learned to hate the sight of books, seeing them as mockeries of life as she knew it.

One afternoon she sat watching the customers as they fingered stained and creaking pages. One by one, they replaced the books and climbed the staircase to the street, and she pictured them marching away to their private destinies. The vision of anonymous feet moving away from her central self affected her like a nightmare in which she was left deserted. In her desperation she found herself missing her father, whose death from cancer had been a merciful release for them both. It was true she had friends, but poverty consumed time and energy, and she saw little of them. "Here I am, twenty," she reminded herself, and shivered. Twenty! Young, active, intelligent, she saw her future encompassed by the four dingy walls of Dockett's bookstore and by the further adamant walls of uncertainty and fear—the gray fear of perpetual loneliness, of sickness and age as she had watched it, year after year, consume her father so he had been glad enough to die, and she had been glad for his sake.

Now she watched a mouse start from its hole and embark on a short and fatal journey towards a mousetrap. Old Dockett was always setting traps which she was always springing when his back was turned, for she liked the mice and in her dark moods sometimes identified herself with them. But she had forgotten to spring this trap and now she watched, fascinated, the progress of the mouse. Then a book fell, and the mouse vanished into its hole.

"I wonder," said Alec, "if you have a copy of Dante's *Inferno?*"

He emerged from behind the stacks, a young man with dark hair and dark eyes, looking as if he had spent his life in the open. "I've got to verify a quotation, but of course I'll buy the book."

Stella was staring at the mouse, which had returned; before she could move to save it the bar of the trap fell with a crushing snap, and the mouse's eyes, suffused with blood, fixed her in mute and eternal reproach.

"Perhaps you can verify it for me," Alec went on. *"Nessun maggior dolore, che ricordarsi del tempo felice nella miseria; e ció tuo dottore.* My cousin Miriam Sparrow insists it's from the Purgatorio, but I know she's wrong."

"I'm sorry, I don't understand Italian."

"Well, in English it goes something like this: 'There is no greater pain than to recall a happy time in wretchedness.' "

He stood before her, his brown hands resting on the desk. "Have you the *Divine Comedy?* I can easily look it up."

"You might find it in that stack over there, by the mouse."

"The mouse?" He turned, following her gaze. "Oh, thanks."

She watched him reach down a book, blow the dust off it, and turn the pages.

"Here it is!" He returned, triumphant. "Canto five, as I thought. Miriam's a regular mule about her literary misconceptions. I'll have to buy the book and hold it under her nose. How much? Eighty-five cents?" He plunged a hand in his pocket and showered the desk with nickels and pennies. Slowly, Stella was becoming aware of him, of the vitality in his voice and eyes. She picked up the coins.

"Shall I wrap it up for you?"

"I can put it in my pocket."

Now he would go, carrying his discovery, victorious over his cousin Miriam. They would wrangle and laugh with fraternal good humor, their lives complete, but she must go on sitting here in Dockett's basement, facing the dead mouse and its red tears until Dockett came down the staircase and pounced on it with an exultant: "Another! That'll teach 'em!"

Alec lingered. "Would you like to hear the rest of it?" and without waiting for an answer he perched on the desk and began to read, hesitating over the Italian, translating for her as he went along. Sunlight on the staircase turned the color of rose, of russet, and when he came to the end of the Fifth Canto he closed the book and sat for a moment, looking at it. "Poor old Paolo," he sighed at last. "Poor old Francesca!"

He got up and walked across the room towards the stairs, and Stella's gaze followed him. As if he felt it he turned and looked back.

"Stuffy down here, isn't it? Do you ever come up for air?"

"Sometimes, when I go home."

"Where's home?"

"Round the corner, in another basement." She laughed, biting her lips.

Slowly, as she had become aware of him, Alec became aware of her, and as the vision deepened he saw it all, this basement, its mummified books and murdered mice, the girl with her bright hair tied with a velvet ribbon. He saw the empty room to which she returned at the end of the day, and in which she awakened. Stirred by pity, and perhaps by the cadence of the poem which he had just read, he gazed at her. Afterwards he confessed to her that he could not have brought himself to climb the stairs until he had made sure that he would see her again.

"Listen, I'm having dinner with the Sparrows, Dick and Miriam. We may go to a movie, or we may just sit round and talk. Would you like that?"

"I don't know the Sparrows."

"They're easy to know!"

"I don't know you, either!" She laughed, flushing.

"I'm Alec Harmon."

"And I'm Stella—Stella Tyson."

Stella had always suspected that she was one of those people whose salvation lies in the hands of another being. For her Alec was that being; he changed not only the outward condition of her life, but its spirit also, and the years before she knew him became as remote and as dusty as the second-hand books in Dockett's.

"I don't call it love," Miriam Sparrow declared on the first anniversary of Stella's marriage. "I call it idolatry."

"Not jealous, are you?" Dick teased her.

"Certainly not." Then she added meditatively, "Envious, maybe."

They were spending that first summer in Jarley, the Sparrows blistering themselves in the sun while Alec weeded his strawberry bed and Stella watched the three of them from her point of vantage under an apple tree. At the foot of the pasture the sea rolled in a long blue wave; sheep lifted their heads, eyeing the little group with unwinking agate gaze.

"You do that as if your life depended on it," Miriam remarked, as Alec clipped a vine and set the young plant off by itself.

"It's how I do most things."

"You don't really expect to make a living out of strawberries, do you?"

He squatted on his heels, his bare body glowing in the sun. "You'd be disappointed if I did, wouldn't you? You know, Miriam, there are times when you remind me of our maternal grandfather."

"Not that miserly old bastard!"

"You do incline to share the old coot's notion that pleasure is a variation on a theme by Satan. I'd hoped Dick would educate you."

"She relapses," mumbled Dick, half-buried in the long grass. "Minute I turn my back she relapses."

Miriam tilted a bottle of sunburn oil over her raw arms. Neither she nor Dick ever got used to the country. Both were city bred, incapable of navigating a plank bridge without twisting their ankles. Every year during their summer vacation they blistered in the raging sun or gave themselves indigestion and allergies by eating too many clams. But both were obsessed by the idea of spending their holiday in the country, whence they returned to New York raw, peeling, exhausted, there to boast to their friends about the delights of country existence.

"I admit," she said presently, "I admit that it does amaze me, the way you and Stella enjoy life. I'm all for it, but you don't seem to do anything else, and I don't think that that's quite moral." She laughed ruefully. "Don't you ever intend to take a real job? Don't you want to make money?"

"Certainly. I make money all the time. I made a profit out of these strawberries, believe it or not."

"I don't believe it. How much?"

"Four dollars and thirty-six cents."

"Net," said Stella proudly from under her apple tree.

Miriam laughed shrilly. "Oh God, if grandpa could hear you!"

"Well," said Alec, prodding the moist earth with his trowel, "look: Father and Grandfather made more dough than either of them could use. They left me a tidy piece, and I'm grateful. They had no use for Jarley, and they got out the minute they could. They were ashamed of being country folk. They didn't like the smell of manure, or the smell of the beach at low tide. I do, and they fixed it so I can go on living here and liking it."

"Playing at being a farmer, with your education!" Miriam looked accusingly at Stella. "You encourage him. You think everything he does is wonderful."

"Marvellous," Stella agreed complacently.

"But what was the use of his expensive schooling if he's going to waste it clopping about in sheep manure, planting berries, and shooting ducks? And yes, poaching with that wild man, James Anderson? Why don't you have a baby?"

Alec shook his head. "Don't you know you must never rush a baby? It's apt to be bad for the poor little thing."

"Besides," growled Dick from his hideaway in the long grass, "have you ever thought where you and I would spend our vacations, Miriam, if a baby had our room?"

In August Alec cut the marsh hay with his neighbor, James Anderson, and Stella watched them move two abreast through the grass, disturbing the plover which rose wheeling and crying over their heads. Alec paused in his scything to send a whistle after the birds, decoying them out of the sky. When summer marched into autumn, all bronze and brass, they lighted driftwood fires in the shallow old fireplaces and Alec hung his blue-and-white work gloves on a nail and went duck hunting on the islands with James. Stella harvested the fallen apples and raked leaves over the strawberry bed as she waited with rising anxiety for the men to come home. Sometimes, for company, she took the path through the woods to the Anderson house and spent an hour talking to James' wife, Myrtle, in a kitchen which reeked of diapers and woolen socks steaming behind the stove. Myrtle would see her to the door and send a reassuring cry after her: "Don't worry about them two! They've been huntin' birds since they was weaned!"

Tired of waiting, Stella walked down to the shore and climbed a rock which overlooked the sea. From here she watched the lobster boats pitching against the sky, and once in a while if she was patient she would catch a glimpse of Anderson's gray dory nosing homeward, and the sound of its outboard motor would reach her faintly across the turbulent water. They came at last, bulky in mackinaws and high boots, their faces crimson from the cold, and flung the day's bag at her feet—coot, eider, blacks, old squaw. "Don't you go fretting about me," Alec cried, laughing at her for her fears. "You should know by now that James and I always come back."

In winter the snow piled steadily under the windows, an acrid smell of wood-smoke made their eyes water, and the radio rumbled with news from Spain.

"What's it all about, can you make out?" growled James Anderson, and they discussed it peaceably, their stockinged feet propped on the andirons, their disquiet less vivid than the fire into which they gazed. "God damn," said James, rising at last and knocking out his pipe. "Why can't they leave those folks alone?" He walked to the window and peered out. "Guess I better get going before it drifts in too heavy."

"Give my love to Myrtle," said Stella, and she and Alec watched him shoulder through the darkness towards his own window, a spark of light beyond the thin winter trees.

That was the first summer and the first winter at Jarley, and they followed in undiminished splendor, five summers and five snows; for Stella they were more than changing seasons, they were present and future in one, weighted with immediacy, each day a radiant replica of yesterday and tomorrow. Gravely, she and Alec dicussed the question of having a child "one of these days," and James Anderson, himself a father at twenty, accused them of expecting to find a baby all ready made, frisking among the lambs under the fir trees some spring morning.

"Better make up your minds. Kids would be a help round the place when you get old."

"Plenty of time," replied Alec. "Stella and I intend to live for ever, anyway!"

Anderson thought it over and laughed. "Me too! Boy yes, long as there's women and birds, and I got a charge of lead in one barrel, I'm in no hurry to quit."

But one September night in 1940 the moon rode high above the fir trees, the meadow gleamed like silk, and the wind carried a smell of the salt marsh and the voices of innumerable birds feeding on the mud flats bared by the tide. Stella heard an apple fall from the tree into the grass, the dry rustle of the balm o' Gilead leaves sounded harsh in her ears; then Alec stepped across the threshold and sat down beside her on the granite doorstep.

"They're bombing the hell out of London," he said.

"I don't want to hear."

"They're killing everybody, everywhere."

She leaned against him, feeling his warmth through the thin shirt. She thought of him as she had seen him last night, bronze against the white sheet. Unable to tell whether his eyes were closed or open she had stooped over till her face touched his. Then in panic at his stillness she wakened him. "Alec! Some one's shooting in the woods behind the orchard."

He leaned on his elbow, in the streaming moonlight.

"It's James, after the deer."

"At this hour?"

"You know he'd rather poach than sleep."

There was another shot, and she said: "Alec, don't go to sleep before I do."

"We'll go to sleep together, then."

She laid her hand on his heart. "Just like a clock," she murmured. "Like a clock, going on and on, for ever."

He was silent, and from the woods there came a third shot. "Like a clock," whispered Stella, feeling the steady rhythm of his heart. "Like a clock going on for ever."

Now as they sat together on their doorstep the moon towered above them, trite and monstrous witness to their love, and the advancing tide sent birds wheeling across the marsh. Stella said: "Don't leave me, Alec."

He moved restlessly. "Maybe I won't have to."

"Say you won't!"

He changed the subject. "I was talking with James this morning. I asked him if he wanted to get into trouble with the wardens, hunting deer at night, and out of season. He said what the hell, men had been doing it for a hundred and fifty years round here, and the warden knew it. He said: 'Leave folks alone and their sins don't amount to so damn much in the long run. It's pushing 'em around makes them ugly.' Suppose he'll be telling that to the warden one of these days?"

"What else did James say?"

He hesitated, "He said he was trying to keep his eye in for what was coming."

"What did he mean, keep his eye in for what was coming?"

"You know what he meant."

She was silent for a moment, then fiercely: "Alec, no! Not for us. There's just you and me, and that's all there is, all there ever will be. Our life, Alec. No one can want it as much as we do."

"They might ask for it one day, Stella."

"They shan't have it!"

"Listen, let me say something, then we'll forget it. If any-

thing should happen, if I . . . you . . . should be asked, then
don't ever believe . . ." He broke off, his gaze fixed on the
moon. "If ever it should happen that you hear I've been killed,
don't believe it. Don't ever believe it."

"What are you talking about? We aren't even in this war.
James is crazy!"

Stella watched the skies turn from violet to slate. It became
difficult for her to read the page on her lap: *"Nessun maggior
dolore, che ricordarsi del tempo felice nella miseria; e cio sa il
tuo dottore."*

Symes woke up and passed his hands over his hair. "Getting
dark, isn't it? You shouldn't try to read in this light."

As if the inert mechanism had but waited for the sound of
his voice the lights went on, consigning the outer world to
darkness.

4

A COLD wind was blowing from the Apennines and the color of these mountains huddled under the sky made Stella think of the hills near Jarley. The resemblance ended there. She was not prepared for the desolation which met her gaze as the train carried her northward out of Rome. That there would be ruins she knew—she had seen them often enough in newspapers and magazines, she had heard them described by commentators over the radio all through the years of the war. But with war's end surely stones healed themselves, battered spires were reunited with the sky, and all that was not flesh and blood resumed, somehow, its old appointed place? From the train she watched swarms of men and women laboriously sorting ashes and rubble, and she thought she discerned, as Symes had warned her she might, hostility and indifference in the eyes of a warm people.

Resemblance to home ended with the dark ridge of the mountains, but she surprised it again in the voice of Guido Vitelli when the train finally deposited her on the platform at Montescari. She stood for some moments staring after the departing train, struggling with an impulse to run after it, to cry: "Take me! Don't leave me here alone!" But it answered her with a scornful bellow and disappeared, and she was left gazing at the tin roof and spindly walls of the station. The buildings had been erected after the war, and had already a curious air of permanence. How long would they be permitted to stand? Fifty years? A hundred?

Her fellow passengers were drifting away carrying suitcases, leading children. She thought: "I'm at Montescari!" She trembled, but the ground of Montescari stood firm under her feet, its stones sparkled in the sunshine of an exquisite April day. The station master, who had seen her from his window, now approached her. He was middle-aged, with a detached manner. He had seen at once that she was foreign—American or English —and guessed the errand which had brought her to Montescari. There had been several within recent weeks, and there would, he knew, be more, many more, of these sad pilgrims from overseas. He hoped that the local inn would soon be restored—it now boasted three rain-proof rooms—and that the local caffe would be rebuilt by the time all obstacles to travel were removed. In the past the little town had been the delight of painters and poets, but a different kind of pilgrim was to seek it now.

The station master greeted Stella. *"Buon giorno, signora."* Then, in two of his five words of English: "Help you?"

She hesitated, and he read the terror in her eyes. "I've come to see the American cemetery here at Montescari. At Rome I was told that I would surely find a place to stay a few days. Could you direct me to a hotel?"

He nodded and gestured, and she guessed that he desired her to wait while he went in search of an interpreter. In a moment he was back, accompanied by a young man wearing khaki pants and a flamboyant tweed coat. He greeted Stella with a friendly smile. "My name is Guido Vitelli. Can I help you, ma'am?"

She replied gratefully that he could help her. It was a relief to hear English. Now she repeated her little speech to Guido, who nodded. "My mother has a house at the end of Scarlatti Street. There is a garden. I think we can make you comfortable."

Mr. Bianchi, the station master, who had been listening attentively, said something in Italian, and Guido nodded again. "He says I should tell you I served with the American Army. Since I was demobilized I live here. I have a truck, and I meet the trains for Mr. Bianchi." He picked up her suitcases. "My truck's down the street. I can take you to the house now. Nobody else, is there, Giorgio?"

Mr. Bianchi replied in Italian that there was no one else in search of accommodation, but that Guido had better be on hand to meet the six-twenty that evening. No doubt the six-twenty would be late, it was always late, due to the repairing of bridges all the way south from Florence. He bowed to Stella, who murmured: *"Grazie!"* as she turned to follow Guido across the platform and down a flight of steps to the street.

A line of houses patched with tin and roofing paper rose from mounds of brick and tufa, their originals. The little town, built on an eminence, rose in tiers which culminated in what had once been the church of San Francesco. In the sunshine, among trees which had survived the battle and those that had been planted since, it was difficult for Stella to realize that the whole place was actually a series of ruins. Men were working, on ledges, on ladders, on scaffolds, while women carried baskets of dust and children dragged little carts stacked with scraps of brick and metal.

"There is my truck," said Guido cheerfully. "Now you need to stand no more in the sun."

It was an old army truck painted blue, with Guido's initials on the door. He put her luggage in the rear and invited her to sit beside him on the front seat. They roared up the street, passing a bulldozer and an assortment of vehicles packed with debris and workmen of all ages.

"We shall be out of this dust in a minute. Then it becomes pretty again." He glanced at her. "Green things grow fast, even here."

"What is that building?"

"The Parish House. In the Oratorio of the church—you can see that from the next street—there is a relief by Della Robbia. That somehow was not hit. But most things were. Most of the frescoes. Even now a wall quivers and the plaster comes sliding down in a cascade. People working on the buildings have to be careful. Already some have been killed by the sudden collapse of a roof."

They jolted along, and Guido told her of a town not far from Montescari, where the idiot Germans had destroyed a castle built by one of their own heroes, Frederick the Second. He slowed, and the truck began to crawl with ponderous growlings. "There, that's the town hall. The Germans used it for an observation post, so we shelled it. Then we used it and they shelled it. A lot of the shells missed the town hall and hit the church and the houses near the church. Vasari designed that church. You know about him?" He put on speed once more. "Well, I didn't, because though I am Italian, I lived in the States since I was a kid. I never did hear about this guy Vasari, or about Della Robbia, till I come here after the war. Then I made friends with an old fella, name of Antonio Suli, and you know what Suli

does all the time? You know what he done all the time during
the battle for Montescari? There was two battles—or three, you
might say. First when we drove the Germans out, second when
they drove us out, the third time when we drove them out for
keeps. Well, what old Suli done all that time was carry a sack
and collect bits of statues and stuff and carry them off to a safe
place till after the war. Now he's working on them, piecing
them together bit by bit like those picture puzzles they give to
kids. It was Suli told me all about Giorgio Vasari and Della
Robbia. It was him told me how old this place was. A thousand
years old!"

"And was this your home before you went to America?"

"No, I come from the south. But after the war I married a
girl from Montescari, and now we live here, my wife and my
mother. Also my son." After a pause he continued: "I was with
the 34th Armored Division and it was us took Montescari.
Afterwards some of us was sent back here, and then I met my
wife. Me being Italian and speaking Italian made it easy. There's
others done the same thing. Americans, English, Russians. Lot
of 'em never did go home . . ." He laughed slyly. "They kind of
disappeared. The man in charge of the American cemetery, he's
American. He married an Italian girl, and lives right here in
Montescari."

"The 34th Armored Division," murmured Stella. "Did you
know . . . do you remember many of the men who were with
you?"

"Most of my own bunch, I remember."

"Would you remember their names?"

"You ask me," he said gently. "Maybe I'll remember."

"Alec Harmon?"

"Alec Harmon? Can't say it rings the bell. An officer?"

"He was a private. Private Alec Harmon." Suddenly she wanted to get out of the car, to rush away into the upheaval of this alien country, to fling herself deep into its sunburnt, gunscorched earth.

"There wasn't no Harmon in my bunch," said Guido regretfully. He stopped the car and pointed. "That's my house, where you're going to stay."

Stella saw a white house roofed with tiles, its doors and windows painted the identical blue which disguised Guido's army truck.

"See that bare place beyond? Bianchi's house stood there. We had to blow it up to get the Germans out. Graves everywhere." He glanced at her. "That one, he was your brother, your husband?"

"My husband."

"Ah, *povretta!*"

"The American cemetery, is it far from here?"

"You take the street to the right, there. You can see the sign. It's only a twenty minute walk. I'll drive you there, when you have rested from your journey."

"I'll go there now," said Stella. "It's not far. I can walk."

"Let me drive you," Guido urged. "It's hot and dusty . . ."

"I'd like to walk, thank you. Will you take my luggage to the house? I'll find my way back in a little while."

Guido opened the door for her. "You can't get lost. First you'll come to a cottage. That belongs to Sergeant Curtis. He is the caretaker and has all the records in his office. Ask for him, Alben Curtis."

Stella nodded and watched the truck rumble away towards the house with the red tiles. A child carrying a copper pot stared at her, unresponsive to her murmured greeting; she read an aloof recognition in the eyes of the men and women, who seemed to guess her errand. Dust covered her shoes, sun beat on her head, and the unfamiliar aura of a strange land rose about her. Presently the street became a mere road with the town rising on one side and the green land on the other. She saw paths branching towards houses partially concealed among the trees, and beyond them the mountains, slate and purple against the sky. An unknown bird sang in a hedge, an unknown man driving oxen touched his hat as he passed her.

Had Alec come this way? Had his beloved eyes encountered the gaze of these strangers? She walked on, a sense of unreality increasing with every step. The distance seemed farther than Guido had said, but at last the field ended and she saw the cemetery, its crosses marching in endless columns towards a hill slashed and scarred like the town at her back. Across the road, in a neat garden behind a painted fence, stood the cottage which Guido had told her belonged to the American caretaker. No one was visible. The man with the oxen had disappeared, the road lay deserted under a haze of heat. For several minutes Stella stood watching the bright flag atop its pole flap gently in the breeze which brought her the scent of chestnut trees flowering among the nearer graves. Silence marched with the graves and beyond them to the indifferent hills. Afraid lest she sink beneath this stillness, Stella turned and walked rapidly away.

5

MARK BYCROFT lighted his pipe and tossed the match over the rail. He felt the lift and sag of the ship as it headed into a wind which seemed bitterly cold for May. A bell jangled, a seaman padded up the deck, whistling, and exhilaration swept through Mark. He thought: "We'll get into New York in time for me to take Regan out to dinner after all." He pictured his wife's face framed in the dark fur of her coat collar. Fur in May? Oh well, women pay little attention to the seasons, and fur was the most expensive and the most becoming frame he could conjure up for her at the moment. He marvelled at his own elation, which had mounted steadily since he left Antwerp. Now the wind snapped at him and he shivered, turning up his collar.

"Cold, all right," remarked Lieutenant Perry, joining him at the rail.

"Nerves, I guess," said Mark, lightly. "It's two years since I was home."

"Well, I can't complain. I had thirty days last year. But this time it's for keeps." He leaned on the rail, some puppy instinct making him get as close to Mark as possible. Mark glanced at him with a mixture of liking and impatience. Perry had worked with him for the past eighteen months, and Mark found his limpetlike devotion a bit oppressive. War and exile had bred a hunger for affection in these homesick children, and Mark had resigned himself to playing uncle or older brother. But the role bored him and he was glad that it was soon to be discarded. They would be home tomorrow, and these emotional innovations, these pathetic loyalties would take their place with the shapeless baggage and rusty armor of war. Mark did not say this, and he was sure that Perry, a simple creature, did not share his ideas. No doubt, thought Mark, he is already making plans for a lifelong friendship high-lighted by yearly reunions of a maudlin and alcoholic nature. He reflected rather sadly on the simplicities born of war, on loyalties rarely carried forward into the dull preoccupations of peace. But my God! Perry would bore Regan to death in five minutes.

"Gosh," said Perry. "I hope Lucy got my cable."

"I hope Regan got mine."

"It does mean something, doesn't it? Having one's wife meet one at the dock, and all that stuff."

"You bet."

There was a slight pause, then Perry said: "You know, Colonel, I've been thinking over what you said to me a few days ago."

Mark waited patiently, wishing the boy would leave him to his own thoughts.

"I've been thinking over the advice you gave me."

"Oh, that! Lord, I only told you what I would do, or what I wouldn't do, if I were in your shoes."

"I've been thinking it over, just the same."

"Fine," said Mark heartily. On their first evening out to sea Perry had joined him for a walk around the deck and after a few preliminaries had come out with his problem: There had been a girl in Belgium. Should he tell his wife?

"Better keep your big mouth shut," said Mark without hesitation.

"But that doesn't seem right, somehow."

"Well, suit yourself. All I can tell you is, I regard my sins as my personal responsibility. I have no doubt your wife would forgive you . . . and that she would reassure you on that score, every two or three weeks."

Perry said broodingly that he feared deceit might prey on his mind, and Mark laughed. "A guy's got to have some privacy, hasn't he?"

They had argued, then dropped the subject. Now on their last evening at sea Perry came back to it with a diffident smile. "Of course, you're right. I shan't be in any rush to start confessing. If, some day, Lucy should ask me questions, I'll maybe tell her. But I guess there's no point in trying to cross that bridge yet." He stared at the gray sea running below. "I ask myself how I'd feel, whether I'd rather know or not know."

The problem, as it affected Perry, had long since ceased to interest Colonel Bycroft, but he pondered it politely, and replied with what he hoped sounded like devastating sophistry that if deceit were the order of the day he trusted that he too might be well and effectively deceived.

Perry laughed. "You should worry! Ever happen to hear what they said about you in our outfit, Colonel?"

"What?" asked Mark uneasily.

"They said that if the Almighty had ever put it up to you,

your conscience could have gone bail for the whole bunch of us!"

Mark was not sure whether to take this as a compliment or the reverse, so he merely smiled and let it pass. He knew that some of his brother officers had considered him a freak, that some condemned him for a snob, and that others dismissed him as a prig, but if war had taught him anything it had taught him a grim patience with the impatience of men. Recompense lay in the affection of a few like Perry. These occasionally saw Mark drunk or lost him in mysterious side streets, but he always showed up sane and self-possessed, wearing both his socks, immune to chaff, impenetrable under cross-examination.

The role of conventional hero had made him profoundly uncomfortable; heroism is not the sensitive man's normal role and privately he decided that it was lucky nations did not confer medals and citations on one for his private victories, else such decorations might paint strange rainbows across the invisible heart.

Two years ago, coming home on his first leave, Mark had fallen in love with his wife for the second time. The first time was when he married her. Later, in a mood of doubt and suspicion, he'd had to leave her and his son and go to war, nor had his mind been set at ease by the letters she wrote him or by the hints and innuendoes which reached him through friends. It was in an ugly mood that he had come home on his first leave, only to forget everything on his first sight of Regan. In a letter which he wrote her afterwards, emotion found expression in one of those incoherent testaments which men sometimes bring themselves to write. It was a victory over his pride, but unluckily for him Regan mistook humility for inferiority, and scorn dulled whatever tenderness she may have felt, for a little while, in his presence.

Victory over hatred had been more difficult, a strenuous exercise of patience. He could recall, fairly serenely now, his hatred for a fawning sergeant in his company, his hatred for General Wilmer, and for himself during those scalding glimpses of hypocrisy and expedience uncovered by the strain of the war. There had been too many occasions when patience, stretched fine, had threatened to snap and fling him on the frail mercy of his own passions. He had rejoiced at the fate of Mussolini, yet felt sick at heart when he saw his fellow-soldiers gloating over photographs of the battered and dangling wretch. But the day when hatred almost conquered him came towards the end of the war. It was after Madgeburg, and he stood in a broken street watching a batch of prisoners being led to their cages. A German officer, wounded in one foot, sat resting on a rubble heap. Clean, brash, his cap at an angle, he was eating an apple, wolfing it with great bites, tearing at the flesh, the seeds. His gaunt face and blue eyes, the look of his muscular hand gripping the apple, suddenly ignited Mark, who dropped his hand on his pistol and half drew it forth, hand and blood obedient to the single impulse of murder. But the unsuspecting German rose, tossed the apple core into the dust, and fell in beside a column of prisoners marching past between their guards. Mark took his hand from his gun and stared at his palm. He had killed men during the past few years, but he did not remember ever feeling this rage against them.

Beside him, Perry broke a long silence. "What did you tell me was the name of your kid?"

"We call him Neddy."

"Must be queer, having a kid you hardly know."

"It is queer." And Mark tried to remember the child as he had last seen him. Dark like Regan, quiet, self-contained. It should be fun, getting to know his son all over again.

"I'd like to ask a favor, Colonel."

"Not more advice, I hope?"

"Not advice this time. I expect to be in New York for a while before Lucy and I go west. I wondered whether we might call on you and Mrs. Bycroft."

"Sure!" And suddenly he felt that he meant it, that he would be happy to welcome them, to present them to Regan and to watch the effect of her personality on their artless youth. No doubt they would stay too long and bore her half to death, but she would rise to the occasion, of that he was certain. Mark could see her doing it as he had often seen her in the past; graceful, assured, putting strangers at their ease, making them feel at home, and never, not once, permitting the tick of the parlor clock to intrude on their enchantment. And he could hear her complaining afterwards: "My God, Mark! How could you? I don't want to sound like a snob, but honestly, those *bores!*"

"It would be swell," said Perry eagerly. "I remember your telling me Mrs. Bycroft was interested in public affairs. So is Lucy. She did a wonderful job in the Red Cross during the war. And she's kind of intellectual, too." He produced a notebook. "I'll take your address now. We may miss each other on the pier."

The sea sent a cloud of spray over them. "Let's walk," said Mark.

The ships' bows rose and dipped before the vanishing horizon, and Mark thought of home, of the house to which he would return with Regan and Neddy, and of a life restored to a normal scale. Everything would be in perspective, intense, personal, responsible. He was going back to small-town politics, to run for mayor as he had planned to do before the war. He was sick of existence on a gargantuan plane, sick of society as an anonymous lump, as he had watched it during his years of service. Europe filled him with dread, and he wanted his own country. For the first time in his life he wanted America.

6

REGAN WAS not at the dock to meet him. Mark waited, disappointment and solitude increasing as he stood among a throng of celebrating strangers; then he strolled up and down the damp concrete, musette bag slung over his shoulder, while a porter mounted guard over his luggage near the exit gate. The crowd broke into groups, into couples, and streamed towards the line of waiting cabs and the bright sunshine of the street beyond, but Regan did not appear, nor did he set eyes on young Perry. The porter caught his eye. "Telephones on the other side of the gate, sir, on your right."

Mark thanked him and made his way towards them, followed by the man carrying his luggage. But there was a queue of people waiting outside the telephone booths; with sudden decision he turned and hailed a cab. He had waited an hour, and Regan was always pitilessly punctual. There must have been a mistake; she may have been misinformed by the cable office or by the officials at the pier. Anyway he would be home in twenty minutes. Excitement, which had cooled while he waited, now returned, and he found himself shaking as he pressed against the cab window and peered at the dingy and teeming vistas of Seventh Avenue. "It's standing," he muttered. "Actually standing!"

He told the driver to stop at a florist's, and emerged carrying freesias and late tulips whose fragrance went to his head. It seemed a long time since he had bought flowers for a woman, and he smiled as the driver caught his eye.

On 53rd Street a late sun quivered on the walls. Would Regan guess it was he that had rung the bell, and would she come down the stairs to meet him? The buzzer sounded and he went in, lugging suitcases. Regan's apartment was on the second floor, and the door was opened for him by a Negro maid, small, neat, middle-aged. She stared at him in concern. "Colonel Bycroft? Is Mrs. Bycroft with you?"

"I missed her. I waited, then decided we must have got our signals crossed." He set the suitcases on the floor and felt suddenly limp and breathless.

The woman clasped her hands in distress. "But she went to the pier to meet you! Oh, what a pity!"

He looked at her. "I don't seem to remember you from my last visit."

"I'm Octavia Evans, and I've been with Mrs. Bycroft a little more than a year. Can I get you something to eat or drink? Mrs. Bycroft should be home any minute."

"Nothing, thanks." He gave her the flowers. "You might put these in water before they fade."

She took them tenderly in her black hands. Slowly, his tension began to lessen and he looked round him at a room he barely remembered from his last leave. A square room lined with books in expensive bindings; panelled walls, a blue rug on the floor, everything elegant, studied. He felt that its owner might appear at any moment, unheralded, from its cool, sunlit void.

It was Neddy who appeared and stood silently gazing at him.

Octavia Evans glanced from one to the other, then moved quietly out of the room, closing the door after her.

Mark said uncertainly: "Hullo, son! Remember me?"

"Yes." He looked past Mark at something beyond. "There's your picture," he said, and came into the room. "Over there on the bookcase."

"So it is."

The photograph, taken when he joined the army in 1941, faced him with its frozen smile. Why had he smiled? How inane it seemed now, that smile, the joke forgotten, the occasion past!

Neddy stood beside him. "There's another picture of you in my room. In my picture you're not wearing a hat."

Mark wondered nervously whether he should kiss the child. Would he like it, or would he turn shy and rebuff him as he had done last time? He reflected remorsefully: How little I know him! He's been here in the background, an abstraction almost, one who has had to wait upon the future to achieve substance and meaning.

"I'm glad your mother didn't take you to the pier to meet me because then I'd have missed you both."

"She said I was to stay here and entertain you till she got back."

The words settled into Mark's consciousness with a sort of cumulative shock.

"What? But why should she expect you to enterain me if . . .'" He stopped, thinking: No use trying to straighten it out at this point.

"Show me around, will you, Neddy? It's been so long since I was here. Tell me what's new."

The boy took his hand and they walked towards the book-cases. "Those are new. Aren't they pretty? Mother won't let me touch them because the bindings are very expensive."

"And that picture?" said Mark, coming to a halt before it. "I don't seem to remember it."

"That's a Braque. I gave it to Mother for her birthday."

"I suppose you picked it out yourself?"

"Mr. Symes helped me. He said he knew Mother would like it, and she did like it."

"Who is Mr. Symes?"

"He's a gentleman," said Neddy, indifferently. Mark gazed at the painting, handsomely framed, and, he guessed, a fairly faithful reproduction. Where had his six-year-old son learned to utter the names of great painters with such glibness? Amused, he studied the picture. Regan's interest in art had always fasci-nated him as he watched it develop by what he recognized as a series of happy accidents from the naïve to the esoteric. She was not artistic, nor was she drawn towards the moody companion-ship of artists. Her tastes had been formed by a fortuituous contact with excellence allied with shrewd judgment. But taste, good taste, the very best of taste, was her real creed, her goal in all she did or aspired to do. In the early days of their marriage Mark had alternated between irritation and amusement at what he considered a particular form of snobbery, but he soon dis-covered that it was snobbery which originated in a deep, unfor-mulated need—the need to be admired, to be obeyed. Beauty, intelligence, grace, all of which she possessed, were apparently not sufficient. Mark's own reaction to painting and music was usually inarticulate; he felt things simply, and when moved to express himself, invariably managed to make some stupendous mistake, as when he attributed to Haydn a symphony of Brahms. "Clodhopper!" Regan exclaimed in shamed disgust, and he had laughed, too much in love with her to mind. Now as he gazed at the Braque with his son's hand in his, Mark experienced the old, speechless delight, and it brought its special reward. Imagine caring whether a person's love for beauty were true or false! As if such a question made the slightest difference to beauty.

Neddy was pulling at his hand. "Here are some more books, Papa. And the Chinese Buddha."

They toured the room, and presently Mark saw that it was entirely changed from the time of his last visit. He could not be sure what had been taken from it and what added; except for his portrait and the child at his side he felt that he had little share in its history. The reflection brought a twinge of regret, but no resentment; he had banished resentment, he assured himself —banished it, for ever.

"Now," said Neddy, "we'll go and look at Mother's room."

Like the parlor which they had left, this was filled with light and elegance, but it was so orderly, so self-conscious in its details that Mark hesitated on the threshold, feeling that his presence, and Neddy's, were an intrusion. The boy may have sensed this, for he walked on tiptoe and spoke in a hushed voice: "Mother's clothes are in that closet, and her shoes are in that one, and she keeps throat-lozenges on that table near her bed. Feel the coverlet!" He laid his small rough hand on the gleaming silk. "It's so smooth!" And with curious inconsequentiality he added: "Mother *never* lets me touch her things."

Mark went to the desk and examined a pile of newspaper clippings. Most of these seemed concerned with lectures and discussions which Regan had given or in which she had participated, lectures on the Negro problem and the Jewish problem and the problem of colonial peoples. There were notices relating to himself, with cuts showing him as the recipient of medals and citations. He guessed that Regan had been preparing them to paste in a scrap book which lay open on the desk. Mark smiled at the neat pile of letters, at the calendar heavily pencilled with tentative engagements, at the deckle-edged dictionary, at cubbyholes stuffed with bills and documents of all descriptions —the paraphernalia of an energetic and public-spirited citizen. There was a photograph of Neddy as a baby, another of Regan's parents, but none of himself. There used to be one, he remembered, a small one taken during his last year at High School. He wondered what had happened to it. Moving away from the desk, he felt the sudden subtle presence of his wife, and his glance sought her in the four corners of the room, in the quilted-satin chair beside the window, among the snowy pillows of the big bed.

On the mantelpiece were framed snapshots of people he didn't know.

"Those are friends of mother's," explained Neddy. "In the country, last year."

"Where are you?"

"I wasn't there. I stayed with Aunt Hester."

Mark returned the snapshots to their place between the clock and a corsage of wilted gardenias in a tumbler. Where was the past? What had become of it? He brooded, remembering the house in Connecticut, the wild iris growing between stone walls, cattle standing in the pastures, friends and lovers talking together in the long summers of peace! War had killed the past as surely as it had killed his friends, and now he thought about those friends as he had not dared let himself think about them before. He thought of them laughing and drinking in the garden, or by the fire. Well, they were dead, and the past which had contained them was dead. To brood was morbid. Here in America the buildings still stood unscathed, gardens flowered, trees bore fruit, fires sent their golden flames upward, but the dead who had loved these things were not here to see or to understand, they were denied forever the sun of winter and summer's shade; the survivors moved in another world, and strangers occupied the picture frames.

Why didn't Regan come home? What could be keeping her? How could she have missed him at the pier? He longed for her with a sort of panic.

Neddy took his hand again. "Now let's go and see my room."

There the tour ended, and as the man sat down on the small bed the child set about his own affairs, which involved a cardboard fort and plastic men. "Do I love him?" Mark wondered, watching the preoccupied face. "Does he love me?"

There, half an hour later, Regan found them.

7

MARK HEARD rain beating against the windows and dreamed that he was in Germany and that rain was falling over the land, returning it to a primordial sludge. Out of the rain a Negro woman came towards him carrying flowers and crying: "What a pity, oh what a pity!" Her voice was the echo of many voices, and he wanted to ask her what it was she bewailed, but fear overcame him before he could speak. He woke in semi-darkness and listened to the drumming of the rain as it mingled with the noise of traffic and voices from the street. The sounds made a design outside the boundaries of the room; the quiet within seemed to extend beyond closed doors, and he lay wondering whether he were alone in the house. Regan had dressed and left the room without waking him. The silk coverlet felt cool under his hand, and he remembered what Neddy had said yesterday. "Mother told me I was to stay here and entertain you till she got back."

Yet when she appeared at last and he took her in his arms, she had exclaimed:

"Mark, imagine! I went to the wrong pier!"

Memory roused with a nervous twitching of his body and a further deepening of silence. He stared at the chandelier where light gathered in fugitive gleams, and thought how often he had lain here with Regan and contemplated those radiant spears of light. That was all in the past. There had been little time, last night, to revive the past. They had left Neddy with the maid and had gone to dinner at a restaurant where Regan, laughing, had begged him not to overdo the drinks. There in the midst of strangers they talked of inconsequential matters; they might have been strangers to each other, and Mark had caught himself wondering whether this were not so. But her beauty had come upon him like a moon out of the trees, bringing him the unfailing, fresh experience he associated with her and with no one else—that shock of sweetness which held him in spite of everything. He had said abruptly: "Let's go home."

She had not shrunk from his gaze, nor later from his arms, but her art was not equal to the final deception when he had recognized, with a dull sense of having always known it, that she did not love him.

Now he heard the telephone ringing in the parlor and her voice crisp and clear as she answered it. There was a smell of coffee. In the old days at home they used to breakfast in the kitchen, with Neddy crawling about on the floor. This morning some instinct bade him put on his clothes as if for a journey, and he was glad he did, when he found Regan not only dressed but wearing a hat. She came out of the pantry carrying a coffee pot, which she put on the bridge table between the windows. The table was set with a cloth, his flowers stood in a bowl in the center.

She said gaily: "Neddy and I had our breakfast, and Octavia's taken him to school."

"Why the hat?"

"I must go over to Hester's. She's wretched." He listened while she spoke of her sister's chronic asthma, each attack of which was followed by a psychic depression when the sufferer would permit no one to come near her—no one, that is, except her sister, Regan.

"Did Hester know that I was coming home?"

"Of course, but she can't help these attacks, and I haven't the heart to deny her when she's so ill."

Regan went back to the pantry and returned with toast and an electric egg-boiler. So he was to be abandoned, first by his son and then by his wife, on his first day home. Mark watched her arrange dishes and knives, and he saw that his scrutiny troubled her. He waited till there was nothing more for her to do, then said: "I'm sorry about Hester, but I'd rather not talk about her for a moment, if you don't mind. Do you know what I was planning on the boat coming over, Regan?"

"What?"

"I was planning to go down to the country, to our house, with you and Neddy. It must be perfect there now. I haven't mown a lawn since God knows when!"

She stared at the flowers. "I should have told you. I sold the house."

"You did what?"

"I sold it last year. I should have written you about it. I meant to, but kept putting it off . . . all the tedious details! I didn't want to bother you. But I couldn't bear the place after John Halloran died, and the Severs boy next door. It seemed so desolate. I thought you would probably feel the same way about it."

Mark sat frozenly, thinking that, of course, she had every

right to sell the house. It was hers, left her by her father. But he had been fond of it, and the thought of its being lost left him, for a moment, speechless. Regan said in a controlled voice: "I'd got to hate the place. Everything was different, changed. I could never have gone back there to live."

"A lot of things seem to have changed. I shall have to get used to the idea . . . I'm sorry, though, about the house." Just to speak of it like that, casually, took his breath away. She gave him a swift glance. "It didn't occur to me that you cared for it, particularly. It wasn't beautiful, or even valuable."

No, it was neither beautiful nor valuable, but it was the place where Neddy was born, it was the place Mark had most wanted to come back to after the war. With an effort at calmness, he said: "I don't understand why you didn't tell me, why you have waited till now."

"I should have told you. But I had a chance to sell when real estate was high. I thought I might as well. Do sit down and have your breakfast."

He had risen, now he sat down again and watched her pour his coffee. In the silence which ensued he felt something perilous between them, but when he tried to speak his lips remained obstinate. She was graceful in her little wifely attentions, retrieving his egg from the boiler, fetching him matches. And last night she had lain in his arms, her body responsive to his, her face set in a mask of dislike, her eyes black with protest. In falsehood either the body betrays the spirit or the spirit the body: knowing this, Mark was unable to ignore it, and in his inability to lay the difference between himself and Regan.

He said presently: "There are several things that puzzle me. One is how you happened to go to the wrong pier yesterday."

Here was Regan's chance, another chance, one of the numerous chances presented to her since her arrival at the apartment last evening—her chance to come out with the truth, to extricate herself once and for all from the errors of the past and the hypocrisy of the present. She answered instead: "But I have told you!" and immediately began to tell him all over again, while he broke an egg into a cup and heard at his elbow the steady vibration of rain against the window. Regan's story was simple and brief, but the story which she could not, as yet, bring herself to tell was neither brief nor simple. *That* story began long before yesterday. It began four years ago at the time of Mark's first departure overseas; it began at the moment when she acknowledged to herself how little she missed him, how untrammeled and exhilarating life had become since he went away. If there had been any doubt in her mind, it had vanished during his first leave, but then some vestige of fair play, the thought that this might, after all, be the last time she would see him, had given her the wit to pretend and to send him back to battle happy and reassured. She had the grace to weep a little when she got his first letter. But a month later she met William Symes, and he effectively resolved any doubts which might have disturbed her spirit, if not her head. Regan had wanted to write to Mark and tell him of this development, and to suggest that they get a divorce at the earliest moment, but word reached her that he had been wounded and cited for gallantry. The lovers decided they had better wait. They waited. Mark got another medal and the newspapers carried his picture and the story of his exploits. Friends called on Regan, they praised Mark and praised her for her fortitude. It became more and more difficult to face the truth. Then the war ended and, instead of coming home as he might have done, Mark chose to stay with the Forces of Occupation. In his letter to Regan he explained, with the simplicity she had learned to resent, that he felt it was up to him to remain till his share of the job was complete. The delay infuriated her. She was infatuated with Symes and dreaded the thought that she might lose him.

The interminable year ended, and on the day that Mark was to arrive in New York, she realized, with dismay, that she was totally unprepared to face him. Throughout the preceding day she was consumed with nervous revulsion. What was she going to say? What were the words one used on such an occasion? She was a fool not to have given him some hint of her feelings before this—a fool not to have prepared him for what lay in store. Instead she had written him noncommittal letters filled with details of her life with Neddy, and of her social and civic activities. Now that the moment of decision had arrived she stood in danger of losing her very capable head. The instinct to procrastinate increased with every second. Was it necessary that she go to the pier to meet him? Why bother to fake rapture at the eleventh hour? Why not just let him come back to the apartment alone and talk to Neddy, while she walked in the Park and clarified her own ideas?

Between the moment of arriving at this decision and the moment of putting it into effect she changed her mind half a dozen times. When Neddy pleaded to go with her, she put him off by saying he must stay home and entertain Papa in case she should miss him. But to Octavia Evans she said simply: "I'm going to the pier to meet Colonel Bycroft."

She had walked up Madison Avenue, across Fifth to the Park. There she strolled and sat on a bench for the better part of an hour, trying vainly to get her panic under control. She watched the afternoon light glide down the buildings, and recalled how she had walked here a few weeks before, waiting for Symes, who had just returned from his trip to the Middle East. He was filled with large affairs and surrounded by his usual aura of mystery, but he had brought her a dozen handkerchiefs from Lisbon. Pride in him and jealousy of the work which took him away from her had warred in Regan. Mark *must* give her a divorce, at once. Her anxiety mounted to a fever. She imagined she heard the hollow summons of a ship in the river, and pictured Mark standing at the rail, searching for her among the crowd on the pier. His face formed before her—smiling, eager, and she thought rebelliously: One can't be expected to be faithful when there is no feeling left.

She looked at her watch and saw that she had twenty minutes in which to reach the pier, if she took a cab. But by the time she had gained the street she changed her mind again, and went to a drugstore from where she telephoned her lover.

"Bill? Oh Bill, I can't meet him."

Symes' voice sounded faintly chilling. "He'll be expecting you, Regan. There's no point in building up hostility at the start, is there?"

"But what on earth am I going to say?"

"You must have thought it over."

"Oh God, yes, a thousand times. But it all sounds so feeble."

"You'll find the right words, I know. You're the most mar-
vellously articulate person!" His voice became caressing. "Be
calm, darling. After all, it's not exactly the poor guy's fault,
is it?"

He was thinking of his rival as the distinguished soldier, the
hero, and Regan frowned. "I do wish you'd give me some idea
how to set about telling him."

"I wouldn't tell him anything today. There's no point in rushing it."

"He'll ask questions. He can be terribly shrewd . . ."

"Listen, sweet. Don't be in any hurry. Don't mention us at
all at this stage of the game. Naming names can have bad
psychological consequences. Be conciliatory. Use all your tact."

"But I have got to come out with it sometime, why not do it
right away?"

"Well," his voice took on a slight edge, "tell him anything,
make any excuse, but don't bring my name into it."

"Bill!"

"Darling, try to understand my position. I've got to watch my
step. I can't risk a row and all the inevitable publicity. Nor can
you." The caressing note crept back into his voice. "It's a damned
tragic situation, but you must know how I feel about you,
about us . . ."

They talked for a few minutes in incoherent, passionate mur-
murs, then said goodbye. Reassured, even exalted by this conversation with her lover, Regan glanced once more at her watch.
The boat would have docked by now and Mark be on his way
home. She stepped into the fading sunlight and signalled a cab.

Mark listened to a different story, the story of her journey to the wrong pier, of her fruitless attempt to catch him at the right one, of her grievous disappointment at missing him. When she had finished this second recital, which he had heard once already, he said slowly: "But why, if you were going to the pier to meet me, did you tell Neddy he must stay home to keep me company?"

She had forgotten this. Well, here was the inescapable moment. Mark was looking at her. She temporized: "I lied to Neddy. I had to. I wanted to see you alone."

His voice became formal. "I seem to be rather dense. There are a number of things I find hard to understand. For instance, your selling the house. I'd have expected you to do it differently, somehow. Your taste has always been impeccable."

Was he mocking? She felt a gust of temper. "Listen, Mark. When one is left alone four years, as I was, one learns to make one's own decisions." He remained silent, and she went on quickly: "You must know how time, and separation, bring changes in things . . . in people . . ." she broke off, waiting for some signal that would help her to come out with the statement which she'd spent most of the night composing. But he said nothing, and she began again:

"There must have been decisions which you made yourself, over there. I wouldn't blame you. I'd understand."

"Decisions?"

"Well, changes of feeling, doubts about the past, and about the future. One can't live through four years without something happening to alter one's whole conception of life . . ."

This was very far from the plain statement of fact which she had intended to make, but she had not bargained for his watchful silence, for his refusal to aid her by a question or an accusation. He was letting her do it alone, and she felt that it was deliberate on his part, a sort of revenge for what he must already have guessed was coming. She paused, standing before him in her frivolous summer hat, her linen suit, her air of patient determination. "Surely," she said at last, "surely you didn't expect to come home and find everything exactly what it was when you went away?"

"Not exactly, no."

"Well, then?"

He said irrelevantly: "I was so sick of ruins, of ruined houses, ruined people. I had a craving for something . . . for wholeness, I suppose."

"I don't think I know what you mean."

"No, I don't think you do."

"Wholeness could mean different things to different people."

"It does." He rose and stood before her, and there was something powerful about him, something menacing. "Wholeness, to me, means the past, the present, the future. I admit it's an idea, only. I've never fooled myself it was much else. I've seen it crumble elsewhere. But I hoped that here, at home, for just a little while . . . But you haven't told me what wholeness means to you?"

"You talk about the past, but was *our* past so good? Are you being honest?"

"Are you being honest, Regan?"

"You won't give me a chance."

"Well, I haven't been around to deny you any chances, have I?"

"Nor have I ever denied you yours!" She was on the offensive at last, her voice barely missing shrillness. "Everything is changed, and you might as well accept it. I don't doubt you're changed too. And what is this past you talk about? Our life before the war? Our lives during the war? Four years is a long time. Can't you see?"

He stared at her, his head lowered in a curious, wary attitude. "I think I see. I think I know what you're trying to say, but I'm God damned if I'm going to say it for you."

She came out with it then, a rush of words, not the words she had composed last night, the polished and logical argument which was to have solved everything, clarified everything, which was to have settled, once and for all, lies, discussion, recrimination. Instead she declared loudly that she was through with him; that she doubted whether she had ever really loved him; anyway, four years had changed her feelings towards him; she had found her metier, her separate life, her career. She wanted a divorce, the sooner the better for every one concerned. And she had made all the necessary preparations. She would go and stay with her sister, Hester, leaving Neddy here with his father for a little while, a week perhaps. After that he was at liberty to see the boy whenever he wished—with certain reservations, of course. He was welcome to stay in the apartment until he made other arrangements. She had wanted to tell him this yesterday, but somehow it had proved too difficult. He had taken too much for granted, he hadn't given her an opportunity to speak out.

Besides, she had been unwilling to spoil his first few hours at home, unwilling to wound him. Then there had been Neddy and Octavia, and a scene was out of the question. But now he knew the truth, and there was little more to be said. She was sorry—of course she was sorry. The whole thing was tragic, but perhaps it would have happened anyway, war or no war. The fact remained, it had happened, and that was all there was to it. There was no point in discussing it further. Mark must think things over and try to be reasonable. After all, they were adult people and these matters should be arranged without bitterness. On her side, certainly, there was nothing but the desire to remain friends, and this should not be impossible, for Neddy's sake. And for Neddy's sake, Mark would see that a divorce was the only thing; he must allow her to bring the suit. However, they would discuss the details later on, when he had had time to reflect and to adjust himself to the situation.

Mark heard her out in silence. When she was done he turned and looked out of the window. A procession of umbrellas scuttled along the glistening sidewalk. The noise of the great city was a distant chorus, impersonal and indifferent.

"Well, I'm going, Mark. Octavia will pack my things, and I'll send for them later. She'll take care of you and Neddy for as long as you want to stay. I hope you'll call me up at Hester's. Perhaps we could have lunch together, or dinner, one of these days when we've both had time to take stock."

He turned slowly. "There's another thing I don't understand. Why, considering all this, did you sleep with me last night?"

She had gathered up her gloves, her pocket book, her silk

umbrella; she *became* the room, as though she had called to have her portrait painted in it.

"Why did I? Well, I felt badly. I didn't want to have it on my conscience that I refused you."

"Your conscience?" he repeated, then turned again and leaned against the window, staring at the wet street. Regan waited a moment, then with a shrug of her shoulders she crossed the room and let herself out of the apartment. He saw her a few minutes later, hurrying up the street under her silk umbrella. He was still standing there when the door behind him opened and some one came in. He whirled round, cursing, and found himself staring into the eyes of Octavia Evans.

She said sharply: "Colonel Bycroft, light your pipe!"

"What?" He peered at her. "What did you say?"

"I said for you to light your pipe."

His fingers unclenched and he sought confusedly for his pipe and tobacco. Octavia hung her hat and coat in the closet and began to clear the things from the table—the uneaten egg, the untasted coffee, the cold toast. She said: "Miss Hester is a sick woman. It's got so she's scared of being left alone."

Mark filled his pipe, watching her suspiciously. How much did she know, this black woman with the matter-of-fact manner. She went on: "If Mrs. Bycroft can't fetch Neddy from school today, will you fetch him?"

"Yes, I suppose so."

He heard the rain beating on the windows and thought of it falling in every corner of the city, touching the faces of strangers, touching Regan's warm flesh, falling, perhaps, on her lover. For he had no doubt, no doubt at all that she had a lover.

The sense of total estrangement grew on him, an unreality so profound he feared it might engulf him entirely. He drew a long breath, like the sigh of a dying man, and Octavia, on her way to the kitchen, turned to look at him.

"You won't forget Neddy, Colonel Bycroft?"

He nodded absently. "I won't forget."

8

A FEW days later he wrote to his wife:

"Dear Regan,

I've been considering this whole affair of you and me and Neddy. I am not, as you are, especially good at self-expression, so you'll have to excuse me if this letter seems a bit crude and to the point. From what I recall of our interview on Monday, it seems you no longer wish to live with me, that you want a divorce at the earliest possible moment. No doubt you are better acquainted with the law than I am, but even I know that in this State grounds for divorce is adultery. If I remember correctly it was your idea that I allow you to bring the suit out of consideration for Neddy, whose home should naturally be with his mother, as it naturally could not be if you should be judged the guilty party. You seem to have given the matter your usual lucid consideration but you overlooked two things—first, that I have no wish to divorce you or to be divorced by you, second that I want my son to live with me. There is a third point, though a minor one. I see no reason why you should expect me to connive at a state of affairs from which I am excluded. If you don't want to live with me I see no reason why you can't go on living as you have these past four years without me. A husbandless state may not be the ideal

68

one for a woman of your intelligence and beauty, but no doubt it has its compensations. Neddy, however, remains with me. You must see that there is no reason, moral or legal, why he should not—rather the reverse in fact. Of course, you are welcome to talk to him over the telephone, or to visit him here in my presence. Octavia Evans has my instructions on this matter.

Yours,

MARK."

This letter was the most temperate, the most formal of several which he wrote and destroyed. But the mildness of its language did not reflect his mood, which flamed into rage while he groped for words. When he had put the letter into an envelope and addressed it, he continued to sit at Regan's desk, surrounded by the minutiae of her existence—the existence from which she had banished him for ever, the existence of which he knew so little, suspected so much.

Ransacking the drawers earlier in the day he had found only endless newspaper clippings and a collection of his letters to her from Europe. These last he examined with horror. How could he have been such a fool as to imagine that the future had been up to him alone? He recalled his fatuous remark to young Perry on the boat coming home: "If deception is in order, then I hope to be deceived," or something of the sort. He had not been deceived, not even for one night.

"I didn't want to have it on my conscience that I refused you!"

Her conscience! He shivered, wondering whether certain pas-

sions might, like malaria, infect a man for the remainder of his
life. Her conscience!

Yet last night he had sat in Neddy's room while the child
slept, and had asked himself whether he still loved her, as
earlier he had asked himself whether he loved his son. Passing
from childhood to maturity and marriage do we merely exchange
one imaginary security for another? Sleepless, Mark turned to
a book for consolation and tried to read.

"So here I am, in the middle way, having had twenty years—
Twenty years largely wasted, the years of *l'entre deux guerre*—"

Were the words written for him, or were they written, perhaps, for Neddy? Mark replaced Eliot and found another poet,
one of the French resistance. So Regan read everything, everything. What did it do for her? How did it affect her internal
chemistry, all this indiscriminate reading? Oh, she had taste,
and what taste! *Impeccable*. But the taste of bees was impeccable, likewise the taste of the worm in the heart of an apple.
Yes, Regan had impeccable taste, impeccable ideas, an impeccable conscience. He shut the book and sat thinking. After
all, was it natural that she would let herself suffer in loneliness
and neglect for four years, or four months, or four weeks? Men
found their compensations, as he knew very well; no one blamed
them. Curious but true, old Wilmer's remark that the soldier
facing death thinks mostly of the good screw he'll have the
minute he can get round to it. Are women who face death at
another's remove more delicate? I can see the problem clearly
enough, Mark reflected, but I'll be damned if I can solve it.

Maybe, if I had come back to a country ruined by war, a country physically in pieces like Europe, maybe then I could forgive anything; the plight of all would transcend the plight of one, and forgiveness itself would seem like presumption. And yet what made him so sure that here was something that demanded his forgiveness? All Regan had said was that she was through with him, that she wanted to live her own life—that fabulous *cliché*, prerogative of Americans? She was not one to leave evidence around. Far too fastidious for that, far too clever. Yet the evidence seemed everywhere visible to Mark's jealous eye: in the books she had taken to reading, in the pictures she had bought, in the things which now interested her. All were the signs and signals of a new passion, and he knew that passion forms, that it often directs even the mature and hardened spirit. But why couldn't she be content just to love? Why must she compel beauty, which she did not understand, to state the case for her? Why must she confuse art and conscience with the paraphernalia of sex?

He had fallen asleep with his questions unanswered.

Now he stamped his letter to Regan and went into the parlor where Octavia was dusting the furniture. "I'm going for a walk. I'll pick Neddy up at school on my way back." Already father and son had come to regard this as a fixed habit.

Mark went on: "I might as well tell you, Octavia, that Mrs. Bycroft and I are not on the best of terms. You must have guessed this. It's why she's gone to stay with her sister. I've just written her that she can speak to Neddy on the phone, but I don't want her to see him except when I'm around."

Octavia knelt on the floor, the duster in her hands, and gazed at him.

"What do you want I should do, sir?"

"That's up to you. I'd be glad if you stayed, but go to Mrs. Bycroft if you prefer. Neddy remains with me."

"But will this last? Or given time, will it pass?"

"God knows."

"It's the war," she murmured, nodding her neat head.

"We can't blame everything on the war." To blame the war was to excuse Regan, and he wouldn't have that.

Octavia said obstinately: "Given evil as big as the war, you can't blame it."

"What difference does it make? If people are not equal to things then they're not equal, that's all."

"Who is equal to war? I don't mean the fighting end of it. I mean the living with it, living with the thought of it." She stroked the duster over the leg of a table. "My son Edgar was a sensible boy before he went to the war. He didn't have but just the ordinary amount of bitterness in him. Then he come back from Europe and he's got no use for nobody, not for white folks nor much for blacks either. Nor he hasn't any use at all for his home, for his wife and three little children." She shrugged. "I'm not criticizing. I'm just wondering."

Her voice took the edge off Mark's loneliness. She was a woman, the broad wedding ring bitten deep into her finger, her palms pale and soft from work. There was no servility in her, and for this, too, he was grateful. She went on, absently: "It does seem like everything you hear is a lie."

"Everything?"

"Most everything. Edgar can't seem to tell the truth since he got home. And he acts proud and bitter to cover up the lies . . . and to cover up the truth that's there, I don't doubt. He says there isn't a single decent white person in the world. Not one he'll trust round the corner. I know it makes him feel good to think that way, and he needs to feel good."

Mark remained silent, and she asked suddenly: "You ever stop to think how hate has taken the place of love in everything, Colonel? In people, in religion?"

"Well," said Mark, "hate doesn't demand so much of one, here," and he tapped his forehead.

"Nor here," said Octavia, and laid her hand on her heart. She added: "I'll stay with you and Neddy."

Mark thanked her and went out to mail his letter. Outdoors the rejoicing sunlight mocked him. His sense of outrage returned as he found a mailbox and dropped the letter in it with a vicious snap of the lid. Well, Regan would not get away with her beautifully contrived little plans. Let her scheme and rage as she liked, he would go on living in the apartment and he would hold on to Neddy. She could go to Reno and try to get her divorce there, or she could go to Hades and take her anonymous prancing gigolo with her.

Miserable, brooding, Mark walked down Madison Avenue, and his embittered expression lingered in the memories of strangers. Two soldiers in uniform saluted, and he lifted his hand mechanically in response. He began to think about his impending discharge from the army, and about the future. The simple, straightforward ambitions of which he had dreamed struck him now as being idiotically naïve. Run for mayor of his home town, would he? Well, he had no home town, nor even a home. He could count on a little money, enough to tide himself and Neddy over the next year or two. Perhaps his old publishing firm would take him in. When he left them five years ago old Carter had assured him that they would be happy to welcome him back. He'd have to call on old Carter . . .

He thought shudderingly of old friends, of the explanations, the excuses he would have to furnish the inquisitive, and of the pitying silence of the observant. Well, there were some who were not alive to ask questions. Tom Nesbit for instance, Alan Severs, John Holloran, all were dead. He wondered about those who had survived. Were their wives faithful? Did they still have homes, and children they could talk to, as he seemed, as yet, unable to talk to Neddy?

"I'm thirty-three," he reminded himself, frowning, and gasped as a racing taxi missed him by inches. The frightened scream of a woman who saw how close he had come to disaster rang in Mark's ears for a whole block. He gave himself a shake and walked soberly on towards Gramercy Park. Perhaps the sense of estrangement would pass and he'd find himself reconciled and at peace. At forty-three he would be old, unless he got himself killed by a taxi or stepped on by a horse. He watched the shiny buttocks of one ridden by a policeman, clopping along the pavement, and remembered another horse which lay on its back in a German street, maggots crawling in and out of its eyes. Quickly, his gaze travelled upward to the pale channel of sky, to the vertical tiers of masonry; and presently these physical objects—cabs, buses, horses, policemen, the dazzling windows, all lost their strangeness and sank into the pattern of familiar things. For days he had walked the city, marking its changes since his youth. It seemed as if the architecture and character of the place transformed themselves while one slept. In Europe, centuries had plunged into the pit, but not even an echo of that fall penetrated these bright canyons where the past lingered in strange and fearful innocence. His own hopes for some sort of permanence, shored up by dreams of home, trembled in the ephemeral light. He peered through the railings of Gramercy Park. Here, too, the past lingered beside the statue of Edwin Booth, under the willow trees and among the ornamental urns, and favored children played among the flower beds. He must bring Neddy and show him the house where Neddy's father was born, that house on the corner, worn brick with an iron buffalo head for door knocker. A succession of nursemaids had lifted him so he could touch that knocker; finally he'd been able to reach it himself, and just about that time the house was sold and his parents took him away to the country.

As Mark stood gazing at his old home, the heavy oak door opened and two attendants appeared, manipulating a wheelchair in which sat an ancient figure, like a caddisworm swathed in shawls. With a shock he recognized Mrs. Halloran, the grandmother of his friend killed in the war. The wheelchair, pushed by one of the attendants, passed Mark. He bowed. Unresponsive, lightless eyes—the eyes of the very old, of the forgetful, the forgotten, peered for a moment into his. So she lived here now in the house where he and her grandson had played as children. Mark turned and walked back as he had come, along the Park railings, thinking of the dead boy. Halloran had died at the beginning of the war, at El Guettar, and was buried in the African sand. Mark stopped and gazed for a minute at the willow which he and Halloran had been forbidden to climb. It rose glittering and formal out of the well-kept grass, and a child leaned against it, watching his friends playing nearby.

9

NEDDY APPEARED to accept the situation with a peculiar resignation. He was a self-contained child, and to his father's terse explanation of Regan's absence—Mother had gone to stay with Aunt Hester, who was ill—he merely nodded and returned to his own small affairs. Mark wondered whether he should tell him the truth, but shrank from inflicting such a shock on the unfathomed childish mind. It was obvious that Neddy was used to being left more or less to his own devices. Did he miss his mother? How much did he know, how much had he seen? The grave and mysterious eyes gave Mark no clue. There were moods when he seemed to come close to Mark, and then they frolicked together, but as suddenly as he came to life Neddy would retreat again, and Mark thought in despair: I shall never really understand him!

Coming home one day from the Zoo, they sauntered for a little down Fifth Avenue. Mark felt a sudden tug at his fingers and looked down in time to intercept a smile, a glance of recognition. It vanished at once, and the recipient, whoever he was, vanished also into the streaming afternoon crowd.

"See some one you know?" Mark asked, and after a slight hesitation Neddy replied: "Mr. Symes."

"Why didn't you speak to him?"

Neddy made no answer, and stopped at a window filled with

knives. Mark released his hand and lighted a pipe. "Was it the Mr. Symes who helped you choose that picture for your mother's birthday?"

"What?"

Mark repeated the question while Neddy pressed his nose against the shop window. "Yes," said Neddy. "Bill Symes and Mrs. Leighton."

"Mrs. Leighton? You told me it was Mr. Symes who helped you choose the picture."

"Mr. Symes and Mrs. Leighton. Will you buy me that penknife?"

"I'll give you one I have at home."

They walked on and Mark thought: What a fool I am! Regan has scores of friends. What do I care whether the favorite is named Symes or Grimes? What the hell difference can it make to me?

But he was disturbed by the incident, for it seemed to him suddenly as though not only his own son but the whole universe was leagued against him. He signalled a cab and they drove home. Octavia let them in. "Lieutenant Perry and Mrs. Perry are here to see you."

They rose from the two corners of the sofa, and Perry bounded towards him like a welcoming dog. "The maid told us you'd be in shortly, so we thought we'd wait. We had hoped to find Mrs. Bycroft too, but the maid said she was nursing a sick sister." Still clutching Mark's hand he turned to his wife. "This is Lucy."

Mark affected a cordiality he did not feel. Thank God, Octavia had spared him the embarrassment of having to explain

Regan's absence. He asked his visitors to be seated while he went in search of whisky and glasses. Perry followed him into the pantry. "Colonel Bycroft, it's so good to see you! I hope you don't mind our dropping in like this? I was keen to have you meet Lucy."

"I'm sorry you will miss Regan," said Mark. He arranged the glasses on a tray, avoiding Perry's fatuous gaze.

"There is something I want to tell you, Colonel. You were dead right!"

"Eh?" he muttered unhappily.

"You remember on the boat coming over you gave me a bit of advice about keeping my mouth shut? Well, I've kept it shut. Lucy's marvellous, but she's got a rigid code of morals, and if I'd told her about that girl in Belgium . . . if I'd come out with it as I half thought I ought to, I'd have bitched everything. I don't think Lucy'd ever have gotten over it. I can't thank you enough."

"That's O.K.," said Mark. How could he ever have thought of this amiable puppy as anything except a bore? He set the whisky bottle on the tray with the glasses, and Octavia appeared carrying the ice pail. "Mrs. Bycroft called you, Colonel. I told her you and Neddy would be back later, and she said she might call again."

"Thanks, Octavia." His hands shook as he picked up the tray.

In the parlor Mrs. Perry and Neddy were standing in contemplation of the Braque.

"I say it's upside down and Neddy says I'm wrong." She gazed at Mark with carplike eyes. "Am I wrong?"

"I'm afraid you are."

Neddy turned away. "Any one can see it's right side up." He looked at his father. "You said you'd give me a penknife."

"You'll find it on the mantelpiece in the other room. See you don't cut yourself." The boy ran out of the room, and Mark poured the drinks. He lifted his glass to the Perrys. "Here's luck!"

Lucy sipped her whisky and made a face like a child's. "Ugh, it's strong. May I have some water?" Mark watched her with amusement. She was, he supposed, about twenty-three but gave an impression of adolescence.

"Colonel Bycroft, Neddy told me he chose that painting himself to give his mother for a present. Is that right?"

"I think he probably had some assistance."

"That explains it. It seems like such a sophisticated sort of thing for a child to have picked out by himself." She continued with animation: "I do wish Mrs. Bycroft was here. I admire her immensely."

"Then you know my wife?"

"Oh no, but I heard her talk last year. She has the best taste in clothes!"

"Impeccable," agreed Mark.

"And I suppose when you're clever, as she is, you're bound to have a queer streak or two."

"Lucy!"

"Don't be a dope, honey. Colonel Bycroft knows what I mean."

"Sure," said Mark, laughing. "You're referring to my wife's taste in pictures. Well, cleverness is a kind of queerness, when you stop and think of it."

"That's not what I mean. I mean when one is really clever, like Mrs. Bycroft, one is entitled to one's own ideas about art and things of that sort."

"We live in a clever age," said Mark amiably. "What with the atom, and everything."

"Mrs. Bycroft is not only clever, she's *good*. Look how she loves people! All kinds of people. That takes character; you know it does. I'd like to love all kinds of people myself; I try to! But I guess I'm not like Mrs. Bycroft. I haven't got her sincerity."

"You seem to know a lot about her," said Mark. "I wish she were here to listen to you. It might embarrass her, though, to find herself in the presence of such an ardent admirer."

"Why should it? Don't you admire her?"

"Naturally."

"When your maid told us that Mrs. Bycroft had gone to nurse her sister, I said to Sam: 'That's what I'd expect of her! Here's her husband just returned from Europe, but does she hesitate when it's a question of someone's welfare? Not she!' "

Mark's smile was glued to his face. Lucy went on earnestly: "And it's not the sentimental kind of goodness either. You can tell that just by seeing her once, as I have. She has a real sense of proportion. Listening to her talk I thought to myself: That woman would never make a muddle out of anything. She would always know exactly what to do and she'd go ahead and do it."

She's right, he thought. Regan would never make a muddle out of anything. She has always known exactly what to do and has gone ahead and done it. That's Regan for you—a biographical note adduced by one who had seen her just once! Nothing, nothing must stand in Regan's way. Possessions, those insidious reminders of a previous allegiance, were quietly discarded; nor was she apt to quibble over the sale of her own home. The disasters of war would not cramp her style, for the tide which had obliterated half the world had served merely to carry her in triumph nearer her self-appointed goal.

Mark said presently that he hoped the Perrys would be staying in New York long enough to meet his wife. "We must fix up something. Dinner, cocktails? I'm sure Regan will arrange it, the minute her sister can spare her."

They beamed. "We shall be here a couple of weeks. Sam wants to stay for some sort of banquet. Tell Colonel Bycroft about it, honey."

"Will you come, Colonel? It's to be at the Rotterdam Hotel, the end of next week, in honor of General Wilmer. A sort of farewell. There'll be a lot of the old outfit present, and God knows when we shall meet again." He looked wistfully at Mark. "It actually gives me a pang . . ."

God, thought Mark. I knew it. Reunions!

He shook his head. "I always hated Wilmer."

"So did most of us, but you should see him now. The old boy looks about a hundred. Now the shooting's over he feels he has nothing left to live for. Told me so himself. Practically wept on my shoulder, didn't he, Lucy?"

"Sweet old man," said Lucy, nodding.

"And he was damned touched to hear we were giving him a farewell party. He asked especially for you."

Mark allowed himself to be persuaded. After all, he could

always get out of it at the last moment. "All right, put me down for a plate. The Rotterdam, you said. When?"

"We haven't fixed a date. I'll call you up."

Mark said that would be fine, and they went on to talk of other things. Perry was full of plans for the future. The minute he got his discharge from the army he and Lucy were going to his father's ranch in Texas. Mark listened while the pair rhapsodized over the steers they would raise, the children they would have, the friends who must come to visit them. They charmed him into sharing their absurd vision of golden dust and violet hills and the beryl waters of the Pecos. He felt that a guitar was all that was needed to complete the picture.

The telephone rang and it was Regan. "Mark? I got your letter."

He stood beside the windows at the far end of the room and held the receiver close to his ear, hoping her voice would not carry to his guests. They murmured tactfully and tinkled the ice in their glasses, but to Mark it seemed as if her voice must be ringing in every corner. "Mark, I never would have believed that you could be so vindictive!"

He said stiffly: "I'm sorry."

"For heaven's sake, are we children? Surely there's some way of working this thing out decently and calmly. Can you give me a rational reason why we can't?"

"Do you mind if we go into this later? I have guests."

"Then I'll call you tomorrow. We've simply got to meet and discuss everything like adult beings."

"Would you care to talk to Neddy?"

"Not now. I'm too upset. Your letter was horrible."

"How is Hester?"

He heard her angry laugh. "As if you gave a damn about Hester!"

He hung up and came back to his seat. "Sorry for the interruption. How about another drink?"

But they rose. "We must dash." Perry gripped his hand. "I'll call you up about that banquet."

Lucy turned her absurd gaze upon him. "And perhaps while you and Sam are entertaining the General, Mrs. Bycroft and I might have dinner together. I'll write her a note."

"That would be very kind of you."

He accompanied them to the door and waited with a fixed smile until they had disappeared down the staircase. Back in the parlor Octavia was clearing away the glasses. He said roughly: "Leave mine! I want a drink."

When she had gone he felt ashamed of his brusqueness, ashamed of the whole ignominious role he had elected to play this afternoon. Oh, he'd make Regan pay for this, he'd make her pay if it took the rest of his life to do it.

The doorbell rang, and when he went to open it he found Perry standing in the hall, alone. The young man seized his arms. "Mark, forgive me . . . I couldn't help hearing something over the phone, and then I saw your face. I couldn't go away without asking whether there was something . . . anything . . ."

"Where's Lucy?"

"I told her to wait for me outside." He stared at Mark. "Something is wrong, isn't it?"

"I should have explained at once. My wife has left me."

It sounded, somehow, less tragic than ludicrous, but he was not prepared for the effect of the simple statement on young Perry. His eyes widened, he clasped Mark in his arms. "I guessed it!"

Mark released himself gently. "It's all right, kid. The heavens are not going to fall. You better run along to Lucy. Convey my apologies."

"Your apologies? How could your wife have done it? How could any woman? Doesn't she know the kind of guy you are?"

He went away at last and Mark returned to the parlor. There he found Neddy sharpening a pencil with the penknife. "It's sharp," said Neddy, with satisfaction. "It's almost as sharp as a razor."

"You be careful," Mark warned him, and added inconsequentially: "That's a German knife." He had picked it up on a battlefield, and it was the only souvenir he had brought home. Neddy gazed intently at the knife. "Did it belong to a German?"

"Yes."

"Did he die?"

"Yes."

"Did you kill him?"

"Yes," said Mark.

10

MIRIAM SPARROW strolled along Fifth Avenue in the spring sunshine, enjoying the weather and studying her reflection in the store windows. She smiled impartially at the youths and maidens who passed her, and at a dowager with corrugated visage, leading a dachshund on a silver chain. Miriam's thoughts were alternately anticipatory and reflective; she enjoyed the sense of peace as she saw it mirrored in the imperturbable American scene. Once more the future had become—or was in process of becoming—private property, and battle the personal concern of individuals. This morning at breakfast Dick had said: "It begins to look as if we'd banked too much on—what shall I call them?—the imponderables. Symes tells me that Colonel Bycroft has returned from overseas and that he flatly refuses to consider a divorce."

"Whose move is it now?"

Dick frowned uneasily. "Ours, I suppose. But it's got to be a cautious one. Bycroft has too much on his side."

But Miriam's thoughts were elsewhere. "Does this mean you won't be able to lunch with Stella and me?"

"I'm afraid I can't. I've got to see Symes. He's in a state, though of course he won't admit it."

"Scared of the gallant colonel, h'm?"

"Not personally, no. But you know how he feels about scandal."

"Well, we'll have to get along without you." She gazed at him with an absent-minded air. "I'm so anxious to see Stella. I wonder whether Italy will have made any difference."

"Well, give her my love."

Stella had telephoned the evening before and they had arranged to meet near the Plaza before lunch next day. Walking up Fifth Avenue to meet her friend, Miriam reflected: "The trip to Italy *must* have made a difference. Maybe I have a melodramatic mind, as Dick tells me. But what was the purpose of her journey if she herself hadn't some idea that it would make a difference? She forced herself to go . . . and that took courage, considering everything. Considering Stella . . ."

Crossing the street towards the Plaza, Miriam caught sight of Stella waiting on the opposite corner. Both waved. They greeted each other affectionately, then walked arm-in-arm towards the Zoo.

"Dick couldn't come," Miriam explained, breaking the ice with trivialities. "He sent you his love." She glanced at her friend. "It's good to see you. How was your trip? Was it warm in Italy when you left?"

Stella's appearance troubled her. Dressed in a nondescript fashion, without make-up or any incentive to beauty, she inspired Miriam with the old impatient pity and dread.

"The violets were gone, but the chestnut trees were in bloom." As Stella spoke she smelled the white flowers of the chestnut and heard the voice of Guido Vitelli exclaiming in bewilderment: "The train for Rome? Sure, it leaves a little after six. But you've only been here a day."

The leaves in Central Park quivered in the breeze, and

Miriam said: "It's too early for lunch. Let's sit down and talk."

They found an untenanted bench. "So you came by ship. How was it, better than flying?"

Stella replied that the voyage home had been uneventful, and as Miriam listened to the familiar voice she tried to penetrate its listlessness, to surprise something unusual in its utterance, but it told her nothing. Why wouldn't Stella speak openly of her visit to the Italian town where Alec had died? She had not even written her friends. With so much to confide, all one got now was a dull catalogue of descriptions . . . the hunger of the Italian people, the rags of the children, the kind of clothes women wore in Lisbon, the smell of chestnut flowers! And I was Alec's cousin, his friend, thought Miriam, resentfully. Surely I have some right to know. "Let's walk," she said abruptly. "It's chilly when one sits down."

They walked beside the brightening grass where men and girls were sitting. Miriam reflected with increasing bitterness: We know each other too well for this absurd reticence. Why won't she say something? She must know that I'd want to hear about Montescari. Alec belonged to all of us in different ways, and she has no right to monopolize his last memory, or to exclude us from that final experience. As her jealous grievance intensified, it assumed the guise of a selfless responsibility. Why in God's name didn't Stella pay some attention to her looks? How Alec would have hated this apathy, this dullness! He had always despised the trappings of grief.

The silence became unendurable, and Miriam said: "I had a letter from Myrtle Anderson, from Jarley. She said she had

written you but that you never answered her letters, not even
the one in which she told you about James' home-coming and
his wounds."

"I know. I meant to write, but I found it too difficult."

"She spoke of your house, said it was in bad shape. The roof
leaks, the walls are stained with water, the floors need attention. And the road, she says, is full of holes, the culvert washed
out, weeds everywhere." She looked accusingly at Stella.
"Myrtle says that another year of neglect, and the whole place
will fall to pieces."

Stella stared at the rich light fingering the leaves, at the gay
summer figures. A child hurled a scarlet ball, a young sailor fed
squirrels peanuts from a paper bag.

Miriam continued doggedly: "Myrtle wrote that the house
seemed to breathe of Alec, that she expected any moment
the door would open and he would come running out. It was
hard for her and James to believe that he was dead."

"How do we know that he is dead?"

The scarlet ball spun through the air, and the sailor, over-
hearing Stella's words, looked at her curiously. Miriam said:
"Myrtle Anderson's letter reminded me how much Alec cared
about things. Nothing was commonplace in his eyes."

"Then why doesn't he come back?"

"Stella . . ."

"Why doesn't he come back?"

Miriam gazed at her; it seemed now as if a perverse sequence
had reversed a normal trend, that the future, not the past,
was imposing itself on Stella's features. What finally revealed
itself, frighteningly, fleetingly, was the face of age itself—age

grown cynical, age defrauded, peering through a living mask into the present. Then the lips quivered and Stella said: "Miriam, can't *you* tell me why he doesn't come back?"

It was the eternal echo, and it silenced Miriam, making her happier convictions wither as if autumn, not spring, had touched them with a pitiless finger. Arm and arm, though strangely divided, she and Stella walked till they stood beside the little pond, where they paused and watched a toy sailboat move across the water. "He's not coming back. You know it as well as I do."

"We never saw him die. How can we say some one is dead when we don't know?"

"But my dear! It's true."

"Death can be a sort of absence, can't it? Going on for a long time, then ending at last and the dead returning. As long as we don't give up believing . . . expecting."

"Alec couldn't have borne to hear you talk like this."

"It was he who told me never to believe he was dead."

"But that was not what he meant!"

"Yes, he meant it."

Miriam's eyes filled with tears. "You went to Italy. You found him there."

"That was not Alec."

"It was Alec, Stella!"

"One of those thousands of crosses? No, Alec was not there. I know."

Miriam thought desperately: something has happened, and she must tell me. I've got to make her tell me. "Listen, Stella, you went to Montescari, you saw the place, the buildings, the fields, the roads where he walked. The place where he died. You saw his grave." Her voice slipped from her control, and Stella turned to gaze at her. "You're mistaken, Miriam. I did go to Montescari and I saw the places he must have seen, the houses, the hills, the people. But he wasn't there. He was not one of those dead white things marching . . . marching . . ."

"But Stella, if he was not, then you'd know. Life doesn't hide itself for ever. You'd know if Alec were living now."

"I know that he was not at Montescari."

Miriam gripped her arm. "Look at me!" she said harshly. "Look at me, Stella! Did you go to Montescari?"

Stella averted her face.

"Stella, answer me."

"Yes, I went to Montescari. Of course I went to Montescari."

"And you found his grave?"

She was silent, and Miriam shook her arm. "You must tell me!"

"I didn't find him."

"What? But you had all the information from Washington . . . from the registration bureau. You must . . ."

"I didn't find him."

Understanding dawned on Miriam. She said slowly: "You mean you didn't intend to." Then, sternly: "You mean you ran away . . . you turned your back—again!"

Stella made no reply, and for several minutes the two women stood watching the toy boat as it veered before the wind. The murmur of the city reached them, its shining ramparts rose above the green of the Park, the tallest shafts standing in a gesture of supreme indifference against the spring sky.

11

DICK SPARROW met his client in a shabby restaurant in the
West Forties. It was one of those places which he had learned to
associate with William Symes—faded awnings and flowerpots
outside, inside a smell of garlic and sour wine. It would be
crowded, stuffy, and remote from the formal exigencies of
Symes' public life. One of these days, thought Dick as he
stooped to enter the narrow door, one of these days I'm going
to make him take me to the Ritz, where he can introduce me
to his important friends. What the hell! Do I always have to
meet him for garlic soup in one of these dives?

Symes was waiting for him in the tiny entry. "Dick! I've got
a table, and Regan is here. We decided it was about time you
and she met, since you'll have plenty to talk about sooner or
later."

Dick said he was delighted to meet Mrs. Bycroft, whom he
had seen at a distance. Symes' reluctance to bring about a meeting was, he had felt sure, due to a characteristic mixture of
embarrassment and caution. Dick could imagine him commun-
ing with himself and deciding that it simply would not do for
the three of them to be seen together and he wondered what
could have occurred to make Symes change his mind.

Regan greeted him with her charming smile. She's even
better looking than I realized, thought Dick, and sat down with
a pleasant sense of anticipation. Despite the stifling heat, the

crowd, the smells, Regan radiated a wonderful air of freshness and elegance. Dick noticed her intense self-consciousness and the agitation which lurked just beneath the surface. He saw too that she was in love, and that she did not share her lover's nervous propensity for concealment, for when Symes seated himself beside her she immediately took his hand.

"I've asked Bill again and again to bring you to lunch, Mr. Sparrow, and now at last he's gotten round to it." She looked at Symes. "Tell me, darling, why do you always insist that we eat in these loathsome joints?"

"Do you really mind? The food is very good and the liquor isn't too bad."

Dick knew that the food would be mediocre and the liquor would be liquor. *I wish he'd remember how often he repeats that line, or that he'd content himself with admitting that he likes to eat in dives because they're good places to hide in when one is in the company of one's mistress and a fairly well-known divorce lawyer.*

Regan gave Dick an amused look. "Bill's such a coward! He's afraid some one respectable will see us together before we're properly married. I'm surprised you don't wear a false beard and smoked glasses on these occasions, darling!"

"Or a cloak and dagger," suggested Dick, liking her spirit.

"Regan's talking nonsense," Symes protested. He assumed a genial air. "I suppose I am inherently decorous, though I try not to be. One's upbringing has a way of sticking, and mine was horribly strict."

"Strict! They practically kept you in a strait-jacket, didn't they, my poor sweet?"

"I was a difficult child, in addition to being an only one."

The words were followed by an uneasy pause, and Dick thought of Regan's son, Neddy. Thus, in a single unpremeditated step, all three were drawn closer to the subject uppermost in their minds. It was left to Regan to broach it, and she did so with a directness which usually manages to conceal more than it reveals.

"Well," she began, "I have no intention of putting a straitjacket on *my* son, nor do I intend to let any one else do it." She glanced at Dick. "Bill has told you about my little boy, Mr. Sparrow?"

Dick nodded, and Symes gazed at the tablecloth.

Regan continued: "I can see that I have a fight on my hands, but I've got to go through with it for Neddy's sake. It's quite evident that he cannot be left indefinitely in his father's care."

"Just a minute," Symes interrupted. "Let's order lunch, then we won't have the waiter hanging round listening." He intercepted a waiter, who took their order and departed. "Sorry, darling. Now, perhaps you'd better tell Dick everything from the beginning."

Regan shrugged. "My husband is behaving inexcusably— I mean it, inexcusably! I expected he'd be hurt and angry—I was prepared for that. But I did think that he would accept the inevitable and that he would behave . . . well, like a gentleman." She laughed bitterly. "He has always seemed to me to be a man of unusual delicacy of feeling. When, in the past, situations like this arose between our friends, Mark was always sensible and broad-minded—often more so than I. Of course, one's point of view changes when one faces such problems oneself, but I confess I never bargained for Mark's attitude. For his down-right *brutality!*"

Dick murmured something about the effect of war on a man's nervous system, and she nodded. "Of course I appreciate that. As I say, I expected difficulties. But I did not expect brutality." She turned magnificent eyes upon Dick. "Mr. Sparrow, Mark won't allow me to see my child!"

"But I gathered from Bill that Colonel Bycroft had no objection to your seeing Neddy, or to your talking to him over the phone."

"That was in the beginning, when he wrote me a hateful letter. Since then I've called up the apartment—my apartment, mind you!—It's in my name and I pay the rent!—I've called up, and Mark always answers, or Octavia does, and it seems obvious to me that Mark has somehow influenced her in his favor. Bribed her, probably. Between them they frustrate every move I make to see Neddy. I've had just one little conversation with him, and it almost broke my heart. Since then, whenever I call up to say I'd like to come to the apartment I'm told that Neddy is out." Her voice trembled. "Of course I could go to the school and see him there, but I'd rather not risk it, for I have no idea what Mark may have said to the teachers, how much he may have poisoned their minds against me. Last night I called again, and Mark told me Neddy was asleep. He added that on second thoughts he did not care for me to see the child. He said . . ." She flushed. "He said he was not at all sure that he approved of my influence. And he hinted that he didn't approve of my friends, either. Meaning of, course, just one thing."

"Then you think he knows about Bill?"

Symes said quickly: "How could he? You and Regan's sister, Hester, are the only people in our confidence."

Dick reflected that although he was often in the company of people who knew Symes, he had never heard them speculate unkindly about the man's private life, nor could he recall hearing anything to the discredit of Mrs. Bycroft. One had to concede that outwardly, at least, the pair had behaved themselves. That they could be lovers for two years and the fact remain undetected in an inquisitive and loose-mouthed society was, in the lawyer's sardonic opinion, a feat nothing short of miraculous.

"What about Neddy? Does he know anything, suspect anything?"

Regan shook her head. "He's only six! And naturally, I've told him nothing, nor allowed him the slightest glimpse into this part of my life."

"But he knows Bill?"

"Certainly, but whenever they meet it is in the company of other friends."

"I see. You don't mind if I ask a few more questions? It's important that I understand the situation. You say you're quite sure Neddy has never intercepted any signal between you? Children can be very observant, you know."

"Not a chance of it," declared Symes. "Neddy knows me merely as one of his mother's friends. I've taken him shopping, and to the Zoo, and that sort of thing, but I've always invited some one else to come along, another child or some woman, so that Neddy's associations with me would not appear too concentrated." He hesitated, frowning. "I wonder, though, whether I made a mistake the other day. I was walking up Fifth Avenue and met Neddy with his father. It was at an intersection and there was a crowd waiting to cross the street. Neddy saw me and for a minute it looked as if he would run to greet me. I acted instinctively, out of surprise, and I suppose out of embarrassment, and passed them pretending I had not seen them." He looked anxiously at Dick. "Regan thinks I may have made a psychological mistake, and that it would have been better to have stopped and spoken to the child."

"You've never met Colonel Bycroft?"

"That afternoon was the first time I had set eyes on him."

"Did he see you?"

"I'd say no, but I can't be sure."

Dick shrugged. "Well, I can't see that it's important. The only reason for your keeping out of the way, at the present time, is that we can't be sure of the Colonel's reactions, and we don't want any unpleasantness. Isn't that just about it?"

Symes gave an uneasy laugh. "We certainly don't want any unpleasantness. At any rate Regan and I don't. But making all due allowance for the man's injured pride, it does seem as if this affair could be settled without . . . without vulgarity."

Dick repressed a smile. "He'd be superhuman if he didn't harbor some resentment!"

Regan objected sharply: "I don't see why he should! He knows I have no intention of living with him. He has no idea that I'm in love with any one else, or that I plan to marry again. He knows that Neddy's place must be with me, and that Neddy must be protected from scandal. He knows that a child, especially a boy, will forgive his father on a question like this, but that he will never forgive his mother. When I ask Mark to let me bring the suit, he knows it's only because I'm considering Neddy. However, I doubt whether Mark cares much for Neddy or for me. He is acting out of wounded pride, in the spirit of revenge. I'm sick to death of all these stories we hear, and have heard, about the effect of their wives' infidelity on soldiers. One would suppose the war was wholly to blame, when the chances are that many marriages would have gone on the rocks, war or no war. And what about the men? Do you mean to tell me that *their* morals have been so exemplary?" She finished on a metallic note: "All these hurt feelings, these accusations, the outraged virtue and all the rest of it. Blackmail, that's all. Men using war, and their medals and their wounds and their breakdowns, for blackmail! The fact remains that when men and women are through with each other, they're through, and that's all there is to it."

The waiter brought them another round of cocktails, and Dick asked Regan how far she thought she could trust the Negro maid, Octavia Evans. "I don't have to trust her. She knows no more about my affairs than Neddy does."

Dick felt a twinge of pity for Mark Bycroft. Regan's beauty struck him now as something cold; he guessed that in certain men such beauty might excite the instinct of Midas, for she was like gold. He thought he could understand, too, how a young and exceptionally sensitive man could also fall under her spell, for her charm was as insidious as any precious metal can be.

As the liquor moved through their veins it served the purpose for which it was intended, erasing the barriers which exist between people who do not know each other well, easing communication and disguising emotion behind a pleasant, equivocal haze. To Regan, Dick advised patience. "You must give your husband time—time to get used to the idea, time to realize that your decision is irrevocable. No man can live in a temper for ever, and if you're patient he may come round to seeing things your way sooner than you imagine."

"I've waited two years. I just wish there were a quicker way . . ."

Symes interposed hurriedly: "Dick has the right idea. You must remember that we cannot afford to be put in the wrong. Isn't that right, Dick?"

"Dead right," agreed Dick. A din of people eating and drinking rose about them. At the next table a young man drunk on beer was exclaiming loudly: "That's just a lot of ——! I've been out of a job a whole year. Low wages or no wages, that's their ticket. That's what I fought for. Low wages or no wages just so some bastards can keep up *their* standards of living. I'm telling you that's the ticket. It's what we fought for, and don't let them fool you otherwise. It's what they're going to ask us to fight for again. You'll see. They'll sick us on the Russkies next. Why? Because there ain't anybody else to sick us on. Because why? Because it's what always happens, see?"

A waiter approached and tapped the speaker primly on the shoulder. His voice subsided into a grumble as his friends began to argue with him in low voices.

Dick said: "Hold on for a few months and see what happens. After all, he's human! Anything might happen."

Regan looked at him narrowly. "What do you mean, any-thing?"

"Well, it's just conceivable that he might get tired of living alone."

She frowned. "Yes, he might. He's very . . ." she hesitated. "He's very much of a man. In that case, we'd have something to bargain on, wouldn't we? I mean, if he were to put himself in the wrong?"

"There's always that chance," said Dick, and lifted his glass. "Here's hoping."

Her face glowed like some brilliant artificial flower. He noticed the exquisite line of her shoulders, the firm and delicate texture of her skin, and felt his impartiality crumble somewhat.

The argument at the next table had started again. "All right, all right, then there won't be no more wars. But if a suitcase full of atomic bombs was to go off in a Moscow subway, what'd you call that? And if another suitcase was to go off in Grand Central, what'd you call that?"

Two waiters squeezed between the tables and bent over the speaker, who had begun to shout. Once more his voice sank to a grumble, and Regan looked reproachfully at Symes. "Darling, what do you say that next time we eat somewhere else?"

12

LATE THAT afternoon Symes went to Washington and Regan accompanied him to Penn Station to see him off. These partings had become, for her, an unbearable nervous strain. Waiting beside him for the gates to open she talked calmly enough, but her eyes were restless, and her hand kept seeking his.

She said: "I think Dick Sparrow is a good person to have on our side. I'm glad he is your friend. If any one can help us out of this hole, he can."

Symes' glance had travelled rapidly over the crowd at the gate; there seemed to be no one he knew, and he began to relax. He had thought it unwise for Regan to come to the station, but she insisted and he saw that in her present mood she was not to be denied. More and more as time went on, these moods seemed to prevail and he found himself remembering his mother, the implacable woman he had loved with a frightened and helpless passion.

"Dick's fine. I trust him. Anyway there's not much we can do except follow his advice."

"It means waiting."

"Well, we're used to waiting, aren't we? And maybe it won't be for much longer. I can't believe that Mark . . ."

They sauntered to and fro on the edge of the crowd, under a blare of loudspeakers and the hollow roar of the great terminal.

Regan listened to phrases worn smooth by repetition, knowing well enough that she never would get used to waiting, that the delay might last much longer than either of them dared to contemplate. She murmured suddenly: "You do love me, don't you?"

"Regan!"

"I know I'm a fool, but the thought of losing you . . ."

"Silly."

"Bill, why not make a clean breast of it and let Mark bring the suit?"

He stared at her incredulously. "Are you crazy? Have you any idea what a smart lawyer could do to us if we tried such a thing? Besides," he added, "Mark might not come across. Don't you see, he has all the cards?"

This fact, grim and inexorable, dimmed for a moment her view of the hideous amphitheatre were they resumed their walk in company with the milling, anonymous horde. Symes pressed her arm against his. He had one cure for his own ennui at such moments, and that was to visualize her in bed. "Regan, I'll be home Thursday. Meet me, will you?"

An inexplicable hostility died at once. "Bill, darling, darling . . ."

"There go the damned gates. I won't kiss you."

"Yes, kiss me."

The crowd sucked them in its undertow toward the gates. Symes drew her to him and kissed her hastily. "Thursday, remember!"

"Thursday!" She let him go. At the gate he twisted round and she saw his harassed face, heard him cry above the tidal wave of bodies: "Not Thursday! I forgot . . . Going to that dinner for General Wilmer!"

Then he disappeared, his brown suit lost among other brown suits, his straw hat among all the other hats. She lingered a moment, thinking: "I could get on the train with him and go to Washington, take a room at the Willard, see him when he isn't busy. Why not? If we were married that's how it would be."

Now the subterranean atmosphere of the station engulfed her, and the crowd, drawn by invisible currents, drifted in separate directions. She pictured her lover sitting in the club car, reaching for his cigarettes, unfolding his newspaper, falling into easy conversation with strangers. His world had claimed him, that world from which she was excluded. She shook her head in fierce protest. She would not endure this state of affairs much longer—it was absurd, inhuman, indecent.

A shapeless woman carrying a baby paused to question her in unintelligible English. "You better ask a porter," Regan advised her impatiently, hating the fat brown face with its moles and moustache, hating the stupidity of anything that allowed itself to become so gross. The woman blinked in bewilderment, the baby whimpered, and Regan turned to the escalator. Something made her glance back, and she saw the woman still standing there, clutching the baby. She looked utterly stranded; one of her stockings slipped slowly down a gargantuan leg, a tear dripped down her cheek. With a shudder of disgust Regan gained the escalator and was borne upward to the fading light of Seventh Avenue and a cacophony of traffic.

She looked at her watch. She had told Hester she would be home by six. There was time to spend on herself and she decided to go to the Metropolitan and look at the El Grecos. She boarded a bus and thought of the time she had last gazed at El Greco's livid faces, at his draperies of electric blue and chartreuse. That had been just before Symes left for Lisbon. They had lunched at Longchamps on West 57th Street, then walked to the Museum. The thought of Mark's homecoming had hung heavy upon them, but they avoided the subject and engaged instead in a silly quarrel over El Greco—the kind of quarrel she might have had with Mark but which she never expected to have with Symes, who usually shared her enthusiasm. Yet that day he said: "El Greco bores me. Look at those angels! They remind me of your sister Hester."

His tone hurt her. "But when you saw the St. Martin in Washington, last year, you agreed that it was one of the most beautiful things in the world!"

"All I said was I liked the horse."

They argued, and Regan lost her temper. They had parted in an atmosphere of bitterness, but made it up again on the eve of his flight to Lisbon. She had not wanted him to go to Lisbon, though she knew he had to go. She did not want him to leave her for a day, though she knew this was absurd. She did not want to differ with him over the merits or faults of El Greco or over anything else. Time was running out and the two marvellous years of their love affair were approaching a crisis. Mark's return was bound to make everything complicated, even dangerous. And what, after all, Regan asked of herself, what do we gain from restraint? We are past our youth, we can at best look forward to twenty years of comparative vitality. Oh, if Mark would only act reasonably. . . . She frowned and made room on the seat beside her for an Italian carrying bundles and reeking of garlic. *"Grazie,"* he murmured. "Tenk you!"

The bus moved on and she thought: I'll stay on it and take a taxi across the Park to the Museum. That will give me a few extra minutes before I go back to Hester. She brooded on her sister. Strange that Hester should have shared so much of the character and life of their mother, while she, Regan, had taken after their father. The first two were hypochrondriacs, but she had her father's temperament, self-willed and strong. She had early come to the conclusion that the weak, the old and the sickly are intolerable burdens on society. How she had resented her sister and mother! And with what speed she had made up her own mind that she would never be an old maid, or poor, or powerless. Beauty had taken care of the first contingency, her father's favoritism of the second, and her own character of the third. Since their mother's death, Hester, plain and pallid and ill, had assumed a sort of composite personality—at once servile and didactic—so that there were occasions when Regan confused the living woman with the dead. It sometimes occurred to her that Hester must hate her for being what she was, just as she despised Hester and often hated her for being Hester. And yet, mused Regan, she is the only person I have ever trusted. Can it be that hating each other as we do we dare not betray one another as we might if we loved? We are afraid of each other, and fear is the bond between us. How strange Hester was, when one came to think about her like this, in cold blood. How perceptive, intelligent, bitter, with such incalculable humor!

Regan reconstructed the occasion when, leaving Mark, she had gone to her sister's apartment on Riverside Drive. Hester was lying as usual on her couch by the window, surrounded by cushions, books, magazines, paper handkerchiefs and vitamin tablets. The room had the peculiar smell of an asthmatic's chamber, and it always made the robust Regan feel a trifle sick until she had got used to it. When her sister entered, Hester switched off the radio and said: "Here you are at last! I expected you last night. Did you actually take the bull by the horns?"

Regan saw this as a deliberate indelicacy which she decided to ignore. Hester's pale eyes followed as she walked to the window and gazed at the river. She went on quickly: "I must say I don't see why you come here instead of going to Bill. However, I suppose that would be a bit indiscreet, in view of everything."

Her speech was that of one who talks to herself, continuous, fluent, erratic; for a few moments Regan stood without answering. There's no use in getting mad at her, she thought. She never will forgive me for having two men dangling round when she has never had one and has learned to hate the whole sex.

Behind her, Hester sneezed. "Reach me the Kleenex, will you? It's fallen under the couch."

Regan reached her the Kleenex. One found it everywhere, tucked into corners of chairs, sofas, under pillows. Waste baskets overflowed with it, so did Hester's pockets. Her progress through life was one long paper-chase of damp little wads of tissue. Why, Regan wondered, if they are determined to suffer, don't they suffer silently and invisibly?

"Where's Neddy?" asked Hester. "Wouldn't Mark let you bring him? By the way, how is Mark? Handsome as ever? Oh, not to you, I suppose, not now anyway, since you've gazed so long at Bill Symes. Not the same type at all, are they? I marvel at your switching as you do from one type to another. But I always rather admired Mark. That integrity! Tell me what he said about Germany. Has he got to know the Russians? Does he think we shall have to fight them after all?"

God give me patience, thought Regan. "We didn't talk much about anything," she said with an effort at calmness. "Aside from the wear and tear of his experience Mark looked pretty much the same as when you last saw him."

"It's been such ages since I saw him. He never came near me during his last leave, you remember. No reason why he should have, of course. He never gave a whoop about me, though he was always sweet whenever we met. A real gent, in other words. Something your Bill is not, my dear—if you'll forgive my frankness!"

Regan lighted a cigarette. "Go on. I'll wait till you're through, then maybe we can talk."

"I wish you wouldn't smoke in here. It hurts my lungs. I thought I was in for an attack this afternoon, but it passed off. This dry weather must be good for me, after all, though it didn't make much difference last summer, when I thought I was going to die! But to go back to Mark. I keep thinking how sad this homecoming must be, for him. I never did understand why you married him in the first place, aside from the fact that you would have married any one to get away from Mother and me. But why did you choose *him?*"

"Why shouldn't I have chosen him?"

"Because you never actually cared a button for him."

"Must we discuss it again? It's all water over the dam anyway."

"So are lots of things—Mother, Father, the war, the house . . . You've junked it all, haven't you? Now it's Mark's turn. I wonder why he married you."

"What do you mean by that?"

Hester smiled. "I've always had a suspicion that Mark saw through you, but that he deceived himself because he was—what shall I call it? Infatuated."

"You don't have to call it anything."

"Of course, as you say, it's all ancient history. You're through with him. I keep asking myself whether Bill Symes is the last on your list. But it isn't so easy to write off ancient history, and I'm surprised that you should want to. The past must have some meaning for you, with your pretensions towards art and letters and all the rest of it."

Regan thought: How long am I going to stand it living here with her?

"Mark must have had a kind of stupid streak, though," Hester continued in a musing voice. "I suppose one might call it honesty. He really believed that all that glistened must be gold. But you haven't told me how he acted. What did he say? What did he do? Did he try to hit you?"

"Oh, for God's sake, Hester!"

"Well, he might. He's full of violence, I think. I've always suspected that he has had to work harder than most men to control himself. And I've wondered how he endured your hypocrisies, how he kept his hands off you when you were being so *darned* superior!" She paused. "I kept wondering and wondering, last night, why you didn't show up as you said you would. You had it all planned that you'd meet his boat, take him back to the apartment, give him a drink, and break the news. After which you'd come over here. But you never came. Why not?"

"I changed my mind."

"Then you spent the night there, with Mark?"

Regan turned her back and stared out of the window.

"Whew!" whistled the invalid. "That's going some, even for you, my dear. How would Bill like that?"

Regan whirled round. "Now look here, God damn it . . . ."

Hester was laughing, her pale eyes brimming with tears, her thin, pointed nose raw and pink. "It's very funny, you know! You don't see it, but it *is* funny, Regan. All these things you and Bill take so tragically, think so important—they are really a scream!"

Regan stared at her in silence. There were moments, and this was one of them, when she wished quite simply that Hester might die, and it did not lessen the intensity of her wish to realize that Hester was fully aware of it.

"So you spent the night with Mark. Does that mean you slept with him?"

"Yes, it means I slept with him. But I don't expect that you would understand. Why should you?"

Hester sank a little deeper into her pillows, what color there was in her face drained away, leaving her to look more than ever like one of El Greco's women.

"Why," she whispered at last, "why did you sleep with him?

Hating him as you do, unfaithful to him as you've been all these years, determined to be rid of him at the first possible moment, why did you sleep with him?"

All her life Regan had thrilled with victory over this woman. It was upon this febrile but stubborn spirit that she had exercised her wit and her talents; now a familiar sense of triumph tingled through her, and she replied coolly:

"No woman who has not slept with a man can understand why I slept with Mark last night. But since you are so morbidly curious, I'll tell you why I did. I felt I owed him something, that I would have had it on my conscience if I'd refused to spend that one night with him."

"On your conscience?"

"Precisely; on my conscience."

"Your conscience," Hester repeated. "Your conscience!"

She repeated it as Mark had repeated it that morning, with a note of incredulous wonder, and Regan turned away in a rage and left her.

Now, riding uptown on the bus, Regan thought about Hester and Mark. They should have married, she decided savagely. Mark, the chivalrous, would have made an ideal mate for the meticulous Hester, and when he went to war Hester would have asked nothing better than to languish on her couch until his return. Yes, Hester would have made him a perfect wife, though of course she could never have produced Neddy. Remembrance of her son roused further disquiet in Regan. She stared out of the window at the teeming sidewalk. All she asked was to be allowed to spend the rest of her life with Bill Symes.

War, which had levelled other lives, other destinies, had made hers worthwhile. War had brought her a lover. She would give up every thing, every one—yes, she would even renounce Neddy, if that would insure her future with Symes. She brooded on the vision of life as she had always yearned for it, as she never ceased to yearn for it, and to strive towards it. Her dull middle-class family never had an idea beyond their own tiny orbit. The world of art and literature, the exciting world of society, politics, public life, held little or no interest for them, not even for her father, with his obstinate, single-track mentality. They had not even troubled to give her a decent education; hers had stopped when she graduated from high school. For the rest she had had to shift for herself, and shift she did, to good purpose. She read, she went to lectures, to picture galleries, to concerts. She listened to the conversation of people she believed to be wiser and better informed than herself. Unobtrusively, industriously, she had soaked up a kind of education and it had made her restless. Something was always lacking—that something which the prostrate Hester seemed to acquire by merely lying in bed and gazing at the ceiling. But it eluded Regan—that creative impulse without which in one form or another all wisdom and all effort are fruitless and unillumined. Passion for Symes had unleashed her energies and given them direction. She took her cue from him, as he quite often took his from her; and talents and insights which could not find expression in art, or solace in contemplation, sought their level in the espousal of causes lost and found, and in a calculating and shallow radicalism.

Hester had looked on with the eerie amusement she always

brought to bear on her sister's activities. "What a self-deluded thing you are, Regan!" she had exclaimed more than once. "As though you really gave a damn about Jews, Negroes, the labor movement, about anything or any one except yourself!"

Regan had retorted with the candor which remained her only weapon against this discerning Sibyl: "All right, I don't give a damn about them. But to love humanity as you pretend to doesn't help it much these days. Legislation—compulsion, if you like—is what moves mountains." She added with a sneer: "But then, idealism never was your strong point, was it, my dear?"

Hester had shrugged. "The trouble with your brand of idealism is that it doesn't spring from love of people but from scorn of them."

Old clapperclaw, Regan thought, and dropped the subject.

At the Museum she had El Greco to herself, and as she went from one canvas to another, observing the marvels of paint and conception, her intelligence demanded frantically: "What does the artist *mean?* What is he trying to say? Why is he wonderful . . . or is he wonderful, after all?" She didn't know. Uneasily, she told herself that perhaps she was one of those who might die without finding out. Hester would know, and in his simple way, Mark would, too. The thought filled her with disquiet. She paused for a moment to exchange a glance with Don Fernando, but his eyes behind their absurd glasses stared past her with an expression of sardonic indifference. Regan abandoned El Greco and wandered from one room to another in a growing desolation. The thought of returning to Hester was repugnant, but where else should she go? Already her own apartment, Mark,

Neddy, Octavia Evans had assumed an unreality in her thoughts. Now she suffered from a frightening sense that something was happening to her among these ancient canvases and statuary, that some malign influence flowed from them towards her, pressing upon her flesh and spirit. The strange idea persisted, became a conviction which made her heart beat uncomfortably. It's claustrophobia, she assured herself, and the glib explanation bore her safely to the staircase and into the open air. But her legs still trembled and she hated herself for her superstitious weakness. Leaving the Museum, she walked slowly up the Avenue in a flickering dance of leaves. Children were going home with parents and nursemaids, couples lounged on the stone benches against the wall, an old man walked ahead of her, leading an old dog on a leash. The city's life seemed to be repeating its patterns, endlessly inhaling and exhaling a variegated breath. Would the scene have inspired El Greco? Was there anything inspiring in this frenetic era, or was it doomed to obsolescence, like its favorite cult? Well, for better or for worse, I belong in this era, Regan thought, and shivered. I belong in it and I'll be forgotten with it. . . .

She walked till the sun had gone, then took a crosstown bus to Riverside Drive. There were several empty seats, but obeying a self-conscious impulse she chose one beside a young Negro sailor and almost immediately regretted it. He had been drinking, and she felt his eyes move upon her face, her breast, her knees. Had he been white she would have moved to another seat, but he was black and it had become one of her tenets that one must never wound the sensibilities of a black man as one might risk wounding those of a white one. The boy, aware, probably, of her dilemma, and enjoying it, took advantage of the movement of the bus to sway against her. His breath brushed her face; uncrossing his long legs he allowed his knee to press hers. Regan stared before her at the rows of heads, and at the brawny shoulders of the Irish driver. There were other Negroes on the bus. If she were to move away they'd suspect her of prejudice, if she remained the sailor might become reckless and she be compelled to make a scene. His little white cap fell off and landed in her lap. "My cap in your way, ma'am?" he murmured. Regan handed it to him without speaking. It fell off again, and in leaning over to retrieve it he dug his elbow into her thigh. Her face crimsoned, her lips set. She felt, at her side, the boy's body shaking with noiseless laughter.

She got off two blocks before she needed to, and the sailor got off with her. Without turning her head Regan knew that he followed her, a lithe figure absurd in its navy costume and white cap. The sense of persecution which had assailed her in the Museum now returned, and she struggled with an instinct to run. Damn him, she thought furiously. Damn him! At last she was at Hester's door, and as she stepped into the entry he passed by on the sidewalk without glancing at her. Then she lost sight of him, but the sound of his laughter, soft, derisive, pursued her into the apartment, into the elevator, and all the way up to her sister's rooms.

13

MARK PUT down his paper and watched Neddy whittling a piece of wood into the semblance of a boat. It was Sunday. Rain slanted against the windows, bringing freshness and a rumble of thunder. Difficult, he mused, to deduce much sense let alone grandeur from the day's headlines. Here were all the old hatreds, the old deceits, the old hypocrisies. Here were the intolerance, the pretense, the prejudice unresolved by victory. As Octavia had reminded him, religion itself had ceased to preach love; it raised, instead, a threatening finger. New terrors had been added to the old; fat slugs were gnawing at what was left of the world's heart. As for him, he felt about as effective as that child in the corner, whittling a toy out of matchwood.

"When I've made this boat," said Neddy, holding it up for him to see, "can we take it to the Park and sail it?"

"When it stops raining. If I hired a real boat this summer would you like to come sailing with me?"

"Honest?"

"Honest, as soon as they let me out of the army."

Neddy thought it over with his customary thoroughness. "Shall we ask Mother to come with us?" he asked at last.

Mark winced. "Do you think she'd care to?"

"I don't know," said Neddy, and picked up the penknife again.

Mark watched him for a minute. "Neddy," he said, in a care-

115

ful voice, "do you miss Mother? I mean, would you care to go to your Aunt Hester's and visit her for a few days?"

The boy shook his head. Mark persisted: "But don't you miss Mother?"

"She often goes away. She'll come back."

It was said with such assurance that Mark glanced at him sharply. A question rose to his lips, but he did not ask it. He longed for some glimpse into the child's mind, but the instinct of chivalry was strong—he could not bring himself to cross-examine, to coerce, or to bribe the boy to betray his mother.

Restless from inaction, he rose and went to the window. Sabbath inertia hung upon the city, even the sound of traffic seemed no more than a prodigious half-stifled yawn. Mark found himself resenting this coma, just as when he was a child he used to resent the thought of other people sleeping while he was awake. Below him a woman carrying a blue umbrella walked with a graceful stride that reminded him of Regan, and from some unexplored corner of himself longing for her rose up and clutched him. He thought of Sunday mornings in the country, and of long drowsy hours in bed. How beautiful she was in bed, smiling when he turned towards her, her voice husky with sleep, her eyelids trembling under his kiss. How could such things be forgotten or counted trivial, once they had been? What had happened to the world, to his world, to everybody's world? Why, if Regan could respond to one man could she not respond to him, who knew her better than any one else could? He was not a prude, he was not a fool; he had not demanded fidelity, but he had expected that they could live out their lives together with passion, good-humor, tolerance. Whenever he thought of her in another man's arms hunger for her clawed at him.

He watched rain falling against the buildings across the street, painting the sidewalks in the pale colors of a clearing sky, and thought: Suppose I call her up now and suggest that she join Neddy and me for a walk in the Park? We could have tea together, talk. We could be friends. And perhaps from that point we could start all over again with the excitement of strangers, turning at last to love. But to be friends is what really matters. To be friends! He hesitated. It's for me to make the first move, for me to say: 'Look, let's call it a day. You're free to come and go as you please, so am I. Divorce me if you want—I'll help you. Who knows, perhaps even after the divorce you may change your mind and come back. While we live we must, in some measure, be related.'

Generous emotion coursed through him. He would call her at Hester's, now, this minute. He turned in a sort of frenzy, startling Neddy. An exclamation burst from the child and he held up his hand, from which the blood dripped in a stream on to the chair. Father and son stared at the trickle, then Mark went to him quickly. "Come to the bathroom. Hold it under the cold water faucet while I get a bandage."

Neddy was white. "I'm bleeding," he whispered. "Look, I'm bleeding!"

Mark saw that the wound was not serious. "Sit where you are and I'll get a bandage."

He ran to Regan's room and found a fresh handkerchief in her bureau drawer. Kneeling beside Neddy, he shook out the square of white linen, but Neddy snatched his hand away. "Not that! You can't use that. It's Mother's best handkerchief. She'd be very angry."

"It'll wash. Here, give me your hand."

"No," said Neddy. "No, I don't want you to. Mother wouldn't like it."

"Give me your hand—do you want to get blood all over everything?"

Neddy was shivering. "Go away . . . I don't care if I am bleeding. Go away!"

Mark seized his hand. "Little idiot, let me tie that up." He started to wrap the handkerchief round Neddy's hand, but the child shrank from him and began to scream. "Leave me alone! Don't touch me!"

"God damn it! Stay still, will you?"

The boy drew one foot back then shot it forth, striking the man in the chest. Then he was out of the chair and across the room, screaming.

Mark rose. "Come here," he said. "Come back here."

But Neddy fled through the door into his mother's room, his screams tingling through Mark's nerves. For a moment he hesitated, at a loss, then he followed the child and found him cowering in a corner by the bed. "If you touch me I'll kill you," came the threat, choked and sobbing. "I'll kill you with this penknife, I will!" Mark saw he held the knife open in his hand.

"You won't kill me. You'll put that knife down and come over here so I can bandage your hand. Come on."

"No!" shrieked Neddy.

Something cruel and exultant swarmed through the man's

brain. "Then I'm coming to get you," he said, and started forward. Neddy's screams stopped. For a moment he stood motionless, his eyes dark with fear, then he hurled himself at Mark, the knife uplifted. Mark caught him, twisted the knife from his fingers, and held the hysterical body close to his breast. His own anger passed as he felt the boy's helpless trembling. "Neddy," he whispered. "Poor little Neddy."

In a little while Neddy drew a shuddering breath and murmured: "Look, the blood's stopped."

"So it has. Better go in the bathroom and wash it off."

When the child had gone he picked up the knife and snapped it shut, then slipped it into his pocket. In the parlor he found Regan's handkerchief lying on the floor. It was a fragile affair embroidered with her initials, and bearing a gilt label marked Portugal. A present? And from whom? Mark crumpled it in his hand. The excitement of the past few minutes had left him feeling chilled and lucid, and his original impulse to call Regan on the telephone had quite vanished. He no longer wanted to see her or to talk to her; he felt again that the distance between them was impassable. And from now on he would have to attend to Neddy. How little they understood one another, but how mysterious, how indissoluble the bonds which held them! Mark closed his eyes, seeing the small, cowering figure, its arm uplifted, clutching the open blade. Would Neddy have to kill a man some day, as his father had had to kill the owner of that knife? The German was rotten in his grave, rotten and forgotten. Had he left a wife, a son, somewhere among the ruins of his town? Mark remembered the pity he had felt for the dead man; he had kept the knife not as a souvenir, but as a memorial. We are bound to our enemies, he thought, almost as closely as we are bound to our loves.

Neddy came into the room and Mark turned to see a tranquil face.

"It's stopped raining," said Neddy. "Can we go to the Park now?"

"Here's your mother's handkerchief. Do you want to put it back in her bureau?"

Neddy glanced at it without interest. "Where is my boat?" He spied it on the chair and pounced on it. "Will you buy me some paint, Papa, so I can paint my boat?"

Mark smoothed the crumpled handkerchief. "You were quite right not to let me use this for a bandage. It's a very fine handkerchief. Did you give it to Mother?"

"Mr. Symes gave it to her. He gave her a whole dozen. He brought them from Lisbon on the clipper." Neddy drummed his heels impatiently. "When will you hire a boat so we can go sailing?"

Mark answered absently. Then he carried the handkerchief back to Regan's bureau and replaced it among the others. Neddy was right, there were several still unused in a corner of the top drawer, among odds and ends of jewelry, perfume, fragments of lace and ribbons. Their femininity, their fragrance, hurt him. He shut the drawer quickly and went back to Neddy.

14

FATHER AND son went for many walks, up and down the great avenues, west and east to the rivers. If there was a growing understanding between them it remained tacit. Neither spoke of Regan, whose personality became a sort of will-o'-the-wisp, glimpsed and lost in the course of their pathetic, disjoined communion. But as the weather became warmer Mark was invaded by nostalgia for the country. He hired a car and they drove to Connecticut and ate their lunch in a field beside a farmhouse. An elderly Pole came out of the house and spoke to them. The sound of his broken English mingled with the sound of cattle stirring in the barn, with the crowing of bantams and the rattle of milk cans. The sun shone on the farmer's gray hair and brown arms, and in Mark's eyes he appeared as a creature grown out of the earth itself—procreative, passionate, independent of speech. Later, as he drove back to the city with Neddy he remembered other men of that kind, men who had moved incredulously amid the ruins of their farms, men who eyed the dead and bloated horse which had once drawn a plow, men who gathered in their rough hands the fragments of china dishes and the wedding portrait of sixty years before. As the glittering spires of the city rose before him, Mark smelled again the acrid odors of cattle urine and rank grass, the scent of hay, of sweat on a flannel shirt—tincture of humanity sprung from the earth and from the ruins of the earth. Patient, ponderous, lyrical, would it resurrect itself among the ruins of some future time?

All faint blue and fading gold, the city claimed them, its windows pricked with flame against the summer sky. Pausing for a traffic light, Mark listened to music coming from the radio of another car. Overhead a plane swam with a soft throbbing of motors and he had a glimpse of its lights, an emerald, a ruby, drifting among the stars. Beside him Neddy curled like a puppy fast asleep, and a melancholy happiness stole upon Mark. Then the music was drowned in an uproar of horns and motors, and he drove on. Entering his own street he saw a figure which reminded him of Regan. Should he overtake her just to make sure? And what then? He stopped the car at the curb beside his door and sat for a few minutes watching the figure grow dim and vanish in the gloom. Then he wakened Neddy and went into the house.

In the parlor the child, still half-asleep, blinked and looked round him.

"Mother's been here," he said.

"What makes you think so?"

"I can tell."

Mark started to speak; then he spied a note lying on the table near the telephone. As he crossed the room towards it he thought he smelled the perfume she always used, as, perhaps, Neddy had smelled it. The note was brief: "Mark, You probably forgot that I have a key and the right to enter my own apartment whenever I want. I would have come before this, but hated the thought of a scene before Neddy and Octavia. It has been almost three weeks since I saw Neddy, and a full week since you let me talk to him over the phone. How long do you propose to continue this cruel performance? I have already suggested that we meet and discuss matters, amicably or not, as you prefer. But the sooner the better. Heaven knows what Neddy must be thinking, but I know that this separation from his mother cannot be good for him. He and I have always been very close. How can you be so spiteful? Regan."

As Mark stood with the note in his hand he felt the tension increase between himself and his son. The boy looked as if he were about to cry, all life seemed to drain from his slender body. Mark thought helplessly: If he should say he wants her, if he should break down, what could I do? He recalled, with horror, the afternoon of Neddy's mishap with the penknife. Silence gave way to the ticking of clocks, to the sound of voices in the street, the music of a radio from somewhere in the building. Mark gazed at his son. He wanted to touch him, to say something tender and consoling which might bridge the gulf between them, but before he could speak Neddy had turned away to read the comic papers which were strewn on the sofa.

Next morning Mark tore the month of May from the calendar on Regan's desk and tossed it in the wastebasket. Three weeks had passed since his return from Europe. A letter from the War Department informed him that his discharge from the army was under consideration—the letter, like the date on the calendar, struck Mark as being symbolic. He left the desk and walked to the mirror, where he stood grimly examining his features. Well, there he was—Mark Bycroft, American, aged thirty-three, whole and healthy, survivor of four catastrophic years of history, heir to all the horrors of peace. He felt that the recent past had left him almost indecently unchanged in appearance. Even his wounds were invisible; decorously clothed, they ached a little in bad weather exactly as old wounds are supposed to do.

The telephone rang in the parlor, and he thought: That's probably Regan. Let her ring. Let Octavia take the message. He had no wish to hear the precise accents reminding him that there were greater things in life than his own petty concerns.

The telephone rang on and he pictured it where it stood between Webster's dictionary and the pencil sharpener. Webster, fat with words, remained silent; the pencil sharpener did not stir, but the telephone rang on and on, monotonously, insistently. "Don't imagine you can ignore me," it jeered in its shrew's voice. "Don't imagine you can escape! I'm not what you think I am—on the contrary I am a Personality, a Charge, a Responsibility!"

He had been standing all this time before the mirror on Regan's bureau. Now the expression on his face startled him into keener scrutiny. Had he thought himself unchanged? The distraught image quivered into familiar lines. My God, he thought, turning away, am I nothing more than a dumb jealous fool, one of the million other cuckolds in the country? A bleached Othello toying with his wife's handkerchief, flinching before a flock of bat-eared suspicions?

Octavia called from the parlor: "Lieutenant Perry on the phone, Colonel!"

He had forgotten young Perry. "Mark? I wanted to call you before, but I was afraid I'd bother you. How are things?"

Mark replied that things were about as usual. "Look, Mark. That dinner for General Wilmer. It's this week—Thursday, at the Rotterdam. You're coming? It's going to be a madhouse, but the old boy's tickled to death. I called just to make sure you'd be there."

"Sure, I'll be there." A sudden craving for masculine society came over him, a nostalgic longing for the rough physical contacts of army life, for the disciplined, unimaginative companionship which he had hated unremittingly for four years. "Six-thirty at the Rotterdam?" said Perry. "I'll watch out for you. How's Neddy?"

"Fine, thanks."

"And you?" asked Perry, diffidently.

"Fine. And you?"

"Lucy and I are going west the second I'm out of the army." He paused again, then eagerly: "Mark, you wouldn't come along with us?"

"What?" He laughed.

"I'm serious. There'd be lots of room for you and Neddy on the ranch. It's the swellest country. You could live with us till you got the—the future straightened out. The kid would love it. Think it over. Christ, you don't want to spend your life among these skyscrapers, do you?"

"I'll think it over," Mark promised, to get rid of him. He hung up, and turned to meet Octavia's gaze. "I've just been offered a job, Octavia. Herding cows in God's own country."

She picked up the Chinese Buddha, dusted it, and replaced it on its stand.

"Colonel Bycroft, may I speak my mind?"

"All of it?" he asked lightly.

He stood filling his pipe, and she thought: Here is a man, simple, natural. No hero, though they'd like to dress him up like one. If I was young I'd like him for my husband. I'd like him now for my son instead of the one I've got, the bitter, bright, strong son who looks down on me for being a servant.

"Why won't you let Neddy go?" she asked at last. "Wouldn't it be better, in the end?"

"Better for whom?"

"Better for all of you. Let him go! He'll come back to you."

"After she's poisoned him against me, as she's poisoned me against most things?"

"You're not acting after your real nature, Colonel."

He sat on the arm of a chair and considered her thoughtfully. "You think I'm putting on an act, don't you? Maybe I am, Octavia. Maybe my wife is, too."

"Neddy isn't."

"He can do a pretty job when he wants to. For instance when he wants to hide something, or some one."

"What'd he be trying to hide?"

"His mother, perhaps, or his mother's lover."

She frowned. "Ah! What difference can it make?" And then, with a bitterness that astonished him: "The war goes on, doesn't it? It goes on and on, everywhere, in everybody." She folded her hands against her white apron in a gesture which seemed to exclude the world, to renounce any responsibilty for its disorder.

He stared at her curiously, thinking: She's black, a Negro, flesh separate from mine, her past lost in the darkness from which my kind carried her away. And he had a queer flash of insight into himself. Why, he thought, I am obliged to remind myself of these things! Could it be that he was as ordinary a person as he imagined? His education had not been altogether different from every one else's. He had lived in a society compounded of tolerance and intolerance. He was fully aware of its complexities and contradictions. Yet perhaps, after all, something had been left out of his individual chemistry, or something had been included, for he knew that antipathy was not in him. His sense of equality was innate, his democracy alive and effortless, but this knowledge, far from reassuring him, left him lonely in the center of his universe.

Octavia went on in her quiet voice: "Why will you let this thing hurt you so? Isn't it maybe pride more than anything?"

"Maybe it is. Didn't my wife ever hurt you? Or did she go to extraordinary lengths not to?"

"Because I'm a Negro? Yes, she went to great pains to spare me. She was so considerate, neither of us ever had a chance to remember much of anything except that I was black and she was white!"

He laughed. "Yet you admired her, liked her?"

She considered this seriously. "No, I can't say as I did." She gave him an uneasy smile. "It was because of something happened . . . a slight thing, but I never did get over it, coming as it did from her. When I applied for this job, Mrs. Bycroft was wonderful. Just like I expected she would be, and like what I read about her in the papers. Then, just about when the interview was over she suddenly asked me had I taken a Wassermann test." Octavia hesitated. "I know it's supposed to be a routine question, but it kind of threw me. I'm old enough to be her mother. And I couldn't help but wonder what she'd have said if I'd asked *her* that question."

"Well, why didn't you ask her? You had every right."

She shook her head. "I know what you mean—I took it from her, and said nothing, and now I hold it against her."

Both were silent, then Octavia turned with an air of primness and he rose, barring her way. "Octavia, you've been a good friend to Neddy and me, so I feel entitled to ask you a question. Is my wife in love with some one else?"

"I don't know, sir. How should I know?"

"You've worked here two years; you've seen people come and go. You must have seen . . . suspected . . ."

"They was just names to me. I give you my word I never saw nor heard anything you could call unusual."

"And Neddy?"

Her face hardened. "That's a question you got no right to ask *him!*"

Mark moved aside and let her pass. He felt that he had been very properly, and not too tenderly, put in his place.

15

THE LOBBY of the Rotterdam Hotel was a vast rectangular space illumined by what is called indirect lighting, that indistinct glow which makes people look as if they were in the last stages of jaundice. The floor was several inches deep in purple carpet interrupted at rigid intervals by outcroppings of furniture of a size and shape better suited to behemoths than to men. Mark's first impression was that here was an ideal spot for the assignation of lovers, murderers, bank-robbers, or political spies, for in addition to a confused decor—the walls were covered with a combination of fumed oak and embossed leather, with here and there an avalanche of fake tapestry—the place swarmed with humanity in varying degrees of physical and spiritual agitation, as amorphous and unrecognizable as the background upon which they moved. Some lounged in the elephantine chairs reading newspapers and time tables, or casting eager glances at the revolving doors which seemed never to stop sucking in a victim or ejecting one. Others seemed glued to the dial telephones which stood alongside an elegant cave reserved for room clerks, managers, and switchboard operators. While most of the occupants of the lobby stood about in forlorn knots, others rushed towards one another with outcries and claspings and were promptly caught in the slip-stream of a revolving door and spewed out onto the sidewalk, or they were drawn, chattering like toucans, into the dim caverns of dining-room or cocktail lounge. Still others stalked or skulked in the wake of liveried

129

adolescents carrying suitcases, and were wafted upward in cages of gilt and bronze.

It was a microcosm of the city, and Mark perceived, in these people, in this place, the soul of the city itself—squamous, self-obsessed, impermanent. A strange revulsion swept over him: he had seen enough of crowds, the crowds of homeless, crowds of prisoners, crowds without identity or destination. *What is the human spirit?* he asked himself stupidly, as he stood in the lobby of the Rotterdam Hotel, watching the human beast rush panting past him on its way . . . where? Why? A memory of other faces surged towards him out of the past; he felt that he might be thrown down and trampled under the weight of sheer human sensuality.

"Mark!" Perry seized his elbow. "Gosh, I'm glad to see you." Mark was turned deftly away from the revolving doors towards which he was headed.

"Sorry to be late," he murmured in frustrated accents. "I thought you said seven."

"Doesn't matter. Every one's going to be more or less late. The others have started on the drinks, and we have the privilege of being as late as we please, provided we pay for it." He squeezed Mark's arm. "You never saw such a gang. Quite a few civilians too, and most of our crowd are out of uniform. They've most all shown up. I never thought old Wilmer rated so high, did you?"

Mark decided that he must get drunk. It was the only way to survive the evening, the only way to escape from the sense of suffocation which he already felt creeping upon him. Perry looked at him anxiously. "You all right?"

"Sure I'm all right."

"I've been worrying about you, ever since that afternoon when you told us . . . told me . . ."

"Forget it."

"Lucy and I felt like hell."

"Well, you can forget it now."

"It's like you to act as if nothing had happened. You were always like that. When the rest of us beefed and whined you went on acting as if the whole show was quite normal."

"Forget it, will you? Just to oblige me."

"Then listen, what about coming out west? We could fix you up on the ranch, you and Neddy. God Almighty, we're friends, aren't we? We're buddies. You've helped me out of holes. And you don't have to be proud when a friend tries to help *you*. You'd be doing us an honor. You'd be doing the State of Texas an honor!"

"What in hell are you talking about?"

The boy stammered: "You make it so damned difficult for a guy to say anything. I'm just trying to show my gratitude, that's all. If it hadn't been for you, Lucy'd have walked out on me." He snapped his fingers dramatically. "Just like that, she would have!"

Mark laughed. "I can't go west with you, Perry. I've got to stay here and look after my kid and try to find a job and make some sort of life. It's just as dull as that. I'm not cut out for the great open spaces. To be perfectly honest, I loathe great open spaces! I'm ordinary, see?" He tried to sound jocular. "Besides, I've never got along well with cows, and I'm jealous of bulls."

Perry was incapable of taking offense at his idol. "O.K. Then let's go on up. We've got a suite reserved for the evening."

They took an elevator to the fourteenth floor. The suite was crammed with men, and Mark recognized a typical American atmosphere, faintly guilty, faintly scurrilous—adolescents out on a spree. His hand was seized and wrung, his shoulders smacked, his hair ruffled, his neck embraced by half a dozen brothers-in-arms. They bawled in his ears and shoved drinks at him, and little by little his equivocal mood began to soften. He had not admitted to himself how lonely he was, how hurt. Now he felt the stirrings of affection for these simpletons, some of whom he had actively disliked in the past and who, he felt sure, must certainly have disliked him.

A commotion occurred in the center of the crowd which parted to exude the small, virile figure of General Horatio Wilmer. This one-star comedian with his rubber legs, this absurd creature notorious for his courage, his bad judgment, his worse language, his appalling mistakes and spectacular good luck, was this evening tearfully enjoying what must have been the happiest and proudest hour of his career. Men who had execrated him and wished him dead a thousand times now hailed him with emotion and told him to his face what a fine fellow he was. They gazed at him as if they believed he really deserved the triple rows of ribbons on his blouse, as if they had forgotten, if indeed they had ever known, what a complete and dismal ass he had made of himself in the past.

Spying Mark he advanced and attempted to embrace him, not very successfully, since he was easily a head the shorter of the two. "Marcroft! Old Pal! How are you, Marcroft?"

Mark patted the little man gingerly, remembering the occasions when it had been his fate to suffer under the General's scatologic broadsides.

"Scotch," whispered the General in his ear. "Scotch, boy, Scotch! Two cases of it. They chipped in and bought it for me, bless their—hearts! This whole show is in my honor. Thought it up themselves, damned if they didn't!" Tears filled his eyes. "If you know what this meant to me, Marcroft! If I could find words . . ."

He was seized and led away by other adorers and Mark turned, trying to fit names to the vaguely familiar faces round him. "Remember me?" inquired a man standing nearby. "You and I were at Madgeburg the morning news came of Roosevelt's death."

Mark remembered him, and they talked about that death which had seemed so remote from their immediate experience, reminding each other now how they had tried to place the moment in history, how they had argued about the stature of the dead man and of his epoch. Another man broke into the conversation: "You were in Germany, but I was on leave in New York the evening the news broke about the President. I was in the Ritz having a drink with friends. A guy was sitting at the little piano at the farther end of the room, playing something. *The Moonlight Sonata* I think it was. I saw a waiter go up to him and say something, and he closed the piano quickly and went out. A woman at the table next ours said: 'Tell him to play some more. We like it.' And the waiter turned to her and spoke in a harsh sort of whisper: 'Madam, there is no more music—the President is dead.' After that we all sat and looked at each other in a sort of desperate silence. I remember think-ing: This is going to hit all over the world. Not just here among the whisky-swiggers at the Ritz, but everywhere—all over the world. And I saw the same thought written in everybody's face. I'd voted for him four times but I knew darned well there were many in that room that hadn't! And yet it seemed as if we all stopped breathing, just for a minute. It was a strange tribute—involuntary, terrible. Afterwards I walked about the streets alone. It was a warm, still evening. The fact of his death seemed to hang over the city like a presence. You know? Saks had a corner window lighted with his picture in it, and a black wreath. I saw people carrying newspapers rolled up, sort of like college diplomas. Extras, they were. Every one was walking slowly, aimlessly, carrying that rolled-up newspaper. Then I went across to Rockefeller Center and watched the flags being lowered to half-staff."

A fourth voice chimed in: "When I got the news I hadn't slept since God knows when and it'd have taken an 88 mm. shell to jerk me awake. But there was a young Jew in my outfit, came to me crying like a kid about the President's death. Crying, he was. He seemed to think it was just about the end of the world. He said to me: 'Look, because that guy died today millions are going to die tomorrow, and the day after, and years from now. All over the world they're going to die.' I remember saying to him: 'O.K. boy, O.K. Go away and let *me* die in peace!' Remember that Jew kid? One with the pop eyes? He was killed two days later."

The talk soared with a humming sound punctuated by bursts of laughter and an occasional crash of breaking glass. Remini-

scences flew back and forth. Old battles were fought again.
Small pools of silence welled up around the names of the dead.
Mark thought: This is a precedent, and it will recur year after
year whenever a bunch of us gets together. We'll relive the war
and our share in it, the occasions which brought us together, the
memories which bind us to each other, but as the years go on
we shall see less and less of each other. Peace will claim us at
last, peace and the preoccupations of peace. Our children will
grow up in a world of atomic revolution, emotion will become
out-dated over night, we ourselves will grow bald and fatuous.
This war will join the long catalogue of wars which began in
the ninth millennium B. C. And our heroes, like a trillion others,
will be leafmold then."

The General had just completed one of his famous anecdotes
and was being roundly applauded. He was succeeded by a handsome major who described the occasion when he brought a lady
friend to the Rotterdam one night when he was on leave from
the war. "I managed to inveigle her through the revolving doors
and across that God-awful lobby, into an elevator. We rose to
the nineteenth floor—and there, by God, I lost her!"

"*No!*"

"I did. We'd agreed to proceed separately, not to rouse the
suspicions of any hotel dick who might be snooping round. But
you know what this place is like? Every corridor exactly like
another, every door just like its neighbor, walls, ceilings, rooms,
furniture, all counterparts of each other. Even the people who
run the place look like quintuplets multiplied by ten. Well, so
help me! I chased my girl up and down the corridors, in and
out of elevators, into the lobby, through the revolving doors

into the street, back to the nineteenth floor—and I never did catch her. I never found out what became of her. Next day I was alerted, and that was that."

"That reminds me. My first leave home—'43 I think it was—I had a date to meet a girl at Penn Station . . ."

Mark felt a touch on his sleeve. A young man smiled at him. "Colonel Bycroft? My name is Osgood. We don't know each other, but I've heard your wife talk on the radio, and I just wanted to tell you how much I admire her."

Mark became conscious of Perry standing rigidly beside him. "I do envy you," said Mr. Osgood. "I envy any guy who comes home and finds a fine wife waiting for him. Mine didn't wait. You know, I never did think I'd care a hell of a lot. I'd married sort of late, and I'm the happy-go-lucky type . . . and I'd seen enough, one way and another . . . so I discounted the emotions and all that. You see, I'd been in the army nearly ten years before I married. The army had always taken good care of me. When I married, my wife took care of me. Now I'm on my own, and do you know, damn it! I've lost the knack of taking care of myself. Or maybe I never had it." He peered at Mark. "Finding a place to live in, finding some one to do my laundry, get my shoes mended." He shook his head. "You wouldn't believe what it's like, not having some one round to attend to those things. You wouldn't believe!"

Mark felt wild laughter rising in him, but before he could offer condolences Perry broke in. "I've got to have another drink. How about you, Mark?"

They moved towards a table set with refreshments. Mark felt

the liquor in his blood, but his brain was wide-awake. Liquor telescopes events, translates reality into a multiplicity of sounds and actions from which, eventually, only the unexpected is retained and recalled. Perry was replenishing their glasses when Mark heard a voice behind him: "Bill Symes! How are you? Last I heard you'd gone to Lisbon."

The name plummetted through the gay confusion in his mind. He waited till his glass was filled, then moved slowly to one side and looked round. Heads, shoulders, backs swirled before his gaze. Men in uniform, men in civilian clothes, the familiar and the strange. The voice which had just spoken was drowned in the uproar, and the name's owner had, himself, melted into the throng. *Or did I imagine the incident?* Mark wondered. *Was it an echo stirred by the whisky he had drunk, or some prevision due to a decreased tension of nerves?*

"Anything wrong?" asked Perry.

"You wouldn't know any one called William Symes, would you?"

"Never heard of him. Friend of yours?"

"Friend of my wife's." Mark had intended the words to sound inconsequential, but his voice betrayed him. He added quickly: "I'm probably drunk. I thought I heard the name Symes."

"I heard it too."

"Well, it doesn't matter."

"I can find out easily enough," Perry said. "I'll ask the General. He knows all the guests."

"Never mind. It's not important."

Mark turned away and Perry watched him speculatively. He was nudged by the bereft Mr. Osgood. "They tell me you married since we last met! Lucky, or are you?"

"I'm lucky all right," said Perry. "Listen, do you know any one here called Symes?"

"Never heard of him." His eyes became glassy. "Say, you know I've got ulcers? Ever since I got out of the army and into advertising I got ulcers. I'm not supposed to touch this stuff. Where's the can?"

Perry gave him the necessary directions, then drifted in search of some one who could tell him which figure among them was Mr. Symes.

Mark, moving through the crowd in the opposite direction, experienced an extraordinary elation. It increased as he persuaded himself that he was being watched and studied by a pair of unknown eyes. What had he against Symes? Nothing, actually. Yet the elation persisted, and he knew that he was spoiling for a fight. Intelligence warned him that it would be stupid to make a scene in the midst of this gathering. And besides, just what did he expect to gain from a scene? He had no idea. All he felt was a racing, tingling excitement, the tension of months —of years, perhaps—seeking relief in violence. Somewhere in this crowd was a man who might be Regan's lover. Mark began to argue with himself, deliberately relegating his own role, and that of his wife and his imaginary rival, to a sort of newspaper vulgarity. He assured himself that all that was necessary now was for him to encounter Symes' glance, that was all. Then I shall know, he assured himself, with a drunken nod. Either he'll meet my eyes with an excessive candor, or he'll refuse to meet them. Then I'll know.

"They're going down to dinner," said Mr. Osgood, appearing, somewhat pale, from an adjoining room.

People were moving towards the door. Mark said: "Osgood, do you know any one here called William Symes?"

"You're the second fellow that has asked me that. No, I don't."

Symes, on his way to the door, heard his name, and for a second his eyes met Mark's. Taken unawares he half smiled, then turned away. "Gorgeous party," he exclaimed to the man nearest him. "Simply gorgeous!"

He disappeared into the corridor, and Mark found Perry at his elbow. "That was Symes," Perry said excitedly. "One in the brown suit. Just went out."

They were in the corridor now, in a turmoil of sauntering figures, loud voices, laughter. Mark saw Symes about to enter an elevator. Possessed by a strange agitation he strode in pursuit, Perry at his side. The young man read his intention and a sympathetic demon sprang to life in him.

"Quick," he muttered, "we'll get him in the elevator."

It was easy enough to shoulder through the careless mob and to reach the elevator immediately after Symes had stepped into it. Mark followed him, and thereupon Perry took matters into his own hands. Seizing the operator he pushed him out of the elevator into the corridor. He then threw the switch, the gates closed, and the machine began to climb. The performance was executed with such deftness that for a moment the three men stared at each other in silence. Then Perry spoke in drunken glee: "I used to run one of these things when I was a kid in Dallas. There are supposed to be thirty or forty floors in this building, Mark. Take your time!"

Symes stood braced against the bronze hand rail. He looked coldly at Mark.

"Your friend seems a bit out of hand, doesn't he?"

"My name is Bycroft. I believe you know my wife?"

"I believe I do. My name is William Symes." He held out his hand. The gesture, intended to disarm, and perhaps to gain time, enraged Mark. He struck the hand aside and lunged forward. But Symes had drunk very little and was in full command of his senses. He struck back hard and surely, and the blow, catching Mark in the face, flung him against the wall of the elevator, whence he sagged slowly to the floor. Symes reached across Perry's arm and threw the switch, bringing the elevator to a smooth halt. While Perry knelt besides his bruised and prostrate friend, Symes stepped out of the elevator and into another which had paused to take on passengers for its downward journey. In the lobby he paused long enough to reassure a posse of hotel clerks and bellhops. "Just a drunken joke. No harm done!" After which he rejoined the genial throng of guests who were headed, more or less erratically, towards the main dining room.

16

"WHAT DO you think of it, Stella?" asked Miriam Sparrow, turning her head from side to side as she appraised the new hat, while the saleslady stood ecstatically to one side.

Stella murmured that she thought the hat terribly becoming.

"That's what you have said about every hat I've tried on today. I don't believe you really care at all. I don't believe you've even *noticed!*"

"But I have! I think they are all becoming. You seem to have that effect on hats."

"Very true," crooned the saleslady. "Very, very true! There, just a teeny bit lower over the eyes, and what a difference!"

Miriam, studying herself in the triple mirror, caught a glimpse of her friend seated nearby. Stella wore an abstracted expression, and her clothes looked more than ever as if they needed pressing. Miriam thought impatiently: She ought to get herself a new outfit. My God, how any woman can go round looking as she does . . .

"Here," she said abruptly. "You try it, Stella. It's more your style than mine."

"I really don't feel in the mood, Miriam—please!"

The saleslady assumed an expression of incredulity, and Miriam rose, sighing.

"Well, I can't say that I do either. Let's eat lunch, then maybe we'll feel better."

On Madison Avenue the sun poured mercilessly on their heads; walls and sidewalks shuddered with heat. "June!" said Miriam, as they paused for a traffic light before crossing into the shade. "Do you remember how we used to head for the country in June? Seems like a hundred years ago."

"When does Dick intend to take his vacation?"

"Oh heavens, he's up to his ears in work. Says he probably won't get off, now, till August." She fanned herself with her gloves. "I may not wait till then. The Gormans have asked me to join them at the Cape. If it gets much hotter I shall." She glanced at Stella. "What are your plans?"

"I haven't any."

"You don't intend to stew in New York through the summer?"

"I may."

"Stella!"

"I don't mind the heat."

"But what's the point? You look absolutely washed out. Yes, I mean it—you do look washed out. And washed up too. For God's sake! What's come over you? You used to adore going to Jarley. The war's over, everything is normal . . . or nearly so!" Then, irrelevantly: "Stella, why *won't* you buy yourself a new hat?"

The lights changed and they crossed the street. Miriam's question remained unanswered, and as they walked down the Avenue she felt ashamed of her petulance, aware that it was inspired less by concern for her friend than by concern for herself. Stella made her feel uncomfortable and she hated to feel uncomfortable. There was rising in her, as in many of her generation, a profound revulsion against the remembrance of the war. True, one had to remind oneself that peace was here, and that the butchery had ceased for a while at least . . . yet peace wore an unfamiliar face. Miriam reminded herself that life was an affirmative thing; one had a right to make the most of what was left. Far from making the most of it, Stella seemed determined to make as little as she possibly could. Though she uttered no complaint and asked for no pity, her manner and appearance were more piteous than ever; like her silence after that mysterious Italian journey, there seemed to Miriam something obstinate, something almost perverse in this inconsolable widowhood.

"It's hot." She signalled a taxi. "Let's go to Philippe's on Third Avenue."

In the cab she turned to Stella. "There's something I want to ask."

"Yes?"

"Would you consider selling the house?"

"The house?"

"The house at Jarley. Dick and I would like to buy it."

"I don't know," Stella said slowly. "I never thought of selling it."

She had not thought about selling it. She had not been near it since Alec went away. There it had stood year after year, grass flooding the doorstep, birds building in the chimneys, worms devouring the apples. Another few years, and it would crumble into the earth. Miriam thought of old houses she had seen as she drove along country roads, houses side-stepped by modern highways, houses abandoned to the woodchucks, the squirrels, the weather. Walls fell in, windows slid askew, and wild, tough, little trees thrust through the floors while mildew spread like forgetfulness over everything. Was this to be the fate of Alec's house?

"Stella, do let me buy it! After all, I'm Alec's cousin. It would remain in the family, and perhaps if Dick and I owned it you would feel more like coming down there."

"I don't want to sell it."

"Aren't you being selfish?"

"It's Alec's house."

An angry protest rose to Miriam's lips, but she remained silent. She felt she hated Stella at that moment. Then the taxi stopped and they got out. Miriam paid the driver and they started towards the restaurant in a welter of heat and noise. Stella took Miriam's arm. "Forgive me! I can't explain. Try and understand."

"You don't make it easy," said Miriam. She saw the despair in her friend's eyes, and remorse moved her to add quickly: "My dear, never mind it now. You and I mustn't quarrel."

They entered Philippe's and a waiter led them to a table at the far end, where they commanded a view of the room. It was not large. A bar occupied part of the opposite wall, and the tables were arranged with an eye to space and privacy.

Miriam chatted to break the tension: "They have a veal casserole here that Dick says is wonderful." She deposited her gloves and purse and lighted a cigarette. "Ever since Dick's been seeing so much of Bill Symes he's become a gourmet. He never used to care what he ate." She signalled the waiter, "Two Martinis, if you please."

They watched him slouch away to the bar, and she went on: "Another reason I'll be glad when Dick retires is on account of his stomach. All these years of fretting over other people's troubles and helping them drown their connubial sorrows is making him dyspeptic."

The waiter brought their cocktails and a menu. They sipped and smoked, and friendliness was re-established between them. Venetian blinds were drawn against the glare of the street. A little black cat leaped on a shelf behind the bar and began to pick its way gingerly among the rows of bottles.

Stella asked what Dick intended to do for amusement when he retired.

"He talks about farming!" Miriam laughed. "Farming! Probably because it's the farthest removed from his present job. I tell him he'd do better to settle in some civilized country spot and write his memoirs. He could do a book on marriage and call it 'Unhappily Ever After.' I've got two of his characters all lined up for him—Bill Symes and his girl friend Regan."

"From what I remember of Mr. Symes I wouldn't suppose he was the type to put up with unhappiness, or even with inconvenience, for very long."

"Well," Miriam said, "speaking for myself, I think I'll be glad to get out of New York."

"But you know you don't really enjoy bugs, and bushes, and heat—and sunburn!"

Miriam shook her head. "I'm tired of eating in restaurants and walking on pavement. There's something else, too—something psychological: I've always identified life in the country with a state of innocence." She laughed again, lightly, but her eyes were serious. "You see, I'm at an age when one looks back, and if one is frank enough one acknowledges that one has wasted one's time—wasted it criminally, deliberately. I should have had children, or I should have taken a job. Something constructive . . . but as it is I've lived like a contented parasite, and now I feel—rather vaguely, I admit—now I feel an urge towards penance."

Stella regarded her with amusement. "Penance or expiation? And are you being serious?"

"Perhaps it's the Martini. I have to be a teeny bit tight to face things. The trouble is the mood usually passes off with the alcohol. Then I feel as if I'd accomplished something, and return to my parasitic existence with a salved conscience." She frowned. "I wonder how many there are like me. Women married to hard-working men, women who started out by being intelligent, passionate, generous. Women who put off having kids till it was too late. Women who fiddled about with committees and boards and this and that out of purest ennui. Women who came to life for a little while during the war, when they were made to feel that they had to have some excuse for surviving . . ." She took another sip from her glass.

"And now that we are at peace you think that life in the country is the answer?"

Miriam shrugged. "It's a symbol, at any rate. It always has been a symbol to Dick and me. Just as you and Alec were symbols . . . of youth, I suppose. Of the continuity of familiar things." When Stella remained silent Miriam went on in a level voice: "I often think of that first time I ever saw you, the evening that Alec brought you to have dinner with us at the

Lafayette. It seemed as if the light, everywhere, became brighter when you both came in. Alec was carrying a book, and he quizzed me about some poem or other."

Stella watched the restaurant cat as it crept along the shelf among the bottles. It was apparently headed towards a corner beside the window where a man sat drinking beer. The cat moved adroitly, though it had no more than an inch of latitude between the shelf and the bottles. Miriam murmured: "I'm just a teeny bit tight now, so I don't mind confessing that I was filled with envy of you and Alec that evening. There is a quality of happiness which comes only to certain people. . . ."

The waiter took away their empty glasses. A train roared by on the elevated, and the cat, coming to the end of its journey, paused, then leaped on to the table where the solitary man sat finishing his beer. It was Mark Bycroft, and as the cat landed at his elbow he stroked it, his profile turned for a moment towards the two women. Miriam noticed him and caught her breath.

"I don't know," she murmured, in agitation. "Maybe I'm wrong, but doesn't he look like . . . doesn't he remind you of some one?"

Stella glanced up from the menu. "Doesn't who remind me?"

"The soldier there, in the corner by the window." Miriam stared at him. She was short-sighted, but too vain to wear glasses. Stella followed her gaze.

"Alec?" The name formed on her lips, a question first, then repeated with audible certainty: "Alec."

Mark rose and turned, facing them as he walked to the bar, where he paid for his beer. He picked up his cap and went out, the door swinging after him, and Miriam said breathlessly: "He *was* like Alec! Heavier, and I'd say older. But what a weird resemblance! Stella . . ."

"I'm all right," said Stella. She was pale, the hand which Miriam clasped felt like ice.

"I shouldn't have spoken," Miriam said contritely. "But he startled me . . ."

The waiter came to take their order and she asked him whether he knew the name of the gentleman who had just left, the officer who had sat by the window drinking beer. The waiter shook his head. "He has come two or three times, but I do not know his name. There are so many people, they come and they go." He tugged a pencil from behind his ear. "I recommend the veal casserole for Mesdames. Not too much onion—just a little!" He pressed thumb and finger together eloquently. "And the meat—so tender!"

"We'll have the casserole," said Miriam distractedly. She was almost afraid to look at Stella, who sat gazing at the empty table by the window. The cat was pursuing a fly round the empty beer glass, and for several minutes the two women sat silently watching its antics. Then Stella drew a long breath and as the color crept back to her face, Miriam saw that she no longer resembled a sad pieta, but one restored, inexplicably transfigured.

17

NEW YORK languished in the June heat. Poetic denizens dreamed of the country, of cattle reclining in the shade like great furred fish in a pool, of fields dim with grass, streams covered in yellow cow-lilies, and killdeer fluttering from weedy banks. Wind from the sea mingled with the harsh breath of stone and asphalt to create a separate climate in which the spirit failed and ambition flagged, yet somehow men and women labored on, computing and deducting, making love in their crannied apartments, sleeping, wakening in hope that tomorrow the wind might shift and rain dissolve the iron skies. In the warehouses downtown, those whose task it was to shunt and carry crates moved doggedly, shirts black with sweat, nostrils filled with fumes from exhaust pipes, ears ringing with the crescendo of Business—that inelegant, indispensable, massive performance which, pursuing its charted course upstream disgorged at last on the counters and showcases of Madison Avenue and Fifth. Here the vendors—trained poodles superfluous as most of their wares—lifted wrist and eyebrow languidly amid the opulence, and the shoppers, marked by an acquisitive curse, ogled and fingered the treasure.

The hat lately coveted by Miriam Sparrow was borne away on another head, and Octavia Evans coming to work one morning on the subway met and admired it from her seat. There would, she guessed, be a replica at quarter the price on 14th

Street, and she wondered whether the style would become her daughter-in-law, low in spirit since Edgar's desertion. Might a bright green feather, and perhaps a new hairdo, lure Edgar home? Octavia remembered her son with fear, but with pride also. How should she ever forget the things he said, or the wrathful dreams he previsioned for her? He had spoken of the men he'd seen tearing each other to pieces in Europe, and now he declared that the white man was an intellectual beast, an enslaver, destroyer! Edgar had elected to measure himself against the pale monster and in her heart Octavia felt pride and the chill of fear.

Mark thought restlessly: In a week Neddy will be through school, and I shall have him on my hands all summer. What then? Maybe I better send him to camp. But if I do Regan might find him, and once in her possession it would be impossible to get him back without a real fight. June sunlight blazed against his windows and he saw the crystal conglomeration of the city dissolve and re-form before his eyes. He thought of the country and the sea, of the ardent, active life which he had planned. Yet here he was, chained to New York, to these rooms which had become a cave in which he could bury his pride and his failure, avoiding old friends, old habits, old haunts as if all had the plague. He was haunted by the fiasco at the Hotel Rotterdam, strive though he did to dismiss it as nothing more than a drunken brawl. Closing his eyes he saw Symes' expression of outraged amazement, and the blow resounded in his ears like an echo crying: "You blundering fool!"

Recovering his sense in the hotel lavatory he had found Perry bending over him. "Where's Symes?" he mumbled between bruised lips. "Where is he? I've got to explain . . . apologize . . ."

Perry laid a wet cloth on his mouth. "You can forget it, Mark. He's gone."

Perry had helped him into an elevator, across the lobby, into a cab. Next day the young man called up to tell him that Symes, evidently a decent sort, had declared himself satisfied that the whole thing was due to a mistake, and had even gone so far as to square it with the hotel, where he was apparently held in great respect. Mark, Perry declared over the phone, could now dismiss the whole affair, unless he wanted to call Symes himself and offer his apologies.

"We got the wrong guy, all right," Perry finished, with a rueful laugh. "I was sure, when we chased him into the elevator, that you must be on the right tack. But boy, that wallop never came from a guilty conscience!"

Mark groaned. "And old Wilmer? What must he think? I never even got to the dinner."

"Wilmer doesn't remember anything. He was crocked himself. So was every one, except Symes."

After this conversation Mark meditated telephoning Symes, but his gorge rose at the thought of making a further ass of himself. What was there for him to say? How explain away that unprovoked assault? "I want to apologize, Mr. Symes, for having tried to break your innocent neck. You must forgive me. I was under the impression that you were my wife's lover." Drearily, Mark rehearsed the absurd interview, then abandoned it with a shudder. No doubt Symes would regale his friends with the story; Regan would hear of it, and he would be held up to ridicule—which would serve him damned well right.

Left to himself a man succumbs to the vices of egocentricity, and Mark was no exception to this rule. But though he was aware of what was happening to him he felt powerless to aid himself. Perhaps he was more exhausted than he realized, perhaps the only method by which he could cope with his altered world was to regard it as an implacable enemy, and himself as a not too worthy opponent. Humility or the inferiority complex? By which of these was he—temporarily—distinguished? Or had he lost the art of distinguishing between them?

"What do you think, little cat?" he inquired of the restaurant kitten which leaped, one day, on his table as he sat drinking beer at Philippe's. The kitten squirmed against his hand, he felt the tiny intricate skeleton under its soft fur, and he thought of the tomcats which had fought each other so that this one might be engendered, and of the tigerish, inescapable jungle of the city and the whole snarling tangle of sex which passed for love. His hand tightened on the kitten's body. One squeeze and there would be one cat the less. Then he released the creature, finished his beer, and went out into the crashing heat of Third Avenue, unaware of Stella's resurrected gaze.

A few miles away in her room overlooking the river, Hester lay with the radio playing in her ears. Her thoughts brooded sullenly over the events of the past few hours and she spoke them aloud into the lonely air: "Regan and Bill are going to their favorite inn down in the country, and they could easily have taken me with them. It would have been a change for me. I never get away from this place, or see any one. But what does

Regan care, or Symes? They've got each other. No one else
counts. Nothing else counts."

Symes had called to pick up Regan, and they had treated
Hester with an impatient, perfunctory kindness. Would she be
all right? The maid would come as usual, give her meals and
fix the place up and do errands. And Regan would be home in a
couple of days. Home! Hester smiled at the word. As if a home
was what Regan wanted. She was really at home in an hotel, in
something impersonal, palatial. Ah, they were well suited, Regan
and Symes. Hester reflected on her sister's lover. Symes always
made her think of Strasbourg geese, he was pâté de foie gras
shaped like a man. Then she frowned. It was all very well to
sneer at Symes, and she never missed an opportunity to do so in
Regan's hearing, but the cold fact remained that he was some
one to be reckoned with. If his words—or his faith—could not
move mountains, it was safe to say that they did move other
men, they set events in motion. But a man who looks boyish at
forty is quite apt to behave like a boy, and Hester knew that
boys can be cruel, even dangerous. How limpid, how blue his
eyes, how cleverly he selected his neckties, how well cut his
clothes, how expensive his shoes and his Panama hat! In fact,
how glossy his whole appearance! Today as he had sat chatting
with Hester while Regan packed her suitcase for the trip to
Connecticut, Symes, for the first time in Hester's memory, had
shown a trait which she at first found difficult to name. He was
always affable, she never could get under his guard with her
gibes and insinuations, but today his manner had shown a distinct and extraordinary arrogance. That was it, arrogance. Hester
wondered from what new phase of his private life it may have

sprung. One can judge the men who acquire merit and medals; their actions have spoken for them. Symes wore no medals, but there could be little doubt that his days were spent in the acquisition of merit. But if anything remarkable should happen to him, what might it bode for the rest of the world? Hester had given up questioning Regan on her lover's mysterious activities. It occurred to her that Regan was very likely as much in the dark as any one. But of one thing Hester was sure: Symes and Regan belonged irrevocably to the new era. They were utterly without nostalgia for the past. War had shaped them, it had given them their opportunity. Childhood, youth, the years before 1940 seemed to have been excised from their minds; they were creatures gestated in violence, delivered shrewd and ruthless to their own epoch. And with sudden bleak insight Hester thought: We are at their mercy. We, who are not as they are, who could never be as they are, we are at their mercy.

A ferry tooted on the river and she raised herself to look out of the window. The cliffs shimmered and regrouped themselves in a faint mirage, sea birds fluttered in blue air, and the noise of the city came to her muted by distance. For years she had lain here or walked round this room, an invalid, a parasite; useless in any society no matter how well it might be ordered. She rose and walked to the window, leaning her elbows on the sill. Far below her, leaves and grass stretched to the boundaries of pavement. Buses and automobiles glittered in the sun, figures sauntered. Hester thought: All this could be obliterated in an hour, and I be buried under the ruins. Left to gasp the frightful air of poison, left in the knowledge that there is no escape, with the thought that everything familiar and marvellous in the world, the sinful with the innocent, was perishing with me in a white heat. Memory itself crumbling with all its monuments. The end of life, of exquisite life . . . Her heart began to pound as the green earth drew her towards it, that earth which for ever withstood the assaults of men; they might climb the air and roam under the sea, but the earth withstood them, and in the end it vanquished them, only to renew itself under the eternal falling of leaves. Tears filled Hester's eyes. She had a vision of the world in its youth, of herself at a window of the Ark, the perfume of citrons blowing in her hair. She leaned farther out over the sill, holding her transparent hands towards the green fragment thirty floors below. She had but to push with her feet and the heavenly airs would enfold her for ever. Then it seemed to her that she heard Regan's voice, that attractive, husky voice which managed to utter its owner's ideas with such precision: "Don't be a fool, Hester!"

Hester turned from the window and went back to her couch, where she was overcome with sneezing. Exhausted, she lay among her pillows, mind and spirit completely blank, only her reddened eyes moving across the unresponsive ceiling.

In the meantime, a crimson roadster driven by William Symes was speeding over the white Connecticut highway, and Regan, watching her lover's hands on the wheel, felt a surge of exultation. She was never more certain of her power over him than when they were together like this, the world with its Marks, its Neddys, its Hesters excluded, and, as the miles rushed away— forgotten. Regan saw that he was smiling. His manner these past few days had excited her curiosity. There was a new assurance about him, and, what pleased her even more, a fresh possessiveness. She laid her hand on his knee: "I wish you'd tell me what's on your mind."

"You!"

"It must be more than that."

"How could it be?" He lifted her hand to his lips, and she leaned against him. For a moment or two he was tempted to tell her the reason of his elation, which sprang from his victory over Mark. Symes' instinct for secrecy had prevented his speaking of it; even now he hesitated, and decided that he had better wait a while longer before telling her of the encounter. In the first place he was not entirely sure how she would take it, in the second, wanted to savor his triumph in private, to try to understand it. For the truth was he had been badly frightened that night. Recalling all the details of the episode, he realized that the meeting had been inevitable from the moment he saw Mark enter the room. Though he tried to keep the crowd between Mark and himself, Symes had been aware, all along, of the fatal attraction which operates between lovers and enemies alike, and on the second when he and Mark came face to face in the door he saw that the game was up. Panic filled him, and out of it rose the single lucid thought: I won't fight him. I'll let him knock me out. That will be the simplest way. Yet he had tried to escape, making for the nearest elevator and praying he might be missed in the drunken mob. What transpired had all the elements of a dream—all the absurdity, all the horror. He knew he was cornered, he knew that Mark was going to hit him, and as the elevator rose he braced himself for the blow as a timid soul braces itself to receive judgment. Then he saw that Mark was drunk. Here was no avenging Gabriel, but an inebriated clown, and, as such, easily dealt with. Symes had struck with all his strength, and watched his enemy subside like a bag of onions. Not until much later, alone in his own apartment, was he able to appraise his action, and his reaction. Then, anointing his bruised knuckles, Symes experienced a stir of such exultation as he had never experienced in all his life. The unpremeditated blow struck in self-defense had released something long pent-up and inarticulate. A weight was lifted, he felt himself to be, at last, the kind of man he most admired, the kind of man he had never quite become—till this moment. Fear, with its taproot guilt, withered away; in its place flowered scorn for the bruised and insensible figure which he had seen groping blindly at his feet.

Symes felt Regan's body warm against his. He slowed the car, and brought it to a halt in the shade beside the highway. She looked at him. "Anything the matter?"

"You should know." He took her in his arms.

She laughed. "Aren't you afraid some one will come by and see us?"

"Let them," said Symes, and began to kiss her with unusual abandon.

That evening Stella dined alone at Philippe's, but the man who looked like Alec did not appear. She had come early and stayed as long as she could, lingering over a meal she scarcely tasted, her gaze hardly leaving the door. The place was evidently better patronized at night than during the day, for every table was taken. But of the face for which she searched there was no sign. What did she expect? He had been in uniform when she saw him first. Perhaps he had been ordered away, perhaps she never would see him again. But as she pushed open the doors and passed into the warm, dim air of the street, Stella could not control a wild rush of hope. Hope was to become a habit with her in the days which followed, but on the nature of that hope she dared not inquire . . . yet. All that mattered was that she see him again. Would his voice remind her of Alec's? How far could such a resemblance go, how far dared she pursue it? Walking slowly homeward through the noisy reaches of the city, she brooded on her vision of the stranger, and rapture flooded her. Rapture glowed in her face and moved through her limbs, so that the people who noticed her smiled involuntarily and went their way wondering at her secret.

18

A THUNDERSTORM dispersed the accumulated heat of the city, but its denizens, to whom the four seasons are as disturbing as the footfalls of an invader, flung up angry umbrellas or leaped into buses and taxies; others, damp and distraught, took refuge in doorways, under awnings, there to wait the end of the downpour. Returning one day from a journey uptown, Stella felt the rain on her face. She came to an abrupt stop on the sidewalk, struggling to recreate an image in her mind. When had this warmth responded through her flesh to the flooding rain? Then she remembered. There had been a day at Jarley when she and Alec had gone to the village to buy stores. Walking home, the rain overtook them and they began to run, laughing, down the gravel road towards the house. The paper bags became soaked and spilled oranges everywhere. Pelted by rain, they stopped to pick up the fruit, and as thunder crackled overhead, Stella, in mock fright, had flung herself into Alec's arms. Together they sank into the heavy grass, and he made love to her among the fallen oranges. She murmured: "Shouldn't we go under the trees?"

"Don't you know that trees are dangerous in a storm?"

In the past these recollections would leave her stricken, but today as she stood in the rain on a New York street Stella felt vitality, like lightning, sweep through her. Then her arm was taken in a firm grasp, and Dick Sparrow inquired: "Are you

trying to get pneumonia, or do you just want to ruin your hat?"
He propelled her into a spacious doorway, and she saw that
she had been standing within a few yards of his office.

"Come on up and smoke a cigarette," he suggested. "I've had
a lonely lunch and I'd like company."

In the elevator he looked at her inquisitively. "Might an old
friend inquire what you've been up to? We haven't heard from
you for days."

Stella replied that she had been up to nothing in particular,
but she was conscious of his shrewd gaze, and waited apprehensively for further inquiries. Dick said nothing till they were
in his office, and once in that impersonal stereotyped apartment,
with a cigarette in her fingers and Dick facing her across his
desk, she began to derive a certain amusement out of mystifying
him.

He began complainingly: "Why didn't you go to the country
with Miriam? It's stinking in town."

"I like the heat."

"Well," he said grudgingly, "it seems to agree with you.
Miriam was all played out." The complaining note returned.
"God, I've had a tough morning. I called you up, hoping you'd
lunch with me, but you weren't home. I've called you several
times this week but you never seem to stay home."

"What happened to spoil your morning?"

"A client, as usual. You know him, too—Symes."

"He's quite a pet of yours, isn't he?"

"On the contrary he seems to regard me as a pet of *his!*"

Symes had called up and begged for a few minutes in which
to discuss the highly important episode at the Rotterdam Hotel.

The few minutes had stretched into more than an hour, during which Dick expressed himself as horrified by the story. "You shouldn't have hit Bycroft!"

"I had to—it was two to one. He had a friend with him."

"But what made you think he was going to attack you?"

"There was murder in his eyes."

"Hell, he was drunk. You said so yourself."

"Then you believe I made a mistake?"

"I don't know. But you must have fetched him the devil of a blow to knock him out as you say you did."

"It was the devil of a blow," said Symes, with a revival of arrogance. He straightened his handsome shoulders. "Look, Dick. I'm getting good and tired with all this waiting round for Bycroft to make up his mind. There must be some way of hurrying him along. He's acting like a bastard—you know he is! It isn't even as if he were any saint himself. I heard a few stories about him that evening, from guys who knew him overseas. A creeping Jesus if there ever was! Then he comes home and tries to strike a holier-than-thou attitude towards Regan."

Dick shrugged. "I've told you he could spoil everything for you both if he got mad enough."

"Well," said Symes, defiantly, "I'm glad I hit him. He had it coming."

"Have you told Regan about this?"

"No, and I'm not sure I'd better. She has enough to put up with as it is. So you think there is nothing we can do to stir him up?"

"We can give him rope, and that's just what we're doing."

Dick sighed, and turned to Stella. "Sorry to be absent-minded. But you know, I'm getting fed up with sitting here listening to people's problems. The war has made me rich— that sounds bad, doesn't it? But it's the truth. The war knocked the mortar out of more darned marriages than you would believe. My practice has increased to the point where I've got to think of taking on a partner or retiring. At the moment, I feel like retiring, and fast."

"Miriam would like that. She wants to go and live in the country."

He shook his head mournfully. "That's always been her dream. But you know me, I can't walk through bushes that high without losing my shoes." He frowned.

"On the other hand it isn't such a bad idea, the country. Old people ought to be put out to grass, and I'm beginning to feel my age. What do you say the three of us go to Jarley, Stella? Let's grow old together."

She laughed. "I wouldn't believe any one could be so sentimental!"

"It's the privilege of age."

"But I don't feel old."

He looked at her closely. "Well, I must admit you don't look old, either."

"I'm only a trifle over thirty," she reminded him. "And you can't be more than fifty-five."

"Fifty-two," he corrected her sharply, and both laughed. "Do you know why a man of my age likes the idea of having extra-curricular love affairs?"

"It's probably due to the deplorable example of your clients."

"It's because love renews youth. Miriam was quoting the other day, from some poet who said: 'I see in love an ancient aspect touching a new mind.' "

Stella said she thought it sounded like a good poem. Privately she reflected: He looks older. There is a softness about him, the inward decay of a man who has never quite believed in the things he says or does.

"Why are you smiling, Stella?" And with increasing mystification: "What is it? You look different. For the first time since you came back from Italy, you look different."

She smiled, shaking her head.

"But you're changed," he persisted. "When I saw you standing there in the rain I stopped to watch you. I thought to myself: She looks like a woman waiting for her lover."

She replied noncommittally and Dick rose, but as he came round the table towards her she rose also. He took her by the arms. "Stella, tell me something."

"What?" There were little red veins in his eyes, in the flesh of his cheeks. His life was really over and he was just beginning to realize it. "Stella!"

She freed herself gently. "The rain has stopped. I must be going."

"Tell me what's on your mind!"

Should she tell him? Had Miriam mentioned the stranger at Philippe's? He said in a puzzled voice: "You look . . . you look . . ."

She waited, but he found himself without words. Both were aware of some new element between them, something neither could explain. Helping her on with her coat, Dick muttered: "Queer. You think you understand people, you think you know all there is to know about them, then they begin to change under your eyes." He escorted her to the door. "You're looking lovely. It's what I've been trying to say all along."

Was he trying to tell her that he believed in miracles, in resurrection? She did not ask him, and the question hung in the dry professional air of his lawyer's office. The rain had stopped and a gigantic shaft of light slanted down the street. She saw herself as transformed, and as she continued on her way, past the Library, it seemed to her as if the pedestrians through whom she moved were transfigured also, as if they too walked in a kind of celestial procession. At any moment the special figure she sought might separate himself from this nameless throng and come towards her. What would she do then, how would she greet him? She conjured up a memory of his face as she had seen it in the murky little restaurant, and passion stirred her, shaping her lips to endearments.

Every day since that first sight of him she had walked the city streets, or covered it in subways, in buses, pursuing one form then another, only to lose it in the end, or to discover that it was not the one she sought. She ate most of her meals at Philippe's, where the waiters had learned to accept her as a regular customer, and she made a point of going alone, for she could not bear the thought of some one being with her should Mark appear again. She wanted leisure and privacy in which to study him, to make sure that the resemblance was no hallucination. It was true that Miriam, too, had seen him, yet might there not be a chance that both had been deceived? Stella had not found an opportunity—nor had she sought it—to discuss the incident with her friend; and all the cold logic in the world had no power to dim the image she carried in her mind, or to subdue the wild hope in her breast.

Thanks to the ironies of city existence and city geography, Mark and Stella were often within an ace of meeting—on the street or in the same restaurant, where he dropped in for a meal on days when she, in despair, had decided to eat somewhere else. Twenty minutes' walk would have brought her to his door, yet the days passed and she did not see him. But she had seen him once, and her life centered on that vision. How often does one not meet, among strangers, one familiar face? How often is one told that one has been recognized all unknown to oneself? Coincidence? But Stella would have none of it. There was a reason for this meeting. How dared she doubt it? Perilous ideas roamed through her brain, through her dreams. Was it Alec after all, or one so like him that the separate identity became a mere abstraction? She believed that were she to see him again, to hear his voice, she would know beyond the shadow of doubt. What she did not—what she dared not contemplate, was the nature of that doubt—doubt itself, the last mainstay of a heart unreconciled.

19

THE MAID was out when the telephone rang, but Stella ignored it. She was dressing for a Landowska recital at Town Hall, and dreaded an interruption of her afternoon, and an invasion of her solitary frame of mind. Judging by the persistence of the summons she guessed it must be Miriam Sparrow calling up to talk at length about her own visit to the country, to reproach her friend for her inaccessibility, and to make searching inquiries about her activities during the past few days. Stella felt profoundly averse to such a conversation, and to the whole idea of companionship. For the first time since Alec's disappearance she was conscious of a completeness in her life, as if it had suddenly acquired boundaries and perspective. She no longer felt lonely, nor were her thoughts easily communicable. If she could not have silence, she would have music.

The telephone stopped ringing, but when Stella reached the door it started again with renewed stridency, as if it had paused only to get its breath. The sound pursued her all the way downstairs into the street, an insentient voice bidding her return.

"Taxi!" she cried in panic, and waved her white gloves at a cab which ground to a halt beside her. Breathless, she climbed in and gave the driver her destination. The sound of the telephone seemed imprisoned in her ears. She no longer thought of Miriam, impatiently waiting for her to lift the receiver; she thought of the sound as something materializing out of empty air, a mystic tyranny reminding her of the dull core of sense beneath the unreason of life. Let it ring! Let it scream its reminders through the empty rooms—she would not answer. She pictured it perched on the table beside her bed, above the drawer which held Alec's letters. She saw the gay airmail envelopes, his writing in the dry ink of the past. "If you should hear that I am dead, never believe it!"

But the present was what the musician unlocked for her listeners, when, all tall, gaunt grace, half-goddess and half-mother, she stepped across the glowing dais to the harpsichord, there to pause, there to acknowledge their greeting with a smile. Still smiling she made play with the cushion, tested the piano stool for comfort and height and sent, from where she stood, a tingle of mirth across the footlights into the eager darkness beyond. Then she was seated, in chignon and golden gown, gazing at her keyboard as though she expected some signal from it—a word, a tremor of its hidden nerves.

Tears rose in Stella's eyes. She felt an unbearable suspense and sweetness in the pause during which every face was lifted towards Landowska in an unspoken plea to those poised, capacious hands. "Let us be transfigured, let us be redeemed through you!" Creator and created stand in direct relation to each other, but the listener stands alone, judge and victim of his own experience. Those marvellous hands, hovering and striking, invited the human heart to rejoice, and the imagination to accept, humbly, joyfully, the eternal human paradox. "Here is the living heart of the abstraction, here the green germ of the illusion!"

When, later, Stella emerged from Town Hall she drifted

with the homing crowd from which the music had temporarily estranged her. Now each face seemed intimate and friendly; her fellow beings spoke to her with their eyes, with fleeting smiles of recognition. Believe in us, they said; believe in yourself. Humanity is all we know and all we ever shall know.

She walked to Madison Avenue, and, reluctant to go home, decided to stroll for a while. Light played on the familiar buildings, ignited fires in the windows and dyed the limp banners. She walked till dusk, then took a bus up town. They plunged past the demure façades of 36th Street and the Morgan Library, where the spectral maples shed their leaves. Images formed and dissolved in Stella's mind: she saw Landowska's hands, poised like birds; a luminous face in the audience; imaginary laughter mingled with music in peacock gardens, and trembled minute after minute in her ears. It was in this strange mood that she sat in the bus and stared at the people on the street; it was then she saw Mark. He had paused to light his pipe and she had no need to persuade herself that it was actually the face and figure she had been seeking. Desperately, she pulled the signal cord and made her way to the door. But the bus kept on its way, headed towards its appointed stop. Passengers stared at her curiously as she reached for the cord again. "Stop," she begged the driver, "please stop and let me out!"

He paid no attention, and she gazed with hatred at the broad back, the thick Irish profile, the adamant hand on the wheel. He might have been part of the machine itself—deaf, blind, heartless, driven by an inhuman caprice. On and on they went and Stella watched despairingly, as a sea of concrete and hu-

manity flooded the spot where she had seen Mark. At last the
bus stopped and she stumbled out on the sidewalk, pushing
through an opposing group of passengers whom she saw, not
as flesh and blood, but as obstacles fiendishly interposed between herself and her desire. At last she was back on the corner
of Madison and 43rd Street, but Mark had disappeared. Five
minutes before—it could have been no more than that—five
minutes before he had been standing on this spot. She had seen
him distinctly, a newspaper tucked under his arm as he paused
to light his pipe. It seemed that the image she had nurtured
for so long had suddenly intensified in the beam of reality;
what she experienced now was not surprise, but shock at an
encounter anticipated but not designed. Nor had she the faintest
idea what she would do if she were to catch up with him.
Passion assured her she would find him . . . but he was not
here. Instead she found herself staring at relays of strangers, or
pursuing their backs. She heard, falling about her like hail,
idiot, unfriendly voices.

Stella forced herself to walk slowly down the Avenue. He
might have gone into one of the doorways on either side of
the street, he may have walked faster than she had calculated,
and in any of four directions. On the other hand, he might
appear before her at any moment, and with that thought she
stopped. So intense was her sense of imminence that it paralyzed
her limbs, and a man, not seeing her in time, bumped into her.
"Pardon!" he muttered angrily, and the jarring impact brought
her to her senses. What a fool to stand here like a stranded
rock while the human tide flowed around her. Meantime, he
might easily be walking away, west towards Fifth Avenue, east

to Grand Central. Grand Central! Could he have been on his way to take a train? The awful possibility made her shy away at once; she faced the choice of going through Vanderbilt Avenue towards Fifth or following 42nd Street to the river. Afterwards she decided that her body, not her brain, made the choice, and because she found herself near 42nd Street she walked towards it, then turned and followed the stream of pedestrians eastward. On another day she would have stopped and bought a newspaper, but this evening the universe and its obsessions had ceased to exist so far as she was concerned. Life had reasserted its personal claim.

By the time she reached Lexington Avenue the sun had gone, but a translucent memory of it lingered. It was after six, cafés and bars were filled. Perhaps he was in one of them, and with this thought she realized that she would soon be on Third Avenue, a few blocks from Philippe's Restaurant. Dared she hope that he might have been on his way there? It was a chance, the flimsiest of chances, but Stella was in the mood to read meaning into the most trivial incident. When a taxi slowed up and the driver poked his head towards her, she took it for a sign and climbed in, her heart beating hard.

The traffic was heavy and they were forced to wait while trucks crawled across their bows. The driver turned on his radio and Stella listened to jive, while trains thundered and automobiles exuded acrid odors of gas and hot metal. The impulse to scream, to order the driver to go on, go on, almost overpowered her. Impossible that the throbbing world should remain indifferent to her anguish! Would she perhaps make better time or stand a better chance of finding him if she walked? Might he decide not to eat at Philippe's after all, but merely pause there for a drink before disappearing once more? Every second increased the chances of her missing him, whereas if she were to get out of the cab and walk, or even run. . . . Then the lights changed, the cab shot forward, bumping over cobbles, weaving between stanchions, while the radio contributed its discords to the turmoil within her.

When at last Stella's cab deposited her at her goal she stood for several seconds, quite unable to make up her mind whether she should enter. Lights shone behind the glass panel of the door, and she had a glimpse of the waiters moving about within. Her agitation became so violent that it directed attention to itself. She feared she was about to collapse on the sidewalk and die there for sheer want of breath. But how absurd to die now, crushed under the bedlam of one's own heart! It quieted at last, and she walked down the two steps to the door and went in.

Mark was not there. A couple sat at the table where she had last seen him, and she gazed at them with incredulous, hostile eyes. The waiter who always served her approached with a friendly smile. "Dinner for Madame?"

She let him guide her to the table where she habitually sat. Ordering a drink, she gazed round her bleakly, the joyous strains of Landowska's music draining from her consciousness, ending on a long, jarring echo. Mark was not here. Had she really seen him? Had her glance actually plucked him from out of the city's seven million figures? She stared at his table, usurped by strangers talking French and drinking wine in long glasses. The cat appeared and rubbed against their ankles, and her hostility extended even to that creature. The waiter brought her a cocktail; she lighted a cigarette and watched a procession of shadowy figures pass on the street beyond the door. The noise of traffic was muted except when a train went by, then the floor quivered and glasses trembled on their shelves.

The doorknob was grasped from outside, the door swung open, and Mark came in. The thing which Stella had longed for and which she had dreaded came to pass; she stared into eyes that were Alec's eyes, eyes which met hers briefly and without recognition. He found a table and sat with his back to her, and all she could see of his face was its blurred reflection in a corner of the window. A waiter came to take his order and Stella listened, hoping to hear his voice, but all she could catch was an indistinguishable murmur, then he spread his newspaper on the table and began to read. She gazed at his image on the window, an image stirred, broken, restored again by the shifting lights and the gloom of the world beyond. Like a mirage, it faded before the rushing impact of realities, only to reappear whole and marvellous. How serious he seemed, how almost sullen! And she remembered how Alec looked when he was reading without attention, his thought elsewhere. How jealous she used to be of those thoughts, how curious, how envious! What was this man thinking, now? Where had he come from, where would he go? Her own thoughts dissolved and materialized with the restless iridescence of his image in the window. A shadow-play of figures, objects, movement, formed a background for his face, and presently she saw that she too was mirrored there, a distant spectral self colored by life, or by the illusion of life. In this peculiar element their glances met, mingled, drowned; their spirits stayed moored on a weird surface, like ships held fast by invisible chains.

When he left Philippe's, Stella followed him through the dim evening streets to his door. She watched from a distance as he sought for his key and let himself into the house, out of her sight. Then she crossed the street and descended to the narrow entry, and studied the names on the letter-boxes. Symons, Brown, Gerber, Winslow, Bycroft, Glazer, Hume. Which of these belonged to him? He wore the uniform of a colonel in the Air Corps, but no colonel was listed here. Could he be visiting one of the tenants? Was he a newcomer who had not yet placed his card in one of the empty boxes? She read the names over again, endowing each with magic and significance, then she turned and walked slowly home.

20

SUMMER DREW over the city, but for Stella the season had lost its conventional meaning. She moved indifferent as a bird, adding day by day to the paradise she had built for her lover and herself. Now every familiar sordid detail of the city changed, in her eyes, to the colors of enchantment. She revived old tricks of vanity, lingering for hours over the selection of a dress or a pair of earrings. Instinct fused with desire became her instructor, and she studied from afar such of Mark's habits as circumstances would permit. It was a strange pursuit, of which her quarry remained for many days ignorant, for she was careful to keep a distance between them, moving as she did between the twin poles of fear and longing. She walked every morning to East 53rd Street and waited for him to appear, then followed till she lost him. Sometimes a small boy accompanied him, and on one such occasion—a hot, still afternoon—she pursued them as they strolled along Marie Curie Avenue, almost as far as Rockefeller Institute. They walked slowly, the child sometimes taking the man's hand, and though their voices reached her they were too far for her to catch the words. Was the child his? Was he a widower, or divorced? The questions occurred to her, but she dismissed them, since their implications could have no bearing on her paradise.

On this hot afternoon the light lay like pewter over the water, gulls swayed in the air and their cries fell languidly through the assorted noises of the street and the river. To Stella there seemed something solitary and meditative in the man's walk, and she remembered Alec in moods of abstraction, when he excluded his surroundings and her, and all those familiar aspects of himself which she believed she knew by heart. There are in all of us small, dark islands of solitude where we are bound to walk alone if we walk at all; habitations intolerable to those whom we love, and who love us.

Spinning her fantasies round the unsuspecting figure of this man who so much resembled her beloved, Stella felt the resemblance grow more poignant as she recognized in his walk, in his aloof and burdened air, yet another vanished trait. So, sometimes, Alec used to walk on the narrow roads round the house at Jarley, or she would come on him sitting on the rocks facing the sea, and he would be unable to explain his queer, melancholy mood.

Mark and Neddy had turned and were walking towards her. They walked faster than she realized and she had the choice of continuing on her own course or of turning away. But as she hesitated, slowing her step, the man strode towards her, so purposeful, so animated by a remembered vitality, that Stella found herself unable to move. Then they were face to face and as Mark's eyes gazed into hers, she uttered a faint exclamation —greeting, recognition, protest, she could not herself have said which. He responded with a slight surprised smile, then continued on his way, passing her and taking the boy's hand as they crossed the street. Stella watched them go, but they did not turn to look back, and for several minutes she stood trembling with happiness.

What did she expect from the situation? Had a friend asked this question she would have found it impossible to answer. The friend might have ventured to suggest that the man's resemblance had recreated—not Alec—but a figure more portentous, one which entered upon her consciousness at a moment when resignation had reached its final pitiful boundary, the very edge of the abyss.

There are people who cannot accept the inevitable, people who yearn on into oblivion, and a friend would have guessed that Stella was such a person. Instinct and imagination conspired to make her perceive, in Mark, something besides his extraordinary likeness to Alec, to catch in him a reflection of her own defrauded spirit, and bleakly aware that in another year she would have become an old woman—one of those human travesties for which the casual eye finds no excuse and the humdrum heart no pity—to recognize and to worship Mark as her savior, just as she had recognized and worshipped Alec. Stella knew well enough that it was no ghost she pursued through the sweltering hours and in intervals when the sea air blew miraculously through the burning streets. A ghost would have recognized her—yes, in the very center of Babel a ghost would have taken her hand and greeted her by name, but this other, this erect and lonely figure stared at her with blank brown eyes, and passed her without a word.

There were opportunities when she might have spoken to him, once while they waited for a bus and he stood aside to give her precedence, again when she followed him and his small companion to the Park and lingered while they sailed a boat on the pond. But she shrank from breaking a spell which left her free to paint the days that passed and those to come in a panorama of enchantment.

By now Mark had realized that he was being shadowed, and his reactions fluctuated between curiosity and contempt. However, he gave no sign, nor did he alter his routine in order to avoid her. He guessed that the world must be filled with lonely people, and that this strange young woman who trailed him up and down the streets, in and out of restaurants and theatres, was probably no more of a menace than others had been. One evening as he took his accustomed seat at Philippe's he glanced across the room and saw her sitting alone in the corner which he had learned to associate with her rather colorless personality. He was not prepared for the intensity of her gaze, and it startled him into a grudging smile of recognition. Neither spoke, but for Stella the moment had surely arrived. Alec's eyes held hers, they drew her irresistibly to her feet, even while something warned her to fly from the encounter. Instead, she found herself standing beside his table. He rose and pulled out a chair for her, and she felt that she was subject to a will no longer her own.

"Please sit down. I'm Mark Bycroft. Will you have a drink?"

"I'm Stella Harmon. Thanks, yes."

He signalled the waiter and gave his order. The kaleidoscope shifted, its radiant design became fixed. It was Alec who faced her, Alec notwithstanding the voice, which was certainly not the voice of Alec.

"You've been following me," he said.

"Yes, for almost two weeks."

"That long? Will you tell me why?"

"I doubt whether you'd understand. It sounds silly, reduced to words."

"Yet you can't blame me for asking."

The waiter brought their drinks, and Mark stirred his with the glass dibbler. It was not for the usual reasons that she had followed him, he told himself. She's not that sort. So much he could guess easily enough. Perplexed, he waited.

Stella said: "I was here the other day, with a friend. We were seated in that corner. You were here drinking beer and playing with the kitten."

"I often come here for meals because it's within walking distance of where I live."

She said after a pause: "I followed you because of your resemblance to my husband."

"I still don't understand."

"He was killed in the war." It was the first time she had said it. The words echoed in her ears, a hushed, incredulous note. Mark looked at her grimly, and she shook her head. "I know . . . I know what you're thinking. It's a new gag, and not in very good taste. But it does happen to be true." She gazed at him earnestly. "Believe me!" He remained silent and she went on quickly: "You must have seen such likenesses yourself—there are such things. This is really extraordinary. Try to put yourself in my place! Don't blame me for following you, for wanting to talk to you!"

"But you could have spoken to me before this. One day when we took the cross-town bus on 57th Street, another time in the Park, once when we—my son and I—were walking by the river." He looked at her scornfully. "What was the idea, trailing me all over town?"

His voice, his face, were full of hostility, and for a moment Stella was silent, crushed by a reaction she had not foreseen. At last she said: "I don't know what I expected. I just wanted to look at you. I don't see why you should care, one way or another."

"I don't care. But I'm not your husband, you know." He did not intend to sound brutal, but his own words evoked another memory, and Regan's face rose before him, Regan's voice filled his ears. An hour ago she had called him on the telephone and they had quarrelled violently. He would not let her have Neddy. She could take herself to the nearest whorehouse for all he cared. And he had hung up before she could complete her side of the tirade. But as the savage exultation of battle ebbed, Mark felt a weakness, a positive physical impotence. Hatred of Regan was accompanied by a recollection of William Symes, by a stinging pain in his lips, still sore from the blow dealt him in the Rotterdam Hotel. He brooded on the pattern of catastrophe as he saw it affecting his life and the lives of others—of Neddy, Symes, even young Perry, with whom he had quarreled and parted a week ago. Following an ill-advised impulse Perry had suggested that Mark seek the advice of a psychiatrist and get himself "straightened out." The implications of such advice were too much for Mark. Curtly, he recommended that Perry himself go west and castrate bulls beside his native Pecos. Hurt beyond words, the young man had said goodbye, and gone.

Mark saw these disasters, silly or tragic as they might be, as springing from his wife's ruthless egotism. The impulse to hurt some one, to revive his own tumbled ego at the expense of another's, returned as he looked, now, at Stella. "I'm not your husband," he had just reminded this woman, another casualty of the age, a somnambulist in search of a bed. His bed? Not if he knew it.

He caught Stella's gaze fixed upon him. She said sadly: "Don't hate me."

"Hate you? I don't even know you."

"You looked as if you must be hating me."

"I wasn't thinking about you." He hesitated, then went on: "As a matter of fact, I was thinking about my wife. She has left me, and I ought to be grateful, but instead I find myself wanting her and detesting her at the same time. Not loving her, mind you. No, not loving her at all."

What possessed him to confide in a stranger? Unable to stop now that he had begun, he went on to speak of his home-coming, of Regan's desertion, of his own reactions, and of his little boy, and as he spoke of these things, they took a shape entirely different from themselves, they became as distorted as his own mental image of himself. He told Stella of his recent attempt to kill an innocent man; of his torments of remorse, of the fiend of violence which he had often waylaid and conquered in the past. But would he always conquer? Superstition made it impossible for him to name William Symes, the name had become a nightmare. "If I had killed him, they would have blamed it on the war. They would have said that I was psychotic and, instead of treating me as a criminal, they'd have sent me off to some institution for the mentally unstable. The truth is we are all responsible for what we do, and in a sense for what others do to us. We're responsible, all of us." He reflected: I shan't see her again. She's used an imaginary resemblance as an excuse to pick me up, and I'm using it as an excuse to leaven my loneliness. What harm? We'll talk a little. I'll pay for her drink, and we'll part. And he remembered other encounters in Europe, nameless derelicts who had turned to him, their husbands being dead or vanished, like hers.

Stella said: "Tell me about your son."

"I hardly know him. He was a baby when I went away, now he's a person. There are things going on in his head—speculations, decisions, in which I have no share. What can I tell him? What can I teach him, that his own experience won't revise? We move in the same orbit, but separately. Not strangers exactly, but not friends either."

"Like the rest of us—not strangers exactly, but not friends either."

He shrugged. "It's only when I try to find something honest and comforting to say to Neddy that I realize I am in a corner."

"Something comforting?"

"Well, when I was his age my mother used to make me say prayers. I said them unthinkingly, but I relied on them, and on her. When I was fourteen I gave up saying prayers, for by that time I'd formed other allegiances besides my mother and God Almighty. We pass from one attachment to another, don't we? In my childhood we began with the idea of a comforting God who spoke to us through our mothers, or our fathers."

"The voice of love, you mean."

"I suppose so. That's where Neddy is out of luck."

"You and I also."

"Sorry. I seem to have done nothing but talk about myself. Tell me about you, about your husband. When was he killed?"

The echo woke in her ears, "Two years ago, at the battle of Montescari. . . ."

"And this resemblance, is it so noticeable?"

"Very." Her voice trembled. "It's extraordinary."

Pityingly, he touched her hand, envying the dead man who had been so well-loved and who was so deeply mourned, then something she had said recurred to him: "You and I are also out of luck." He had no wish to be included in her bad luck, for he had his own, and it was more than enough. Pity for her was succeeded by revulsion against this likeness between himself and the dead. Our fundamental sense of identity is a subtle and precious thing, not easily shared, even with the living. Contact with Stella's hand sent a current of intimacy towards him, and he recoiled.

"Dinner?" asked the waiter, and laid a menu on the table.

"I'm sorry, I can't stay." Mark paid for their drinks, then nodded to Stella. "I've got to go home. Thank you for talking to me."

"Colonel Bycroft, would you have lunch with me tomorrow?"

He hesitated, but it seemed easier to leave her with an acceptance.

"If you like. Here?"

"Here, at one o'clock?"

"Fine," said Mark, and left her.

21

WALKING HOME, he speculated about Stella. Should he have stayed and had dinner with her instead of running away? It might have been kinder, but he was in a mood to suspect some trick, though unable to define his fear. He began to regret that he had accepted her invitation for lunch the next day. Well, there was time to change his mind; he could easily leave a note for her at Philippe's, expressing regret and saying goodbye. He had found her sensitive and intelligent; she would hardly fail to take the hint and leave him alone. Then he recalled her face, discovering beauty in it, and in her voice. He guessed that it would not have been difficult to make love to her, that she would not have repulsed him. But could that be what she was after—the cheapest of commodities? There had been nothing cheap about her, rather something ardent and pathetic, the friendliness of a child. Remembering the response of her hand when he touched it, he felt a sudden kindling of desire and half turned to go back, but desire brought an image of Regan: he saw her face contorted in a mask of dislike, even while her limbs embraced him, he heard her saying, "I didn't want to have it on my conscience that I refused you!"

Mark walked on, scurrilities filling his mouth, uttering themselves, so that people who passed glanced at him in disgust. He walked slowly in the cooling summer air, and by the time he reached the apartment Neddy was in bed, and Octavia, hatted

183

and gloved, sat reading the paper while she waited his return so she could go home. "Sorry to be late, Octavia."

She rose and looked at him with an air of indecision. "Colonel Bycroft, you've got to do something about Neddy."

"Isn't he all right?"

"Oh, he's all right, I guess. But there's something on his mind."

"I suppose you're getting ready to tell me he misses his mother."

She faced him stubbornly. "He'd be a queer sort of child if he didn't miss his mother!"

"There's nothing to prevent her coming back, you know."

She shook her head. "What do you expect, Colonel? Where is this going to get you, or Neddy? Something is happening in the child's mind."

"Well?" Queer, he thought, how this woman can always command my attention. Could it be that even in age she retained a femininity he missed in women of his own color? If she had been twenty years younger. . . . But she was sixty and respectable.

"Well?" he repeated, relenting.

"Neddy wants his mother."

"We've discussed this before, Octavia. You know how I feel about it."

"But he needs her!"

"I'm afraid he'll have to put up with me instead."

"Ah, let him go. He'll come back to you in the end."

"How do you know?"

"He's trying to love you, only he's frightened. Something

happened today. He must have heard you quarrelling with Mrs. Bycroft over the phone, and when you left the house he went and locked himself in his room and wouldn't let me in, nor answer me. When he came out again I saw he'd been crying. I wanted to ask him why, but I was afraid that if he told me I wouldn't know what to say to set things right."

Mark felt confused and angry. "Why in hell should I let him go to her, probably to be brought up by some man not his father?"

"And you? Do you mean to live alone the rest of your life? If you keep him, won't he be brought up by some woman that isn't his mother?"

"It's none of your God-damned business!"

The austerity in her face gave way to a smile. She looked at him quietly, then moved to the door.

"Octavia!" And as she turned, he asked miserably: "How have I scared Neddy?"

"I don't know. It's easy to scare children." And with that she left him. When the door had closed on her Mark went to the pantry and mixed himself a drink. He came back to the living room and picked up the newspaper, taking the chair Octavia had just left. Here is the world, he told himself sardonically as he spread the paper on his knees, the world beyond my stinking personal one, the world invented by Big Threes and Big Fours and Big Fives, the world which might explode at any moment in shudders of blue light. Regan's face gazed at him from the front page, smiling between a column which dealt with famine in China and another with starvation in Europe. She had delivered an address before a women's club the evening before, on the question of democratic training in the kindergartens of Japan. There were excerpts from the address, followed by a glowing description of the speaker's charm and the excellence of her delivery. Readers would recall that Mrs. Bycroft was the wife of Colonel Bycroft, the distinguished soldier, just returned from duty overseas.

So Regan was not going to have the infant Nips on her conscience, either, thought Mark, and tossed the paper on the floor. He stretched his legs and reflected on the events of the day. First the row with Regan. Where had Neddy been during that highly articulate quarter of an hour? He'd forgotten all about the boy and about Octavia, both of whom must have heard every syllable of his outburst. Later he had gone on one of his long walks, trying as usual to burn off unexpended emotion, and stopping for a drink at Philippe's he had met Stella. The sense of waste, of existing in a vacuum, came over him. Was the remainder of his life to be spent in child-surveillance, in aimless saunterings, chance encounters, with only a dim horizon of hope for something better? Just what was it he wanted or expected, now that he knew he could not return to the old life? *I shall have to hunt for a job.* The thought brought its familiar spasm of distaste. God! A job—office hours, commuting, business luncheons, buying, selling, competition—and behind it all the perpetual shadow of insecurity and age. Original fellow to have discovered it all so late! For several minutes he busied himself with financial computations. He could count on about ten or twelve thousand dollars, enough to tide Neddy and himself over a couple of years if he used discretion. Thank heaven Regan had her own income, which spared him the vile intimacy of money dealings with her. The best thing to do would be to clear out of New York the minute he was quit of the army, and invest in a small place in the country. If he just had the house in Connecticut . . . Longing rose in him, memories of the house, of the smell of the garden in spring, of familiar rooms, of voices hailing him on quiet roads, the give and take and the small politics of rural society.

Darkness filled the room, the lights went on across the street and he sat quietly sipping his drink and watching strangers pull their curtains against his envious gaze. Voices eddied up from the street, he heard the clang of a mail-box lid as some one mailed a letter. The continuity of life was thick and consistent, and perhaps to some all-perceiving eye it afforded a visible design, but all that he could detect were patches of brilliance in the threadbare warp of ruin. What was it Stella had said? "You and I are out of luck." That's right, he brooded, nodding. But I am not your husband, my dear. *He's* dead somewhere under the Italian mud, Mussolini's mud, the mud of the Medicis, of the popes and the Caesars. He died to make America safe for the competitive system, and now death has smoothed away his flesh and his wounds with it. Now only his straight white bones remain to lime the Italian field. But his wife walks in the sunlight, and it wouldn't take much, no it wouldn't take much to bring *her* to life again!

He got up and went to the window. The warm night greeted him and he stood watching figures saunter under the lamps. Then he went to Neddy's room, where the child lay motionless in his narrow bed. Mark had to bend low to make sure the big eyes were closed. He stood pondering Octavia's argument. Was she right? Was this battle over a child worth the price? And what was the price? Should he take it for granted that Neddy must be the one to pay? Only in America, thought Mark, are these questions important. Only in this great lush land where the bitches wear blue ribbons, where children are property, where the crowd has thankfully turned its back on war and the broken pieces of the world, and its attention to the cream pie. How long before the pie blew up in its face?

Poor little Neddy. Mark bent and kissed his hair, but the child slept on undisturbed.

He was late in keeping his engagement with Stella next day, and found her waiting for him at Philippe's. "I was afraid you might have changed your mind," she said as he sat down.

"I did change it, several times."

"Did you? Why?"

"Suppose you tell me why you were afraid I might?"

She hesitated, then: "I was afraid you'd decide I was a fraud. But apparently you didn't, for here you are."

Mark felt a slight twinge of guilt, for the truth was he had not meant to keep the engagement. He had drunk too much the night before and had awakened with a headache. The morning had seemed interminable, walls and ceilings seemed to press upon him, he saw himself a prisoner of his own self-righteousness. The need to escape from yet another situation drove him forth at last, and remembering Stella he thought: I'll leave a note for her at Philippe's, then take a ferry and go somewhere—anywhere. But by the time he reached the restaurant it was twenty

minutes past the appointed hour, and there she was, waiting.

As for Stella, she had spent the morning as she spent most
of the previous evening, scheming for this moment, dreaming
of it, fearful of disaster and interruption. She had directed her
maid to take all telephone calls and to tell friends that she
would call them back. By this means she circumvented the
Sparrows, who had been trying to reach her for several days.
Her mood was all suspense—a touch, a smile of derision, would
shatter it, and it was in this mood that she had come early to
Philippe's, anticipating the joy of watching Mark enter the
room. Waiting, she indulged in all the simple sensuous pleas-
ures of expectation, pleasure in the knowing smile of the waiter,
in the play of sunlight on a checked table cloth, in the gambols
of the kitten as it stalked its shadow across the floor; pleasure
in the smell of food and the rattle of cutlery and the sound
of pulled cork. It seemed to her that she had not heard these
things, or seen them, or felt them, for a long time, and her
absence from them had ended at last in the house of the living.

She noticed that he looked as if he had not slept, that his
eyes were bloodshot, and reading her glance, he shrugged.
"Look like hell, don't I? I got drunk last night, all by myself."

"Have you no friends to get drunk with?"

"I was not feeling particularly friendly." Drawn by the
sympathy in her eyes, he began to talk about himself, won-
deringly, disgustedly, as if he were describing a younger and
a difficult brother. He told her of his stupid quarrel with young
Perry, during which he had said all the quick, sure, unforgive-
able things. "He was young and happy, and he bored me. That's

one friend I'll never drink with again." He went on to recount his argument with Octavia, and his uncertainties concerning his son. "You see, it's no longer a question of love and responsibility being the deciding factors. I find myself living an unloving and irresponsible life."

"I don't see anything contradictory in your wanting to keep Neddy."

"I'm not sure I do want to keep him, if his unhappiness is going to poison me. That's not as selfish as it sounds. The truth is, most men don't understand children the way women do. That's what Octavia meant when she told me it was better for Neddy to be with his mother. And maybe she meant, too, that it would be wiser to let him learn to know his mother for whatever she is . . . after which he might want to come back to me. Yet I hold on to him. I can't help seeing him as a symbol— a reminder of the past and of the future."

"You can't reconcile them. It's something you've got to leave to Neddy."

"Ah, yes, a little child shall lead us, and all that crap." His face darkened with a memory of the children he had seen in Europe. He believed that Christianity had died there with them, while Mama and Papa God were looking the other way.

He said bitterly: "We go on making a kind of sense . . . trains run, cars and buses start and stop, people walk about on two legs, every man for himself remains the morality of our day. Some of us paint pictures and read poetry. My wife, for instance. She makes sense. I make sense. Yet I know that something has gone from us—from all of us. Something has gone from the middle of us."

The waiter returned with their drinks. Mark went on: "The queer thing is that all this doesn't really depress me. I suppose that if it did I'd bump myself off. During the war I saw the naked helplessness of people and knew that it was matched only by their tenacity. What really stops me in my tracks is the knowledge that I have passed beyond despair."

Stella regarded him pensively. "We are in another world, aren't we? Perhaps we're only just beginning to get the feel of it. Another world, a scientific morality."

He laughed. "Scientific morality! That's a nice expression. But if scientists had the gift of prophecy any old morality would be good enough."

They were silent for a little while. Round them rose the voices of other guests, and from the door, left ajar because of the heat, came the noise of the trains. Through this larger, impersonal orchestration moved the small, intense preoccupations of Mark and Stella, drawing their lives together, shaping the invisible and inviolable design of their future.

22

SEVERAL DAYS passed and he did not see Stella, nor did he hear from Regan. Time became a succession of fiery hours, in which he read, walked, slept, and tried without notable success to understand his son. They went to movies and to the Park, on ferry rides to the Jersey shore and excursions to the airport. There were occasions when the boy emerged from a cocoonlike abstraction to ask when Mark intended to hire the sailboat he had once spoken of, and whether they would ever really go and live in the country. "Soon as I am out of the army," Mark assured him, and Neddy accepted the assurance as he did most things, without further inquiry. Why doesn't he rebel, wondered Mark. Why doesn't he quarrel with me, make demands, ask embarrassing questions? He longed for a glimpse at the concealed mirror of his son's mind. What would he have found there, what images of himself and Regan, and how far distorted, or how faithful?

One evening a week after his luncheon with Stella she called him up. "I'm down here at the Village. Will you join me for dinner?"

"Isn't it a bit warm to be moving round?"

"There is actually a breeze down here!" Her voice had a ring of gaiety. For some reason Mark imagined her to be wearing a white dress with frills at the neck.

"All right," he said. "Where shall I meet you?"

"At Longchamps on 12th Street and Fifth Avenue. They have an outdoor café." Mark departed light-heartedly to take a shower. As Stella had said, it was quite cool outdoors, the air had a strange freshness after days of heat. He had ample time, so took a bus instead of the subway, and climbing to the top, watched the city subside in a pink evening haze, and the Washington Arch loom above brick façades and the dusty trees of the Square. Stella was waiting for him and they sat down at a table facing the avenue. Mark said: "I believe I must have second sight. I knew you'd be wearing a white dress. However, I miss the ruffles."

"Ruffles?"

"White dresses should always have ruffles."

"Are you disappointed?"

"No." Far from being disappointed he experienced a peculiar pleasure in being with her. The air was fraught with a smell of gasoline and the vagrant perfume of women's clothes. Mark wondered whether all American cities possessed this aura of femininity—expensive, erotic. The Martini he ordered tasted like nectar, which he had never drunk, but which he now believed must taste like a Martini. And how nice, he thought, to be out on such an evening with an attractive woman, with the expectation of a moon above the Washington Arch. For the first time since his homecoming he felt grateful that the wondrous city should have been spared the fate of Europe, but gratitude mingled with the foreboding which had been his inveterate companion during the past four years. How would New York smell after bombing? He had not smelled Hiroshima, but would this one give forth the sickening odors of Kassel, Ham-

burg, Pforzheim? Would it reek like Caen and St. Lô? How had
Nineveh smelled, and Babylon, and Ur? Thinking of this he
felt a familiar tightening of his nerves as they prepared for
something—for some sound, for an impact which would leave
him, as it had always left him, shivering and incredulous.

"What's on your mind?" asked Stella. Her face emerged out
of a ruck of faces, noises, memories. Her face a shade or two
duskier than her dress, the flesh of her neck and shoulders
faintly visible under the thin material. He told her what was on
his mind, and she shook her head. "That's all finished, isn't
it? Finished."

"Finished . . . *kaput*. But here we are, you and I, alive and
not too decrepit to rejoice."

"I'm glad you came this evening, Mark. I woke up with such
a feeling of optimism, and it's lasted all day. I haven't felt like
this for a very long time, and I wanted to share it with you."
Her words roused a warmth in him, and suddenly he understood why he had known that she would be wearing a white
dress this evening. Memory had been pressing against the edges
of his mind; now it came into the open and he recalled the
early summer of 1941, when he and Regan had come up from
the country for a farewell party with John Halloran, who had
enlisted in the army and was being sent south for training.
They had spent a merry evening in the Village, and Regan had
worn a white dress with ruffles, and her beauty made people
turn to stare at her. Newsboys appeared, headlines announced
the sinking of the British battleship *Hood* by the German
cruiser *Bismarck*. Savagery and desolation seemed to tower above
the carefree diners and to hang there, a giant comber threaten-

ing them all with extinction. Now Mark tried to remember Halloran, but all that came back to him was an impression of some one slight and fair-haired. And why was it always so difficult to recall the color of a person's eyes?

He spoke of this to Stella. "Yours are gray, aren't they? And mine?"

"Brown."

"But you're not looking at me!"

"Brown," she repeated in a whisper, and he put his hand on hers. "I forgot. Sorry!" But the recollection made him uneasy, and to change the subject he began to talk about future plans. "If I don't hear from the War Department pretty soon, I'm going to Washington and beard them in their den. Meantime Neddy is growing paler and paler, and it bothers me."

"Why don't you send him to the country?"

"Because I'm afraid to let him out of my sight."

"Afraid?"

"Afraid of my wife. Sounds ugly, doesn't it? Sounds silly, too. But she might get her hands on him."

"You speak of him as if he were an object, a possession like a piece of furniture."

"Well, what is he, actually? The property of his parents. So long as we don't abuse him too much, we can do as we please." The old bitterness began to rise, and he fought it off. "No, I shall keep Neddy. Once I'm out of the army I'll be able to think, to make concrete plans for both of us."

There was a short silence, then Stella said: "I have a house in the country. It's on the Maine coast, with fields in front and woods behind. The house is old and looks like one of those shells we pick up at low tide. At night, when the windows are open, you can smell the pine trees and the sea. In fall the air smells of apples."

"You're lucky. I had a house once, or thought I did. And I had the usual sentimental feelings about it. But it belonged to my wife and she sold it."

The color had risen in Stella's face. "Then take my house!"

"What?"

"It's there, ready, waiting. Take it, Mark."

"Your house? But why don't you live in it yourself?"

She ignored the question. "You and Neddy. . . . Yes, of course, that's the solution. Why not?" She leaned towards him eagerly. "Why not, Mark? It's there, it's always been there."

He felt an answering excitement. "It's an idea! I could rent it, couldn't I? Sounds ideal. But I still don't see . . ." Then, as he studied her, he did begin to see a little, and his feeling for her—a feeling compounded of many things, attraction, suspicion, friendship, resolved itself slowly into a grudging tenderness. "Poor Stella!" Again he touched her hand. "Well, why don't I take your house, since you're so kind? Would you come and live with us?"

"Do you want me?"

"Of course!" But since he could not bear the thought of a misunderstanding, he added: "I've become a dull guy these past few years. I've not much to offer any one, but we could be friends, I think, the three of us."

She met his gaze, and to Mark it seemed as if she were perilously near to committing herself, and him, to further responsibilities. In another mood, with another woman, he might have welcomed the danger out of sheer loneliness, but while this woman attracted him, she always strangely repelled him. His feelings towards her were not whole feelings, and passion for her died almost at the moment of its inspiration. He had said that they could be friends and he meant it. There was comfort in the thought, and fittingness. But he was through with love for the time being, perhaps for the rest of his life. Regan had attended to that. She had attended to it with her customary efficiency, and he believed that no matter what relationship he might embark on henceforth, there would always be a lack in him, an incapacity for fulfillment, a deep weariness.

"Well," he said, smiling. "What do you say? Neddy and I offer you a handsome rental and our undying gratitude. Shall we drink to it?"

Though she returned his smile, he guessed that she had read his mind, that she forgave him because she loved him. She had reminded him, once, that they were both people out of luck, but in this capacity for love she was less wretched than he; shouldn't he be grateful to her for that also? And how demonstrate his gratitude unless through candor? She seemed to expect that much from him, at any rate. He said gently: "You're finding me a mean customer. But I've been rooked—cleaned out. Do you understand that? Can any woman understand it? I don't want to make a play for your charity. I think if you showed me charity I'd kill you. I saw enough of that in Europe, where all we had to offer those wretches was charity, where every natural instinct dribbled into charity. The return for charity is hatred, and I would never want to hate you!"

She sat quietly looking at him. He went on: "I became very

simple in those days. There was nothing to look at except blasted houses and human beings who looked back at you with eyes like broken windows." He stroked her hand. "Your eyes are not like that, Stella."

"Will you tell me why you said, just now, that women cannot understand men who have been rooked?"

"Because they can't understand how war—I mean the actual waging of war—affects men. It leaves us bankrupt. That's why governments dole out medals, citations, pensions, bribes. They're supposed to take the place of our humanity, to reward us for our impotence."

She looked away, unable, suddenly, to face him. He said: "Perhaps all I need is to see things in a humble perspective! I need the country . . . I need green things, harmless, permanent things." He stared at her anxiously. "Would you say I was ducking the issue?"

She answered swiftly, tenderly: "The house is there, for you, Mark!" And now she talked to him about it, describing the rooms and garden, the pasture which sloped to the sea, the dusty roads threading ancient fields; she spoke of her neighbors, fishermen and hunters like James Anderson, little shopkeepers, craftsmen who made the weathervanes, the coffins, and toys for the children. Mark listened, charmed by her voice and the visions it invoked. All through dinner they discussed the house and plans for setting it in order. "I've neglected it," Stella said. "It needs a lot of work."

"I used to be pretty good with a hammer and nails. Can't say as much for my gardening, though!"

He pictured himself, his son, his home in the glow of a new

life, not life in the sentimental vein, but life which must germinate out of rottenness and death. After dinner they strolled round the Square, where evening glowed on the brick of old houses and all the light in the city seemed to have rushed to the sky and resolved itself into a luminous background for the moon. When at last he took her back to her door he stood for a few minutes, reluctant to let her go with no more than a word of thanks and goodnight. People passed them in two irregular streams, a radio muttered unintelligibly from a parked car.

"Stella . . ."

"Mark, let me come and see you and Neddy. Let's meet again, soon."

"Of course. Tomorrow, next day, the day after—every day!"

Sympathy had brought them close; in that incandescence she moved like a new person. "Every day!"

"Good night, my dear."

He waited till the white dress had vanished through the dim entry and out of his sight.

23

DESPITE HIS friendliness when he asked her to visit him, Stella thought she detected a touch of reserve in Mark's manner. Could it be that he feared, as she did, that such a meeting might force their separate worlds into a conventional mould, and so expose them to all its hazards? An instinct that was part jealousy and part superstition prevented her from confiding in her friends and seeking their advice. Even in the midst of chaos the world she knew managed, somehow, to cling to the formal and the exacting; it still preserved its fatal aptitude for obedience, the enemy of love. So far, her companionship with Mark had had all the enchantment of the thing concealed, the half-real; she knew that the intrusion of others, even of those who were indispensable to both of them, must sooner or later alter their relationship. She thought of Neddy. Would he resemble his father? Though she had seen him, she had not yet had a chance to examine him for any resemblance, and in a strange way she was more troubled by the fact of the child's existence than by Regan's. Yet she knew that there was no avoiding the encounter. She had come into their lives, she had given them her house, yet she knew she was herself the real tenant, and her lease a tenuous one.

Dressing one day to go to Mark's apartment, she was interrupted by Miriam on the telephone. "Where have you been?" demanded Miriam. "Not a word from you for three weeks! Dick and I were considering putting the police on your trail."

Stella sat on the edge of the bed with the receiver in her hand, and smiled at her reflection in the mirror across the room. She took mischievous pleasure in her friend's reproachful tone. "What have you been up to? We've missed you. I was afraid you must be ill, but your maid assured me she had never seen you in better health. She said you were hardly ever home these days. *When* are we going to see you?"

"When? Oh, I don't know . . . soon, I hope, Miriam."

The light coming through Venetian blinds divided her body into bars of dark and crystal; her hair was still wet from the shower and shed cold drops on her skin, making her shiver slightly, as if she'd been unexpectedly kissed.

"Are you alone?" Miriam demanded suddenly. "I mean now, this minute?"

"Of course I'm alone."

"You sound queer. Listen, Stella. Will you come to a party Friday evening? We've managed to rope in a few people who're still alive in this God-forsaken city. The Smiths and Willingdons and William Symes. You remember Symes?"

"Symes?"

"Say you'll come. There's so much to talk about."

"Of course, I'll come. Friday evening? Thanks, Miriam dear."

She hung up and sat for a moment, pondering. The world of the Sparrows and their friends seemed far away, a genial disturbance on the periphery of her own world, yet sooner or later the others must learn of her friendship with Mark and of her plans about Jarley. Sooner or later, the dike which she had built must give way and admit the rough, and perhaps treacherous tides.

It was late afternoon and she decided that she would walk to Mark's. Intricate, immense, the city's life thundered round her, breathed furiously against her ears, the breath of Minotaur: "I am the world, fiery, mechanical, merciless. Ignore me, you might as well, for whether you remember or forget can make no difference."

She thought of Mark and of their last evening together. His face materialized before her, and his voice stilled the voice of Minotaur. In a few minutes she would see Mark, touch him, hear his voice. She walked with quickened step, wondering whether he would be at home. Touched by the fear lest he put her off, she had not telephoned to say she was coming. If he were out, she would do some errands, then come back in the hope of finding him. But her ring was answered, and she climbed the stairs with a fast-beating heart.

Octavia Evans opened the door. "Mrs. Harmon? Colonel Bycroft thought you might call. He asked that you wait for him. He'll be right back."

"Is Neddy at home?"

"They went together, but they won't be long. Will you take a seat?"

Words and manner were conventional, but they seemed scarcely to conceal a peculiar hostility, and Stella glanced at the woman in surprise.

Octavia said: "I'll just remove all those catalogues, so you can find a place to sit."

"Catalogues?" Then she saw them, glossy and fat, piled on the chairs.

Octavia explained: "Colonel Bycroft brought them home this morning, and he and Neddy have done nothing but look at them. Seems they're getting ready to go live in the country." Her voice rose on a harsh note. "They been chattering about the country just like two birds!"

"They're going to live in my house, as I suppose Colonel Bycroft has told you?"

"He told me. He seemed to think it was true."

"Why wouldn't it be true?"

"It would be a shame . . . it would be a crime if this wasn't true."

To Stella everything about the woman was dark, a rampart of black skin upon which her own understanding beat without avail. In a voice intended to be disarming, she said: "It would be a shame if they were disappointed, but I can't see why they should be."

Octavia picked up a catalogue and carried it to the bookcase. Stella watched her, thinking: She's probably jealous or angry because Mark is leaving and perhaps she cannot go too. "Do you care for the country?" she inquired, in a conciliatory voice.

"All I care is that decent people shouldn't be cheated."

"Yes, of course. But we're all free to choose for ourselves, and if Colonel Bycroft . . ." How on earth had she got into such a conversation with this colored servant?

"Free?" Octavia turned and Stella wondered what could have lent her eyes such a gloss of tears. "Free to choose for ourselves?" She lifted her hand and let it fall to her side, as if some weight it supported proved too much for her.

"I don't know what in the world you're trying to say," Stella protested. "Colonel Bycroft and I are friends, and I'm very happy that he and Neddy should want my house."

Octavia looked for a moment as if she would speak again, but no words came. Resignation settled on her features and seemed to descend in a visible mantle to her feet. She gave Stella an impenetrable glance, and left the room. Stella gazed about her, trying to find Mark in these unfamiliar surroundings. The whole impact of his unknown life came home to her now. Here was a privacy which no one, not even a friend, might share; here was that barrier of a previous intimacy which a fresh passion might never transcend. The past holds us, she thought despairingly, and not our past alone but the past of others. She moved round the room, examining books and portraits, pausing a long time before a photograph of Mark in uniform. Why had he smiled? He gazed directly at her and it seemed to Stella as if the room suddenly expanded and the inanimate objects in it grew to enormous proportions, like things seen in delirium. They had the frightful suggestion of witnesses arrayed against her. She turned to escape, but the windows became fiery caverns, the doors cross-barred against retreat. She turned back to the photograph, fastening all her attention upon it. Alec, she cried, though the cry did not pass her lips. Alec, Alec!

There were footsteps in the hall, and she replaced the photograph as the doorknob rattled and Mark came in. "Stella! How good of you to come. This is Neddy."

The boy had followed him into the room and stood quietly regarding her. He came forward and shook hands with inarticulate politeness. Seen close, he did not resemble Mark, and the discovery restored, little by little, Stella's faltering self-control. Mark was looking at her narrowly. "Are you all right? You seem awfully pale. Come and sit down." He led her to the couch. "Stella, I've done nothing but think about Jarley. Do you think I'm fooling myself? Is this going to make a difference?" He went on quickly: "I've felt so damned happy ever since I saw you last. I'm trying to get used to the idea of my life as something personal, composed, durable." He tilted his head back on the sofa and gazed at the painting on the wall above him. "Like that picture! That has a life of its own. It's a complete thing. You and I can't add to it or take away from it without its ceasing to exist. It's man's achievement, yet it has nothing to do with man. But what about us—about you and me and Neddy?"

She looked at the child who lay at their feet, turning the colored pages of a catalogue, his thin legs stretched behind him like a hound puppy. Mark took her hand. "Do you believe we can recapture ideas and values now, at this stage of the game?" He seemed strangely wrought-up. "Do you, Stella?"

"Yes, if they'll let us."

"They?"

Octavia emerged from the bedroom and crossed the floor towards the pantry. Stella gazed after her and when the door had closed upon that slender, indefinably hostile figure, she said: "Your colored woman doesn't seem to believe in Jarley!"

"Octavia? Of course she believes in Jarley. I told her we were going."

"Will you take her?"

"If she wants to come—and if we go."

"If? But you just said . . ."

His fingers crushed hers. "I've got into the habit of thinking in terms of if. All through the war I kept saying to myself, If I don't get bumped off . . . if this and if that. It's the same way with Octavia, I guess. But the whole thing is really up to you and me, isn't it?"

She looked at him mutely. His eyes were furious, intent. "Stella, tell me something." She turned, expecting the kiss her whole body craved for.

"Tell me something, Stella."

"What can I tell you? You know."

"I don't know. Everything is if . . . if . . ." He let go her hand with a brusque, almost a brutal gesture. "Never mind. We'll go to Jarley, you and I and Neddy. May be, there . . ." She waited for him to finish, but instead he rose and stood for a moment looking at her. "We might as well be happy, Stella. It's such a simple matter. All you have to do is look through Sears, Roebuck and pick out what you want."

Neddy twisted round on the rug and cried: "I could make a boat if I just had some of these things!"

Mark dropped on his knees beside the boy and they began to argue about lathes and hack-saws. Stella watched them, passion and uncertainty pouring through her. Why should Mark refuse to kiss her when he had been on the verge of doing so? Why that abrupt transition from friendliness to hostility? What was there in this house, in this room, that generated disquiet like a poison? She remembered their evening together, the walk under the moonlit trees in Washington Square, the restrained tenderness with which he had bidden her good-night.

"Mark," she whispered in anguish.

He turned and glanced at her, then came back to the sofa. "Let's talk," he said softly. "Let's talk about Jarley." His mood changed once more. "You haven't told me whether there is some sort of landing for a boat. You see, I intend to take this house of yours on a long lease. Of course, there is still time for you to change your mind if the idea scares you!"

"It doesn't scare me."

"Then shall we say a lease of fifty years? That'll make me eighty-three. What do you say, Neddy?"

Neddy made no reply. He was absorbed in a page of golden sunflowers.

24

"WELL," said Miriam Sparrow sternly, "where have you been, and what have you to say for yourself?"

Stella, seated at the dressing table, carefully dabbed her nose with powder. She felt Miriam's gaze, the gaze of a small pink hawk. Beyond the closed doors of the bedroom the cocktail party was in full swing. Stella had arrived late, hoping to find her hosts and their guests pleasantly and incuriously drunk, and thus to evade the inquisition she dreaded, but Miriam had seized her at once and led her to the bedroom, ostensibly to repair the ravages of a twenty-minute taxi ride through the city.

"It's been ages since we set eyes on you," Miriam went on, relentlessly, "and now you appear, looking different." She stared intently at the face in the mirror. "Absolutely different."

"Not really, Miriam."

"Don't think you can get out of it by a show of innocence. It's obvious that something has happened to you, and of course any fool can guess what it is."

"Well?"

"You've found some one to fall in love with, and you're being mysterious about it, instead of letting us rejoice with you."

She settled down on a corner of the bed and wrapped her arms round the post.

"Dick and I are your closest friends. Haven't we any right to know what happens to you?"

Stella thought: Should I tell her? Then she shrank from the thought as an old fear asserted itself, the fear which had dogged her since her first meeting with Mark, the fear that to name her love might expose it to unpredictable dangers, to derision, to scepticism. *"What? Can the period of immolation be past? But you had led us to believe that your love was immortal, your grief never to be assuaged!"* Oh, they must find it out sometime, but not yet and not through her.

"You can't keep a secret for ever," Miriam warned her. "How silly, and how unfair to imagine that you could!"

"Unfair?"

"Well, don't you owe us anything? Since your return from Italy we've hoped something like this would happen. There's no use beating about the bush—something has happened. Dick noticed it when he saw you the other day, and I notice it now. Notice! It's written all over you."

"Well, I might as well tell you I am going back to Jarley."

They rose, confronting each other. A gale of celebration throbbed in the living room beyond the doors.

"You're going back to Jarley? Alone?"

Stella lied instinctively, defensively: "Yes, alone."

"When did you decide? I'm delighted, of course . . . but still puzzled. It's not like you to make these decisions."

"Miriam dear, don't ask me any more questions. You've told me often enough that I should return to Jarley, and I am going. There is nothing more to say, now. When there is, I shall say it. As you just reminded me, one cannot keep secrets for ever."

Miriam flushed. "I'm not trying to pry! You seem happy. If you are really happy I'm satisfied."

"Happy?" murmured Stella. "That has a dangerous sound, hasn't it?"

Miriam's natural generosity came to the rescue. "Oh Stella, you used to be happy! You used to be the happiest person I knew." Impulsively, she kissed her. "We better join the animals, Dick will come barging in here after us in a minute."

The living room was crowded with people, and the talk had reached a point familiar to Stella, the point where sense and nonsense become inextricably confused. She heard Dick's voice at its most trenchant, "Given our national temperament of crass sentimentalism and deadly practicality, there is every reason why we should be detested by the rest of the world."

"Oh, lay off," growled another voice. "They have always found our national temperament pretty damned useful when they got themselves into a jam."

"Well, believe me, boy, next time America the beautiful will pop like a great big bloated bedbug."

"Oh dear," murmured Miriam. "They've started arguing. It's Pete Willingdon and Dick. I wish Dick would leave him alone. These idiotic discussions always ruin a good party."

Dick was shouting in a corner: "We're a bloody breed of extremists, incapable even as individuals of elevating any relationship to a spiritual or artistic level! I tell you I'm an expert on human relationships. We pass from good fellowship to bed fellowship at the drop of a hat." He paused and added thoughtfully: "And there are among us those who sometimes neglect to remove the hat."

"What's wrong with that for a national psychology?" demanded Mr. Willingdon. "It's a damned good one, if you ask me. It's made us what we are?"

"And what are we? Tell me that. Just what in hell are we?" Miriam groaned. "Do go and break it up, Stella!"

Stella made her way through the crowd, and was immediately greeted as an ally by Dick. "I'm trying to be earnest," he told her plaintively. "The only chance I have to be earnest is when I'm drunk, then bang go all my inhibitions."

"He's been telling me what he thinks of the Republican party," said Mr. Willingdon, looking as if he had received a body blow.

"You'll admit I've been impartial. Drunk, I spare no one, not even my friends."

"And what then becomes of your professional discretion?" inquired Stella, accepting a cocktail from a passing maid.

"Oh, professional discretion is in a class by itself. It operates on the same principle as the conditioned reflex."

Mr. Willingdon drifted elsewhere in search of sympathy, and Dick turned a penetrating eye on Stella. "You look as if you had been in a far country, but it wasn't Italy this time."

"I've been talking to Miriam. I told her that I had decided to go back to Jarley."

"Jarley? Is that where you've been hiding?"

"No, I've been in town, but very busy getting my ideas sorted out."

"What's his name?"

She shook her head. "No, Dick. Don't go jumping to conclusions."

"I'm in an athletic mood. I've jumped all over Willingdon, now I want to try a few conclusions. And you look lovely. It's all so obvious, even to my jaded eye. Why should you want to conceal it? Or is there some difficulty? Is he married, or something?"

Stella forced herself to meet the merry but merciless eyes. "Aren't you glad enough that I've decided to return to Jarley? You've always urged me to."

"Of course I'm glad! It's where you belong. I have a theory that certain people belong in certain places and should not be uprooted. You don't belong in New York, though I can guess why you have chosen to live here since Alec's death."

She waited, while round them the amiable babble rose and fell. Dick went on:

"It was because you were homeless and New York is a city of the homeless. It's why Miriam and I live here. Our roots don't go deep—they're the kind that draw their nourishment from just below the surface." He waved his glass at her, genially. "But if you had stayed on here much longer . . ."

"Yes?" she prompted.

"You'd have dried up. You'd have become old and withered like last year's geranium."

She laughed, but he went on seriously: "Just remember one thing: if there are difficulties in the way of your happiness, I might be able to help you. I'm a very clever guy, you know. There's scarcely a person in this room who has not benefitted from my advice at one time or another."

She reflected silently on Mark's dilemma and on the fact that hard-boiled professional characters like Dick Sparrow should be called on to alleviate private woe. Mark's refusal to submit to, or to connive at, an automatic version of justice appeared in her eyes as something both right and pathetic. The thought of him brought a glow to her eyes, and William Symes, standing at a little distance, studied her with increasing surprise. He had not recognized her at first, and recollection of that airplane journey to Lisbon revived slowly, as he listened to fragments of this conversation, as he had listened to the one which preceded it, between his host and Mr. Willingdon. It was Symes' practice, on these occasions, to convey the impression of conviviality without becoming drunk, a practice which had saved him from more than one disaster. He rarely missed anything that might prove to be of value to himself and to his profession, although as a trained observer he gave few people credit for subtlety, for he had heard too many men wittingly and unwittingly betray themselves, each other, and their countries in the course of a single conversation, often under the stimulus of the first drink. The instinct of mistrust, bred in his childhood, had become a habit, and one of his favorite pastimes was to speculate on the integrity and patriotism of people he knew. But his speculations were not always on such a sinister level. Discretion rather than integrity was more the order of ordinary times. So it happened that this evening, while he doubted that Dick Sparrow would let fall any inadvertent hint relative to himself and Regan, habit prompted him to loiter within earshot of his host, and he tingled a little at Dick's facetious reference to his guests as persons who were actual or potential clients. It was an unwise thing to say, even in joke; he must speak to Dick about it later. However, as the conversation proceeded more or less harmlessly he dismissed his fears, and fell instead to watching Stella Harmon. Queer that he should have put her so completely out of his mind, and that seeing her again she should appeal to him as being youthful and attractive. Then, remembering the mission which had taken her to Italy, he decided she must have undergone a metamorphosis, and as he sipped his drink he wondered about the nature of it and its possible agent. Had she slept with one of the good-looking pilots of the American clipper, or picked up some robust young Dago, one who peddled consolation to rich foreigners among the ruins and the graveyards? Perhaps even Dick Sparrow . . . Symes gazed with a sudden renewal of interest at his friend the lawyer. Dick seemed ardent enough in all conscience, though that *might* have been induced by liquor.

Some one took away Symes' half empty glass and gave him another. Voices billowed round him, argumentative, provocative, amorous, incoherent. Stella had turned, and he thought her profile charming. He smiled as he remembered the last time he had seen it, when, thanks to Regan, he had come close to missing the plane; now he recalled scraps of the conversation which he'd had with Mrs. Harmon. She had bored him with her air of grief and her totally uninspiring appearance, when all he had wanted to do was sit by himself and think of Regan.

Behind him some one opened a window and a stir went through the room as people regrouped themselves in obedience to some mysterious law, their voices falling, then rising as conversation was resumed at the point where a breath of air had interrupted it. Symes turned to find that Stella was staring at him with unrecognizing eyes. He went forward and held out his hand. "How was Italy?"

He asked it out of pure malevolence, annoyed that she should not have remembered him.

She shook hands. "Italy?"

Dick said: "You remember Bill Symes?"

"Yes, of course." She remembered him then, this well-groomed young man whose personality continuously and perversely eluded her.

"I hope the weather was fine for the remainder of your trip," Symes continued urbanely. "The spring wind can be rough, even for our clippers."

Stella thanked him and said that her trip had been quite pleasantly uneventful. He saw that she was unwilling to continue the conversation, but surprise at her changed appearance, allied to injured sexual vanity, inspired him to further spitefulness. "I haven't been in Italy since before the war," he said. "I was sent there then, on a mission for our government. I must say I dread seeing it again. I often think of Churchill's speech when he promised that the red-hot rake of war would draw the length and breadth of the country! Well, it did, though God knows we paid for it along with the Dagoes."

His eyes, the handsome eyes of a cruel boy, dwelt on Stella as he inquired, with an air of one informed intelligence consulting another: "Tell me, how *was* Italy?"

Dick stared at him in amazement, but Stella had recovered her composure. She believed that Symes must be somewhat drunk and therefore forgetful of the errand which had taken her abroad. She answered calmly that she had found Italy most beautiful, and added: "I should thank you again for your kindness in helping me get there."

"I'm sorry I couldn't have accompanied you all the way to Rome, or to have been of service to you while you were there. You were in Rome, weren't you?"

"I went north, to a town called Montescari."

"Oh yes, the scene of one of the great battles. We lost a lot of men there. It used to be a favorite spot for tourists before the war. I don't suppose there's much left." He offered her a cigarette. "I expect to be sent to Italy one of these days, and frankly I don't look forward to it. I don't fancy ruins in the initial stages! Ruins and cemeteries. I'd rather wait till the grass has grown a bit." He turned genially to Dick. "That was quite a bout you had with Pete Willingdon. No fair, pitching into a guy twice as drunk as yourself!"

Relieved at the change of subject, Dick laughed. "Willingdon just plain refuses to see the United States as anything but a bigger and better National Association of Manufacturers."

Stella listened with a forced smile. Symes' manner had left her considerably disturbed. Was he really drunk, or inexplicably vindictive? She found it difficult to rid herself of the latter suspicion. Yet why should he have wished to hurt her feelings? Might it be a mere trick of her own imagination? She sensed his awareness of herself, and it frightened her. This was a familiar terror, it held her rooted in the center of this noisy and preoccupied throng, just as it sometimes affected her in a subway or at the crowded intersection of streets. Suppose something happened . . . something, anything, and she were to find herself once more alone? I must go away, she told her-

self urgently. I must find Mark. Finding him, she would cast
herself into his arms. "Hold me, save me!" She turned, more
than half expecting him to appear in obedience to her inaudible
summons.

Her companions were talking energetically and she moved
away towards the farther corner of the room, where Miriam sat
beside a large pudding of a woman, the thrice-divorced wife
of successively younger men. The prospective fourth, a wilted
youth with padded shoulders, hovered in the offing. Miriam
drew Stella on to the arm of her chair. "You've met Marie
MacLennan? Marie has been telling me about a marvellous
cream for sunburn. It takes the sting out immediately."

"Costs ten dollars a jar," said Mrs. MacLennan hoarsely.
"My beautician makes it up himself. It's a secret formula, and
worth every cent. Magical, really magical."

Stella smiled vaguely. Two hundred pounds of vanity stared
back at her with feverish eyes. "That's a beautiful coat," declared Mrs. MacLennan abruptly. "A beautiful beautiful coat!
Would you think it rude if I asked where you found it?" She
touched the coat with fat, covetous fingers.

Stella told her, laughing, and a shallow gleam flashed across
the woman's eyes. Then their focus shifted like lightning towards her current betrothed, who was swaying dangerously
in his long, pointed shoes. "Desmond, do sit down." She
shrugged theatrically. "He never knows enough to take his third
drink *sitting!* Desmond!"

The young man subsided at her feet. "I have a headache,"
he moaned. "I have one head of a hellache, Mama."

Stella lingered a few minutes, then got up and moved from

group to group till she had gone the rounds. Glancing at her watch she realized that she had been here almost two hours. The semi-delirium of these gatherings always left her with a creeping sense of depression. People crowded about her, her ears hummed with voices, her mind grappled with ideas half-formed, extravagantly expressed. Time passed, time alone passed pitilessly over these unquiet heads.

She escaped at last, but with difficulty. "I have a headache," she pleaded with Dick and Miriam, taking her cue from the prostrate Desmond. "And it's late, really late." It was after nine and they had been drinking since five-thirty. Miriam accompanied her to the door and whispered: "Have lunch with me next week." Her eyes added accusingly: "You are leaving us to go to some one else!"

Stella promised to have lunch one day next week, and out on Park Avenue she lifted her face to the air, rejoicing in the summer night. But she had not gone half a block when a voice hailed her and she was overtaken by William Symes. Masterfully, he seized her arm. "Mrs. Harmon! How fast you walk! Were you running away?"

"Running away?"

"Oh, I wouldn't blame you if you were." He pressed her arm. "I was so afraid you'd disappear before I'd had a chance to apologize. I could kick myself for having been so crude. It was completely unpremeditated, I assure you. After you had gone Dick lit into me, and quite properly too."

Stella glanced at him apprehensively. "It's all right," she murmured. "Perfectly all right. I understood."

"You're sweet to say so. I have so much on my mind, I tend

to overlook personal things. I had completely forgotten that you lost your husband in Italy, and that you were going to visit his grave, the day I met you on the plane."

"It's all right," Stella repeated, suddenly on the verge of tears. Why didn't he leave her? She had planned to walk a block or two in order to clear her head, then to take a cab and stop at Mark's on her way home. Symes' personality oppressed her unbearably. "Please forget all about it, Mr. Symes. It really isn't important."

"But it is important! You must have thought me an awful bastard. Dick was furious. It hurt him, I imagine, pretty much as it must have hurt you. He's one of my closest friends, as I understand he is yours, too."

Stella thought: I'll get a cab, and perhaps he'll leave me then. But Symes urged her forward, matching his stride with hers, keeping a possessive grasp on her elbow. She was conscious of some strange excitement running through him. He went on: "You see, the trouble was I didn't recognize you when you came into the Sparrows' living room. The last time I saw you, you were not looking very well. You had a sort of sadness, as why not, considering everything? And there was I blatting on and on about Italy and the war and everything!" He shook her arm, then clasped it closely against his side. "Dick told me how fond he was of your husband, too. He should have stopped me when I started to talk that way. Naturally, he was astonished at what he took to be my bad taste. Damn it, I wouldn't hurt him for the world, nor you. You do forgive me, don't you?"

She said coldly: "Yes, I forgive you. Please don't let's talk of it any more. Would you mind signalling a cab? My head's quite bad and I'd like to go home."

"Poor kid! Of course."

Still holding her firmly by the arm, he signalled a cab and handed her into it, getting in after her. "Where to?"

Stella thought helplessly: Mark is nearest. He'll have to leave me there. "East 53rd."

The cab churned down the Avenue, and Symes said vibrantly: "I shall see you to your door." He took her arm again. "It's the very least I can do." He fell silent for a moment, then: "How you have changed! That's what confused me. It's what I told Dick. Do you mind if I tell you also? Don't misunderstand when I say that you make me think of a woman in love."

"I don't misunderstand," she replied bitterly, hating him.

"I'm afraid you do, but I'll take the risk." He peered at her. "I'm devoted to old Dick, myself. In fact I regard him as an older brother. I don't know what I'd do, sometimes, without him."

"He has many friends," said Stella. Before them, apparently interminable, glittered the ruby traffic lights.

"I've never known a lawyer with more human understanding," Symes continued warmly. "You'd suppose their job would make them hard as nails. It does, most of them. But Dick is exceptional."

She managed a laugh. "Are you getting a divorce by any chance, Mr. Symes? I was not aware that you were married."

"I'm not." He wrapped himself in a moment of mystery, then emerged. "No doubt Dick has told you something about my difficulties." It was a statement rather than a question. She answered: "He is very fond of you, and has often spoken of you to me." Her indefinable fear of Symes had spent itself in boredom. She saw him now as merely drunk and lecherous, and she gazed thankfully at the traffic lights as they turned emerald down the Avenue. The cab started forward and Symes said in a charged voice: "I don't blame Dick for being in love with you."

She turned slowly to stare at him. "Dick is not in love with me. You are quite mistaken."

Symes laughed. "Oh, I understand. You and Miriam are good friends. But in these situations, passion always triumphs over friendship, doesn't it?"

He *is* drunk, she told herself again, contemptuously. Drunk like the rest of them this evening. Drunk as Dick himself. What could Dick have said to him? The thought jarred her into wariness. She said: "Dick sometimes talks like an idiot after he's been drinking."

"Does he? I would have sworn he never transgressed the bounds of professional discretion!"

"I think you can leave transgression out of it."

He studied her intently. He was not really much farther along than when he'd started, but it had been an exhilarating inter-lude. Working on the faintest scent, he believed that he had flushed an invisible hare. Reassured as to his own position, he felt that he could safely relax and compose the incident into an amusing story for Regan. But that he had actually flushed a hare, and one of unexpected agility and size, dawned on him as the taxi bore them down Park Avenue towards their destination. "East 53rd did you say? I seem to remember Dick saying that you lived in the East Forties somewhere."

"I do, but I want to stop and see friends who live on 53rd."

"And that headache?"

"They'll have aspirin, and if it doesn't get better I can spend the night there."

Weariness made her say it, weariness and the determination to get rid of him at all costs. Under the circumstances, he would scarcely try to intrude on strangers.

"Here we are, East 53rd."

Stella gave the driver the number of the house and the taxi stopped. Symes climbed out, holding the door for her. Surprise, which moves most people to noisy exclamation, kept him silent as he escorted her to the door. Regan's house! He could have found his way here blindfolded. How extraordinary! Who were these friends, and did Stella by some lunatic chance know Regan? But he knew all Regan's friends and most of her acquaintances, by name if not in person, and Stella was not among them.

Hat in hand he descended the steps after her. "I do hope that headache will be better in the morning. And I am really, truly forgiven?"

Safe at last, Stella could smile without effort. "Thank you for bringing me so far. And don't let us talk any more about forgiveness. You've been most kind."

"I'll wait and make sure your friends are home. Which bell?"

"Two-eighteen. Bycroft, to your left."

"It says Mrs. Bycroft."

"Yes, that's it."

Symes pressed the bell. The buzzer sounded almost immediately, and as Stella pushed open the door he jauntily replaced his hat. The echo of his voice bidding her goodnight fell vibrantly through the air, then he turned and walked back to the waiting taxi.

25

RECOVERING FROM an attack of asthma which had left her chilled and spent, Hester lay among her pillows, watching Regan who crouched at the foot of the bed, manicuring her fingernails; the lights of the bedroom played over Regan's naked body and Hester's gaze shifted from her sister to the window. A slight mist obscured the river, but she could picture it, lead-colored, a few boats plowing against the current. Lying here she longed for a breath of the storm-scented air, but the doctor had warned her she must keep her windows closed in bad weather. The room smelled of the aromatic powders she had burned to relieve the asthma; it smelled also of Regan's favorite perfume, which vied with the powerful tincture of drugs.

"So you've thought of everything," said Hester. Absorbed in her task, Regan merely nodded.

"Of course there's a chance you might be mistaken."

"We've thought of that, too."

Yes, Hester reflected, you would have thought of that, too. After a pause she went on: "A meal here and there, an occasional visit to a man's apartment, don't necessarily constitute adultery."

"No, they don't, but they are very apt to." A gleam lighted, then veiled itself in Regan's eyes. "However, according to our information, Mark and Mrs. Harmon have been seeing each

224

other almost uninterruptedly for the past three weeks. They've dined, lunched, taken walks together. Mark has visited her at her apartment, and I've told you Bill's account of how he escorted her to Mark's door one night last week. Since then, we've learned that they have gone shopping together, sometimes taking Neddy with them." She anointed a pointed nail with a brushload of crimson. "Neddy is in bed by seven-thirty every night, after which the nigger goes home and Mark and his female friend have the place to themselves. Aside from these details we know nothing! We may, as you just reminded me, be entirely mistaken. But if any one knows what really goes on, Neddy does."

Hester pondered, then spoke in her tired, impersonal voice: "Wouldn't you get more out of Octavia Evans than out of Neddy? And wouldn't it be better, really, to question her than that child?"

"You're always so *ethical!*" sneered Regan. "The point is I want Neddy. He's my son. Besides, tackling Octavia is out of the question. I don't trust her."

"You have in the past."

"No, never. And that's lucky, for it's my belief she's sold out to Mark."

"How can you be so sure?"

"I'm not sure of anything, a servant's loyalty least of all. Now that I think of it, Octavia has always been a bit too much on the superior side to be entirely safe. Since I walked out of the apartment, I haven't got anywhere with her, though she's polite enough on the telephone. But then, so am I." She held up one hand, examining it critically. "In fact I've been at some pains not to antagonize the black bitch. We may need her for a witness one of these days."

When Hester remained silent, Regan went on: "Octavia could have proved her loyalty to me by leaving Mark and bringing Neddy over here. I never suggested she do it—I had no intention of incriminating myself in the least degree. Neither Octavia nor Mark, nor any one else, has anything on me. I have not written equivocal letters, and my communication with Mark, as you know, has been by telephone. Now it begins to look as if Dick Sparrow's technique is paying off, as if I really did have something on Mark!"

"Isn't it going a bit far, setting a detective to spy on him?"

"Don't call that poor creature a detective! He's just a down-and-out pal of Bill's. He's worked for Bill before, in an official capacity, and knows how to get round doormen, bellhops, waiters and so forth. For instance, it was he who found out that Mark and Stella have been dining together regularly at Philippe's on Third Avenue. It's an old dive of Bill's, and I took Mark there to supper on his first evening home from Europe. It's only by the sheerest luck that Bill and I haven't run into them there."

"You do seem to have the darndest luck," agreed Hester. "Just the same, I think I'd rather trust to luck than resort to the services of that grubby character Bill has sleuthing for you."

"Grubby characters have their uses," Regan put down her brush and looked at her sister. "Listen, Mark could have spared us this nonsense if he'd acted like a grown man, instead of a jealous vindictive one! If he'd been willing to let me get this divorce, we could have arranged something fair and friendly about Neddy—he knows that, I told him so. He knows that I'm through and that I never will go back to him. And that's why he's determined to make it as difficult for me as he knows how. What am I supposed to do? Sit back and let him spoil my life?"

"You could let him bring the divorce."

"How you love to simplify things! Does it occur to you that he may not want a divorce under any circumstances?"

"Well, what about Neddy?"

"What about him?"

"How is he going to take all this?"

"He'll take it the way thousands of kids take it."

"But what if he should prefer to stay with Mark?"

Regan shrugged. "I've told you what I intend to do. I intend to take him away from Mark right off quick—the minute the coast is clear, I'm going to the apartment and take him away. I shall leave word with Octavia, or I'll call Mark on the telephone afterwards, and put it up to him. Play ball now, I'll tell him, and when the divorce has gone through you can have Neddy back, no strings attached. Refuse, and you may never have him." She paused, meditating. "Of course the whole thing depends on what I can find out from Neddy."

"You told me once that Neddy could have no idea of what went on between you and Bill. What makes you think he'd know more about Mark and Mrs. Harmon?"

"Because I took darned good care Neddy shouldn't know anything. Mark and I have somewhat different temperaments!"

"And you believe Neddy will tell you what, if anything, he does know?"

"He'll tell me. He's my son, and I understand him."

"Yes," Hester said, slowly, "yes, you understand Neddy. You understand Mark, too."

"Just what do you mean by that?"

"However, there's something none of us really understands, and that is the role of Mr. Dick Sparrow in all this."

The words brought a look of uneasiness to Regan's face. She had completed her manicure, and sat contemplating ten sharply pointed, blood-red fingernails.

"It's true," she admitted. "Just what is Dick Sparrow's role in all this? Has he a role, actually?"

"He's Bill's lawyer."

"And he is also, apparently, Mrs. Harmon's friend!"

Hester seemed to struggle, for a moment, with the desire to laugh. "His role may be quite innocent, of course. He may not know of Mrs. Harmon's friendship with Mark. He may be even more in the dark than the rest of us."

"It's what Bill thinks, but I confess I don't know what to make of it. She and the Sparrows are old friends. You'd think she would have confided in them." Regan examined the long, curved claw of her left thumb. "And suppose she had confided in Dick Sparrow, wouldn't he naturally—inevitably, out of loyalty to her—wouldn't he do his utmost to shield *her*?"

Hester's smile was spectral. "From you and Bill?"

"From anybody!"

"While he continues to pose as Bill's legal adviser?"

"Oh, I know it sounds impossible." Regan rose and walked restlessly to the window. "What do we know about people, when you come right down to it? If we really knew what

Mark's relations were with this woman, everything would be simple. We'd have something concrete to go on."

"Why not ask Sparrow?"

"I wanted to, but Bill's against it. He doesn't want to antagonize Dick, or even to embarrass him at this juncture."

"Of course," Hester said, thoughtfully, "faced with divided loyalties, there is nothing Mr. Sparrow could do except abdicate from his role as Bill's lawyer . . . and perhaps even as his friend."

"I've thought of that." Her eyes had a smoky look, reminding the other of their childhood, when a frustrated Regan stood meditating vengeance. "There is just one thing to be done now, and that is for me to get hold of Neddy. Once I have Neddy, I shall be in a position to drive a bargain. Once I have Neddy, Mark will stand to lose everything, or to gain everything. After all, what do I care, really, whether he is in love with this woman or not? When I'm free to marry Bill, Mark can marry any one he wants, and he can have Neddy for good measure. Can you see any flaw in that reasoning?"

"No," said Hester, looking at her curiously. "After all, it isn't as if you and Bill wanted Neddy yourselves. He'd be in your way—a child of six! No, I can't see any flaw in your reasoning. You've thought of everything."

Regan's face cleared, and Hester, watching her, caught her breath. What can it feel like to be so lovely, she wondered. To be so filled with health and passion, so careless of the past, so ardent of the future?

Regan began to dress in a leisurely manner, picking out her underclothes, discarding one in favor of another, eyeing herself in the full length mirror of the bathroom door, her scrutiny innocent of any doubt or anxiety about her appearance. She possessed a rare gift for simplicity, yet though art was far less essential to the enhancement of her beauty than it is for other women, she gave much time and care to her toilette, moving with an objectivity which Hester had learned to recognize as the hallmark of true self-infatuation. I wonder what you'll be like when you're old, thought Hester, as she watched the ritual. When those beautiful breasts have lost their roundness, that throat its texture, that glittering black hair its ebony vigor, that mind its power to deceive and to exploit not only its enemies, but its lovers and itself? No flabbiness for you, my dear. You will never flounder into old age, transferring your appetites to canapes at cocktail time, and mid-morning snacks. And in her mind's eye she saw the radiant figure of her sister dematerialize into a witchlike sharpness, the nose curved like a hawk's, the flesh turned leathery, the mouth a bitter line under cold, preying eyes. What happens when there are no further triumphs, no more lovers, no more tomorrows worth waiting for? As for me, I shall be dead by then. I hope so. I have known what it is to be the victim of your beauty; I would not care to be its last crumb!

While she was dressing, Regan outlined her campaign to the wan listener among the pillows. "I'm going, now, to Bill's apartment. From there we'll get some one to call Mark's number and find out whether he's home. If he should be, I'll have to wait and try later in the day, or even tomorrow or the day after. I don't want to run the risk of finding him and letting myself in for a fight, and the possible ruin of my plans. If

gone to the country without leaving an address. Tell him you've been deathly ill and know nothing of my activities. If, as you say, he's so decent, he won't persist in troubling you. But if you're not equal to it, then just let the phone ring. I shall be back tonight, after dinner. I promise."

She waved, and Hester watched the door close upon her. She heard the soft rumble of the elevator and pictured the slight, purposeful figure as it stepped into the summer rain. Blindly, Hester turned and reached for the telephone. She dialled a number, her mind in a fury of excitement through which there burned a single, selfless intention.

Mark's voice answered: "Yes?"

Hester held the receiver to her ear. Her heart was beating as it did when she had had an injection of adrenalin, but no sound came from her lips. Four lives . . . the words leaped like living things across her gaze. Four lives are in my hand . . . four destinies and all their unforseeable events depend, now, on me, on my word, on my intervention, upon me who have never taken action in my life; upon me whose mere existence has never cast a shadow, nor roused an echo in the void.

"Hullo? This is Colonel Bycroft."

The sense of his proximity overwhelmed her. She could hear the intake of his breath, faint sounds as he shifted some object on the table, fainter, farther sounds from the room where he stood. Warning, saving words dissolved in her mouth. Then Mark hung up, and she let the receiver fall on her lap. Silence settled on the room. The rain had ceased, a dim glow filled the sky. Hester coughed, her eyes dilated, she coughed again and felt the first demon stir in her chest. Slowly she got out of bed.

Her limbs felt hollow like the bones of a bird as they bore her guilty body towards the window, beyond which the sky was slowly pushing through the mist. She stared at the silvery reaches of the river and the distant Jersey shore, then her gaze descended to the trees which lined the street below, and she pursued, with the wondering gaze of a captive, the gay colors of buses and automobiles. There, before her defrauded eyes, creation moved upon its destined way—survivors of catastrophe, while she was merely the inheritor.

"I've always told you things," she heard Regan saying. "I've always tried to share my life with you."

It was true. All the guilt, the scheming, the restless self-seeking, the deceits and hypocrisy; the countless confidences and confessions, orgies of repentance without expiation—these had been Hester's share of that life. Out of this she was expected to make sense and to fashion, somehow, a moral and a reason. What is the bond which ties us to our brothers and sisters? Is it blood? The flesh of our parents? Is it the memory of all the dead persisting in us? Yes, Regan had shared everything with Hester. Regan had more than shared—she had rendered up the evil in herself and placed it in Hester's lap. It began in early childhood, when one, always sickly, lay watching with envious eyes the other's radiant unfolding. Under this vigil Hester had faded year by year, reduced at last to a shadowy mirror, in whose tarnished glass the beautiful sister pondered her own resplendent destiny.

26

THE STORM passed out to sea. In the florists' shopwindows marigolds burned a fiercer gold, and Atlas, straining his sinews, waited the hour when he might hurl the burden from his shoulders and stand erect once more; across the Avenue a threadbare St. Francis crept forth from the Cathedral to feed the pigeons in defiance of municipal law. But the storm which had been rising in Octavia Evans did not pass with the emerging sun. It smouldered in her dark body, stooped like Atlas under an imponderable burden. In the eyes of her own flesh and blood she was just a stupid woman, resigned to her debased condition, and faithful to an idea which had waited a long time for realization. Since there never had been anything else for her to cling to, she had clung stubbornly to the mythology of the white world. She needed to believe in a paramount virtue, and she buried her doubts, if she had any, very deep indeed. Mark had appeared in time to vindicate her faith, and what she felt for him was not less veneration than love. She would have died for him. She was accustomed to the genial condescension of white employers, and resigned to the attitudes and falsities which had driven her son Edgar to extremes of cynicism. But in Mark, Octavia believed that she had discovered the complete human being, a human heart which had rejected all the jailbird fixations of his kind. In other words, Mark made her feel at home, and to feel at home, as Octavia well knew, is to be as near to God as one ever gets.

It was not demanded of her that she die for Mark, but she felt that it was expected of her that she guard him from the catastrophe which she sensed as threatening him from every side. Octavia was familiar with catastrophe in one form or another; suspicion rose in her as naturally as trust arises in the more fortunate. There had been a morning when, reading murder in Mark's face, she had moved swiftly to divert him. Later, in urging him to surrender Neddy, she had done so because she believed in his eventual triumph. She knew, as Mark did not, how little the child mattered to his mother, and how quickly Regan would be bound to tire of the responsibility once she had her way. But now it seemed that Mark was threatened from another quarter. Octavia's suspicions were aroused on the day of Stella's first visit to the apartment, following Mark's casual account of his meeting with her at Philippe's. Octavia had listened to that account with a polite incredulity. It just didn't make sense, or else it made a peculiarly nasty kind of sense, for even if one were to take into account a man's natural craving for feminine companionship, could he be fool enough to fall for such a fantastic lie? True, Stella's appearance did not accord with Octavia's suspicions, for Stella was gentle, even ingratiating. But that, Octavia decided grimly, is because she knows I see through her. I ought to—I've seen through enough of her sort, and smarter ones than her.

As the weeks marched forward and she watched the friendship between her idol and the interloper grow and prosper,

Octavia curbed her more elemental feelings and set to thinking. Though the pair were constantly in each other's company, she guessed that they were not yet lovers. Had they been, she must have come to accept the romantic inevitable; but the fact that they were not—of this she was reasonably certain—caused her to revise her grosser estimate of Stella in favor of one even more sinister. And when the talk started about a house in the country, a house to which the deluded man dreamed of transporting himself and his son, with Mrs. Harmon in the role of benefactress, Octavia's mistrust crystallized into dreadful certainty. Here was a trap vile and cunning to its last detail, devised by Regan and Stella. To what purpose? Simply to put the Colonel on the spot. Once on the spot they'd have him . . . Mrs. Bycroft would have him as she would have Neddy—*cold*. As the diabolical scheme unfolded in Octavia's brain, she set to inventing frantic counterplots to save Mark. I must tell him, she exhorted herself every morning as she boarded the subway on her way to work, and every evening when she rode back to Harlem. I must put him on his guard against this Stella woman before she, too, betrays him. He would not stand another betrayal. Octavia sweated as she recalled the look on his face the day that his wife left him. She found herself reliving the anguish which had followed Edgar's desertion of his wife, and experiencing all over again the nightmares of denial, denunciation, divorce. Yet how to put Colonel Bycroft on his guard? Phrase after phrase rose to her lips and died there. That she must, sooner or later, speak out and save him, no matter at what cost, she was sure. But in the meantime her vigilance became a morose, even morbid thing, proof against Mark's new found gaiety, against the pathos of Neddy, against Stella's conciliatory manner.

Coming to work one morning, Octavia noticed a man strolling slowly past the apartment house door. His leisurely gait, belied by a queer alertness of the eyes, struck her at once. He was there again next day, and the next. Thereafter she saw him often, walking aimlessly with hands in his pockets, his eyes sliding to and fro under the rim of his hat. Of course, there was every possibility she might be mistaken in her fears, but she could not put the ubiquitous stranger out of her mind, and one morning she spoke of him to Mark. Neddy was in bed with a cold, and Mark was eating breakfast alone. Octavia, who had just come up from the street, glanced at him uncertainly, then said: "Have you any enemies, Colonel Bycroft?"

"Why do you ask?"

She went to the window and looked out. "Would that be one of them?"

Mark followed and peered over her shoulder. The stranger was strolling along on the opposite side of the street, apparently oblivious of scrutiny from the upper windows. "Never saw the guy in my life," said Mark. He laughed. "Octavia!"

"You can laugh, but he's been there off and on for the past four or five days."

"Persistent animal. He must like the rain."

"Maybe he's paid to like it."

"Well, I can't think of any one who'd pay him to like it on my account." Mark went back to the table and finished his coffee. A letter from the War Department lay beside his plate.

Presently he would telephone Stella and suggest that they dine together to celebrate his imminent discharge from the army. Next week he would go to Jarley to look at the house. He might even offer to buy it, and that would be the beginning . . . the beginning of something. He was still not prepared to say the beginning of what, for the emotion which stirred him was unnameable and fragile. He found himself treating it with reserve, careful to exclude all dangerous elements. The thought of Regan was one element, thoughts of his undivorced condition another.

Octavia hovered near the table. "A man telephoned you yesterday. He didn't give his name, or leave any message."

"Well, he'll probably call again if it's important." Mark tapped the letter. "See this missive, Octavia? My passport to civilian life." He frowned. "I wonder what happened to my civilian clothes?"

"Mrs. Bycroft would know."

"I suppose she would." But he'd be damned if he'd call her up to find out. He'd be damned if he'd ever call her up again, about anything. Let there be silence between them from now on, silence between himself and the lost years and the lost hope and the lost love. The world might collapse tomorrow, atomic death finish, once for all, the past, the present, and the future. What was he supposed to do about that? Forgive and forget while there was still time? Cast his vote in the next election? He glanced at the letter. Well, he had done his share in the general destruction and they had given him a medal—several medals. Things were about even. And at this moment he was prepared to cast his vote for private life, for the house in Jarley, for marsh grass and the look of a clean sea, and for whatever else might be left of his normal span of three-score years and ten minutes.

Octavia looked out of the window. "He's crossed the street!" she said. "He's walking past our door."

"Shall we fill a paper bag with water?"

She turned, frowning, and he stopped her. "What's bothering you, Octavia? Why not tell me? I might be able to help."

"It isn't me needs the help."

"Your son, then? Some one you care for?"

Here was her chance, but she could not bring herself to utter the words she had rehearsed so carefully. "Maybe it's all right for you to joke. Maybe the man down there means no harm. Maybe Mrs. Harmon is a true friend after all, and maybe I'm as wrong about her as about everything else. But you forget you're on the spot. You forget you're standing in somebody's way, somebody who would never hesitate to hurt you." How silly the words seemed when they were considered like this, and how terrible if she were to say them and he should resent her doing so! He seemed so stalwart, so more than equal to a situation. Who was she to presume he needed her advice, her feeble, stumbling assistance? He might even scorn her as Edgar scorned her, for being a superstitious old black woman relying on her instincts, smelling enemies at every corner.

Mark said gently: "You know I'd be glad to help you, Octavia."

She nodded, and the nod ended in a shiver. "Thank you. But it isn't anything very serious."

She left the room and Mark heard her moving about the

kitchen, setting her small world of pots and pans in its customary order. Then he went to the window, but the anonymous figure had disappeared in a squall of rain and blowing newspapers. Mark stood for a moment watching the rain fall into the street, and longing rose in him, longing for the look of rain falling across fields, falling into the ocean, falling across the purple shoulders of a hill. This longing cleansed the past of bitterness, and mingled with gratitude and tenderness for Stella. He meditated on the evening they would spend together, and on the peculiarities of their relationship. His desire for her was quite unlike the emotion he had always felt for Regan. He did not want to feel an identical emotion towards Stella, for his life with Regan had been unique, and now his unwillingness to repeat the experience with another woman was more than a romantic loyalty to the past—it was based on necessity, the basis of most of our loyalties, the necessity to believe in the rightness, the singleness of our choice. He realized that Stella loved him, and there were moments when he rejoiced in the knowledge, yet whenever he seriously contemplated sleeping with her, all desire expired.

He heard Neddy calling from the bedroom, and went in to read to the child, and to discuss all over again their plans and prospects for life at Jarley. For the first time since his homecoming Mark felt that he had a share in his son's existence; a mutual vision of the future drew them together, warming the boy towards the father, breaking down the barriers of shyness and mistrust.

Towards evening the rain stopped and he heard the telephone ringing. It was Hester, but he did not know it, and after waiting a minute or two for some sign of life at the other end of the wire, he hung up in disgust. Four lives, Hester was thinking . . . four destinies and all their unforseeable events depend, now, on me, on my word, on my intervention. . . . But she remained silent, and an hour later Mark stopped at a florist's and bought flowers for Stella. Coming out on the street, carrying a paper cornucopia, he felt young and elated. The air was cool, and women's dresses blew round them in a progressive ballet which entertained him as he walked. The look on his face won him a smile or two; he responded gallantly, seeing himself as a late arrival to peace and its celebration, still wearing his uniform with its bars and eagles. He wondered again about his civilian clothes, and decided that he must invest in a new outfit. Homespun, gray flannel, corduroy, dungarees and work shirts. The trappings of freedom!

A last beam of sun struck the tops of buildings. The Hotel Rotterdam, spangled like a ballerina, beckoned him from the distance, and he felt a sudden let-down of elation. That damned place! Those walls, covered with chromatic ringworm, that blasted elevator! And Perry, poor Perry! Where was he now? Back in God's country, posturing before a picture postcard sunset, the war behind him, his doubts resolved, the future all rosy red sand, flowering cacti, domestic bliss, prosperity and Gila monsters. And General Wilmer, where was he? General Wilmer who had muffed the capture of one square mile of enemy territory, then gave it as his opinion that "we" should forthwith embark on a conquest of the world. Where were the boys who died because of General Wilmer's mistakes? And where, at this moment, was Mr. William Symes? Mark gripped the paper of flowers a trifle harder, felt a thorn pierce his finger. Changing the flowers to his other hand he sucked the wound, and walked faster to get away from the thought of Symes. Wherever he went he seemed to meet that figure disguised as echo.

Stella opened the door and he took her in his arms. "We're going out to dinner and drink bubbly all evening long. I'm out of the army, and I've brought you some flowers . . ."

He knew there was something false in his boyishness, but felt that it must do for the present, to tide him over certain private uncertainties. As she stood in the circle of his arms, her face seemed to swim up to him like a face seen under water. He was conscious of the desire which flooded her, conscious that it ebbed again before his insincerity. He glanced round him at the room which always affected him rather dismally, as if no one lived here. She seemed so much a person who should be with others that the fact that she lived alone, that she was actually alone, always surprised him. There was a nunnery air to the place, and to her living in it.

She took the flowers out of their paper, and holding them against her dress, which was of some indefinite blue, she moved to the pantry, and he followed her. Light showered on her head, glittered and died there and on the small pearls in her ears. He watched while she arranged the flowers in a vase; the look of her pale arms and of her hands, hovering among the flowers, crept into him, drying his mouth.

"They are lovely," she murmured. "Lovely!"

She turned to pass him, and he took the vase from her and set it on a shelf, then drew her towards him. "Stella, do you—can you understand?"

"I think so." She put her hands on either side of his face, closing her eyes.

"Well, down at Jarley, maybe." He held her against him, then released her, then brought her back. Her warmth was all about him, with the scent of flowers, and the stillness. "Away from the city, where everybody is a reflection of everybody else. . . ." Her hair was exactly like a coin, precious from the centuries. He ached with feelings he could not name. Why couldn't he love her? It had been so easy with Regan, so incredibly easy. Why couldn't he adore this woman whose body rested against his own, as if hers and no other had ever rested there?

They left the apartment, and out on the dimming streets his alien mood returned. He talked with a fluency he detested but could not restrain, telling her funny stories, recounting some of the amusing incidents of his wartime experience. He saw that she was playing up to him, matching him laugh for laugh, her eyes blithe, her arm thrust lightly through his. So one tries to recapture the old spirit, he thought with inward bitterness. Soldiers, artists, live a wholly different kind of life: they are concerned with ends and with beginnings, but we, we others exist between the two, passing from fever to fever in a waste of futility.

They had dinner at the Lafayette Cafe, where they toasted Mark's freedom in champagne. "I should have brought you gardenias," he said. "Gardenias, or maybe orchids, to go with this stuff." He lifted his glass. "And a black lace nightie with pink ribbons."

"Not pink ribbons!"

They carried on the banter, and his heart sank lower and lower. He ordered rich and expensive food and more champagne, and gazed at her caressingly over his glass. She had ceased to move him, and the less he cared, the more he exerted himself, his stories getting dirtier, his voice coarser, his laughter less convincing. Meeting her glance he read tenderness quickly veiled, and thought with a flash of temper: She's being *understanding*. But where is all this going to end? What happens when I take her home? And how long has it been since I took a woman home? He frowned, trying to remember. A year? Hardly that long. Where? Brussels? Munich? Did it matter? They had all been substitutes for Regan, and he was tired of substitutes, and Regan was tired of him.

"What's on your mind?" she asked him. He told her, and watched the painful color rise in her cheeks.

"Well?" he insisted. "What about it, Stella?"

"Of course."

"Of course?"

"If you want me."

"You mean you'd sleep with me? Why?"

"I said, if you want me."

The waiter bent over her shoulder, trickling champagne into her glass. She waited till he'd gone. "There is a quotation," she said, "from something . . . do you know it? Something about happiness remembered in misery."

His surprise increased, and with it the impulse to wound.

He listened while she stammered out the Italian phrases, then smiled. "I had no idea you were so erudite. From Dante, isn't it?" Comprehension dawned on him. "Yes, of course, I see."

"It's what you were thinking too, isn't it?"

"I suppose so."

She leaned towards him. "Mark, I'll do whatever you like."

"Because I remind you of your husband?"

"Does that matter?"

"Maybe not. One reason is as good as another."

She let the remark pass, and as the perverse demon waxed within him Mark made open love to her. He felt that she suffered it out of her omniscient understanding of his plight, and to punish her, he outdid himself in general beastliness. By the time they had finished dinner and he had consumed several brandies he was nicely drunk. Out on the street at last, in the muddy incandescence of lights, he took her arm. "Let's walk a bit, or would you prefer a cab?"

"I'd rather walk." She was pale, but steady. He felt the protective response of her arm, and laughed. Drawing her into a shadowy doorway, he kissed her. Her lips were cool and fragrant. "Stella, aren't you tight?"

"No," she murmured, and steered him out on the sidewalk again. They walked slowly, and as his head cleared a little, an awful depression hovered over him. This sort of thing, he knew, was being done all over the city at this very moment. It was inevitable, stale as the lees in old beer bottles. Why not make up his mind to it that desire, that earliest exuberance, that sharp salt bliss of the very beginning of things, lay buried under the heaped rubbish and the nettles of the past? Neither he nor she would ever recapture it. The world had lost it for ever. From now on it was pretence, all pretence.

He kissed Stella again, with deliberate brutality, and she said: "Mark, you don't love me, but we need each other. I'd be content with that, if you could be."

"No!"

They walked on and came to West 4th Street. "This is where I used to live, before I married." She pointed to the black flight of stairs which led to a basement.

"So there was a time when you and I knew only ourselves, when we were undisturbed by the dead or the faithless." He drew her closer, so that in walking their limbs moved in harmony. Presently she stopped again. "And that's Dockett's, where I used to work."

The sidewalk bookstalls had been cleared for the night and the little shop was in darkness. She peered through the glass of the door, but could see little except the black shaft of the staircase descending from the floor into the deeper blackness of the basement, and she pictured the desolate room with its bookcases rising to the ceiling, its spindly ladder, its dust, its mice, and the dreamy figures which drifted from stack to stack. One of these figures, a young man with a dark, eager face, turned and came towards her carrying a book, his voice startled an echo in her ears. Or was she asleep, or dreaming? She pressed her face against Mark's shoulder, and he said coldly: "We're both drunk and unhappy, and this was to have been a joyous occasion. It was to have been a celebration in honor of the future. It was to have been . . ."

A cruising taxi came to a halt beside the curb, and Mark helped Stella into it.

"Let's go home to Neddy and make some good strong coffee. It's time I let poor Octavia go home, anyway." He peered at Stella, and added roughly: "You can spend the night, if you like."

She made an undefinable movement, but said nothing. The wine had settled in his brain, and his thoughts moved like marionettes to a brittle tune. Stella's hand crept into his and he caressed it with the same roughness with which he had kissed her. If brutality was to be his road to passion, then he would be brutal. Octavia let them into the apartment. She said slowly: "Neddy has gone."

"What?"

"He's gone. Your wife came and took him away."

"What?" said Mark again. He came further into the room, blinking as if the light hurt his eyes. "What are you talking about?"

"She told me to tell you she was taking Neddy, and that she would get in touch with you in a few days. She said she was within her rights. She said it wouldn't do no good for you to try and find him, because she was taking him out of town. She said you'd better think everything over carefully, because you were in no position to do anything else."

"You let her take Neddy? You didn't try to stop her?"

"I tried," said Octavia harshly. "I tried! But she's not one you can stand against. And he wanted to go with her." Her voice quivered. "He seemed happy to go with her. But I did try. I argued, I even put my back to the door and told her she couldn't do it, not that way, not without your being here. I told her it was my duty to stop her, but she called me a treacherous black bitch and pushed me aside. Then she and Neddy left me here to tell you." Her eyes glittered with a savage misery. "Now I've told you."

"Yes," said Mark. He muttered the word over to himself. "Yes, yes." Then he looked at Octavia. "You say Neddy wanted to go with her?"

"She's his mother. Why wouldn't he want to go with her?" Octavia drew a deep breath. "You got to accept it now. She's not one you can stand against. I tried to tell you . . . about the telephone calls to find out if you was home, about the man down there on the street, watching us . . . watching, and reporting back to her, I don't doubt. Oh, I don't doubt! But it didn't seem to be my business."

"For the love of Christ! Why didn't you call the police? Why didn't you send for the watchman downstairs and have her thrown out? What were you hired for?" He rushed to the window, then turned back. "That fellow who's been walking about down there on the street . . . you say . . . you said . . ."

"She had friends enough, maybe he was one of them."

"I'll go over to Hester's. They must be there."

Octavia shook her head. "That's the last place she'd be, knowing it's where you'd think of looking."

"But she's not going to have Neddy!" Mark was shouting to convince himself. "She's not going to have him—not if it takes all I've got to stop her."

Octavia walked to the door. "You can't win that way," she told him in an exhausted voice. "You can bargain, but you can't win." She gave Stella a bitter look. "Maybe Mrs. Harmon can tell you the rest of it. Maybe you better start asking *her* a few questions."

She left them, closing the door after her, and they heard her feet cross the passage towards the stairs.

"What did she mean?" asked Stella. Horror was crushing her. "What in the world did she mean?"

Mark looked at her curiously. "I'm not sure, but I can guess. She meant more or less what I've thought myself, only I never let myself think it out to the end."

"What did you think, Mark?"

"That you and Regan are friends. Are you?"

"Regan and I?"

"You and Regan and Symes—didn't you tell me he brought you home from a party? And then there was that bloodhound out on the street, and the lies about Alec and the house in Jarley . . . the whole filthy, rotten, stinking bunch. . . ." He stopped, and Stella ran to him, her hands outstretched. "Mark! You're wrong, Mark—wrong, wrong!"

He slapped her with all his force and she crumpled on the arm of a chair, her hand to her cheek, her gaze fixed on him. He strode to her and pulled her hand away, revealing the crimson imprint of his fingers on her flesh.

"An elaborate job of it you all did between you, just for the sake of stealing away my kid. But you'd do anything. And there's precious little *she* ever stopped at. Where would you stop, I wonder? How's *your* conscience?"

"Clear," she whispered.

He pulled her to her feet. "Why did you come home with me tonight? Just to gloat?"

"Oh, Mark, my darling."

He lifted her, carried her into the bedroom, and lay down with her among Regan's pillows. "What about your conscience?" he repeated, his voice breaking. "What about it? Would you sleep with me—in what do they call it, expiation? So as not to have this on your conscience? Would you?"

She drew his head down to hers, pressing it against her cheek which blazed from the blow he had given her. Her tears covered his face, and her hair coming loose in his hands felt cool, like mist.

Mark awoke early and went into the kitchen to make coffee, and to face his thoughts alone. Out on the street the lid of the letterbox clanged, and he heard the rumble of traffic in its overture to the new day. There was strangeness in these familiar sounds, and in the appearance of the rooms through which he moved. Events which had transpired here retreated, and he saw them now as one sees details in a landscape—depersonalized, utterly still. He heard Stella in the next room and presently she came into the parlor, dressed, but with her hair loose on her shoulders, like a girl's. Their glances rushed together and flew apart like birds colliding in mid-air.

"I didn't mean to waken you, Stella."

"I was awake."

• "I got up to make coffee. I usually have it there, by the window."

She nodded, and he saw that she kept her face turned from him, so that he might not see the bruise which discolored her cheek. His own emotion formed an abyss between them and he waited desperately for the silence to dissolve itself, for the trivial world to remind them where they stood, and what, from now on, must be their role, and as he waited, it occurred to him that they were no longer alone: another presence stood with them—the familiar, strange, implacable figure of love itself.

Stella broke the pause: "Will you go with me to Jarley, Mark?"

"You know I will."

"Then I'll telegraph the Andersons to fix up the house, and we can leave whenever you like."

Talking made it easier. They smiled at each other briefly, and Mark said:

"There are things I've got to attend to first. I must get hold of a lawyer and find out about Neddy."

"Of course. Let me talk to Dick Sparrow—he's a good friend and I know he'll help us."

Little by little as they talked, the familiar world returned—their world, with its emergencies and its preoccupations, making it a little less difficult for them to meet each other's eyes, concealing, for a time, the deep agitation of their hearts.

27

MIRIAM SPARROW watched her husband as he arranged various objects in orderly heaps on the bed, preparatory to packing them in the suitcase which stood open on a chair beside him. Observing his frown, she smiled. Never would Dick be quite the man he used to be. The events of the past two months had effectively revised him, casting his careful legal mind into confusion, and by the same token restoring something of an earlier, humbler nature.

Autumn was knocking on the windows and sunlight streamed coldly on the traffic of Park Avenue. The flower shops were selling immortelles and bittersweet, and women walked like fur-bearing birds, draped in mink and opossum.

"Where are my mittens?" demanded Dick.

"There," said Miriam, not stirring from her chaise longue.

He rolled the mittens together and laid them in the suitcase with his red-topped hunting socks. "There are moths in this mackinaw!"

"No wonder, after five years." She gazed at him thoughtfully. "Five years! Do you realize it's been five years since we were last at Jarley?"

"Of course I realize it."

"I find it a bit difficult. In fact I find everything difficult to realize, just at the moment."

"Thanks to your harping, I find it quite easy."

"The whole thing is such a mixture of the miraculous and the inevitable. I have to keep reminding myself it is not a dream."

"It's like you to confuse coincidence with miracles!" Dick straightened up, wincing. "Lord, how I hate packing. There was a time when you did it for me, remember?"

"That was when we were young and I knew no better." She smiled. "Shall we recapture it at Jarley, do you think?"

He picked up a muffler and laid it with the socks. "Recapture what?"

She said irrelevantly: "Some people have all the luck, don't they?"

"Who are you talking about now?"

"Stella, for one."

"Because she's found Mark?"

"And Mark for another, because he's found Stella."

"So now you add luck to the miracle?" He turned to look at her. "And aren't you forgetting Alec?"

"Oh, Dick."

"I'm not heartless. I'm just trying to see things as they really are."

"There are some things you just don't seem to see at all."

"If you mean this supposed resemblance between Mark and Alec, no—I don't see it."

They had returned, as Miriam had intended they should, to the subject which had enthralled them for the past two months, from the morning when Stella walked into Dick's office and said, simply: "A little while ago you asked if there was something you could do for me. There is something. Dick, you have got to help me—you have got to help me and you've got to help Mark Bycroft."

Miriam had been summoned by telephone and arrived to find two incredulous people facing each other across Dick's plate-glass desk. "What in the world is this all about?" she demanded, repeating a question to which she had been feverishly supplying answers for the past half hour.

"You tell her," Dick said to Stella. "Tell her from the beginning, so I can listen to it all over again as I sit here pinching myself."

Stella turned to Miriam. "Mrs. Bycroft has stolen Neddy."

Miriam, in the act of lighting a cigarette, paused theatrically. "Mrs. Bycroft? Neddy?"

"O God, O God! Stella means Regan Bycroft, Bill Symes' lady friend, his mistress, his what-have-you. Neddy is her son."

"And will you tell me what Stella has to do with the Bycrofts, or with Bill Symes, or with Neddy?"

"I know Mark Bycroft," murmured Stella. She faced her friends, and Miriam saw that one cheek had a discolored patch, as if from a blow.

"I might as well tell you now, what you asked me the other evening at your party. I have known Mark for some time. I was with him yesterday when he found that his wife had taken Neddy away."

"You know Mark Bycroft? But when did you meet him, and why have you not told us?"

"I don't know why I didn't tell you. Yes, I do know . . . there were so many reasons!" She shrugged. "They don't matter now." She glanced from one baffled face to the other. "You'll understand when you meet him. Miriam has already seen him."

"I?" wailed Miriam. "I've never set eyes on the man!"

"Do you remember one day this summer when you and I had lunch at Philippe's, on Third Avenue? It was you who pointed him out to me. The man who looked like Alec."

"I remember." She stared at Stella. "That was Mark Bycroft?" Dick laughed shortly. "See?"

Miriam shook her head and lighted another match. "I don't see. I see absolutely nothing." Bill Symes and Stella, Regan Bycroft and Bill Symes, Stella and Mark Bycroft; herself, Dick, Symes, Stella—and now all of them together. "I absolutely fail to see," she repeated, with rising shrillness. "I absolutely fail to see and I fail to understand why one of you doesn't *tell* me something that makes *some* sense. Stella!"

Mark's roses were pinned to Stella's jacket and she touched them, stirring their slumbering fragrance as sentence by sentence she led her friends back over the unseen events of the summer, while their amazed minds pursued the sequence of a story in which they, with Symes and Regan, had had each an unsuspected share. There were some things she could not tell them: the story of last night when Mark had visited upon her that savage blow which had been gathering strength within him. Nor could she tell them of this morning, of his remorse and tenderness, of their mute realization of love. But in the end she looked from one friend to the other and said, simply: "So now you see, you have got to help us."

Dick clasped his hands over his face in the gesture of a man trying vainly to dispel phantasmagoria. "Help you? How?"

"First by getting Neddy back from Mrs. Bycroft."

"You forget that Regan Bycroft is by way of being my client. So is Symes."

"I'm not forgetting anything. I know they're your clients. It's why I came to you. I wanted to tell you everything before you see Mark. He's coming to call on you himself tomorrow."

"It won't do any good, Stella. The whole thing is a most God-awful muddle . . ."

Miriam interrupted. "It isn't a muddle. It's as clear as crystal. Why, you big dope—don't you see that you, and you alone, are in a position to help Stella?"

"And I repeat, how?"

"Because you happen to be on the other side of the fence." She laughed. "Because you know all there is to know. Why, you've got Symes and Mrs. B. in the hollow of your fine legal hand!"

"You're crazy. And you can laugh all you want, but it's not going to do you or Stella or me a bit of good. Not a bit. The most I can do is wash my hands of the whole damned business. Resign from the case, and tell Symes and Regan why I am doing so."

"But it isn't a case yet," protested Stella. "And if it gets to be a case, there is no reason why you shouldn't stay on their side, is there?"

He looked at her grimly. "Just what are you trying to suggest?"

Miriam sat bolt upright and thrust her bright, flushed face towards him.

"The trouble with you, Dick, is your utter lack of imagination. You have the legal mind, which is only one degree less

atrophied than the military mind. Of course you can help
Stella! In the first place she's our friend. She comes first, doesn't
she?"

"Naturally, which is why I intend to wash my hands . . ."

"Oh, go and wash your hands and get it over with!"

Dick gazed somberly at his wife. "I may not have a hell of a
lot of imagination, my dear, but I'm willing to bet I've an edge
over yours. Just how well do *you* know Symes and Mrs.
Bycroft?"

"Every bit as well as I need to know them," replied Miriam.
She seemed inspired by an irresponsible gaiety, which she had
communicated to Stella, who now interposed with deceptive
meekness: "It's all quite simple, really. I've talked with Mark
and I believe he is willing to let Mrs. Bycroft have her divorce,
provided he can be sure she will give Neddy back to him afterwards."

"You see, Dick?"

"Pardon me! I seem to be handicapped, as you are not, by
certain ethical considerations . . ."

"Ethical poppycock! Did Regan tell you she was going to steal
Neddy?"

"She did not, but that's hardly the point."

"Was it your idea that Symes hire a professional sleuth to spy
on Colonel Bycroft?"

"Certainly not!"

Miriam gave him an ironical smile. "Knowing Symes, would
you put it past him to do such a thing?"

Dick hesitated, and Miriam laughed again. "You know darned
well it's just the sort of thing he would do. He has never trusted

you. He trusts nobody. And when he learns of Stella's share in this, he'll undoubtedly believe that we were all in collusion."

Dick rose and began to walk round the room. "You think it's all so simple, but it isn't. There *are* ethical considerations. I've got to see him and tell him how things stand, and ask him to relieve me of my responsibility. It's the only thing I can do."

"What then?" Stella asked. "What happens to Mark, to Neddy, to me?"

He shrugged. "Why in hell didn't you come to me in the first place, before things had gone so far?"

"There was nothing to come to you about. I didn't know anything of Symes' relations with Regan and Mark. I had no idea you knew Regan."

"O good Lord! You must have heard me mention her name a dozen times when we discussed Symes."

"If I did it made no impression. I'm not good at remembering names, or people. I never dreamed of Symes' part in all this. The first I heard of it was this very morning when you told me he was Regan's lover. He must have wondered a good deal, when he escorted me home the night of your cocktail party. I stopped at Mark's apartment and Symes saw me to the door and waited till I had gone in. He must have known that Mark lived there, yet he never mentioned it!"

"He didn't?" Miriam repeated, then answered herself, slowly: "No, he wouldn't."

"Are you suggesting that Symes laid a trap for us?" demanded Dick.

She gave him a narrow, catlike glance. "Poor Dick! It does seem as if the whole thing were now up to you. It does seem, doesn't it, as if you were bound to go to Symes and say to him, 'Look here, you son of a bitch' . . ."

"Now Miriam!"

". . . You can have your Regan, but at a price, and only you, Mr. Symes, are in a position to meet that price because you are the only thing she wants in this world. The price is Neddy. You must persuade her to surrender Neddy. Oh, not at once. She may as well enjoy her little triumph, or the illusion of it anyway. But when the divorce has gone through on her terms and you and she are safely married, Neddy must be given back to his father, who after all seems to be the only person really interested in him."

Dick stood with feet planted on the rug. "It sounds easy, but you're taking it for granted that Symes will knuckle down to such a proposition. What would happen if he told me to go right straight to hell?"

"You'd have to go, I suppose. But you could make a graceful exit. Taking your hat in one hand and bowing from the waist, you could say: 'Then all is over between us, Mr. Symes! Rest assured that your secret—your many secrets—are safe with me. However, perhaps I owe it as much to myself as to you to be frank at the eleventh hour. It consorts better with my professional ethics for me to confess that in my moments of weakness, weighed down by legal problems and with liquor, I have at times entrusted some of these highly confidential matters to the wife of my bosom. But have no fear, Mr. Symes! My Miriam is beyond suspicion. She *never* talks too much unless she's drunk, and then nothing will ever stop her talking, nothing!' "

"Blackmail!" groaned Dick. "Sheer blackmail!"

Laughter broke the tension, laughter, the jocose attitude which, in fact, was the only attitude left to them. They knew each other too well—perhaps too long—to venture anything more serious. Strangers may tamper with solemnities, friends dare not. Later, when Stella left them, Dick and his wife felt free to examine the situation from every new and unsuspected angle. Miriam had perceived what Dick refused to acknowledge —the fact that the "case" as he called it could not go through without the connivance of every one concerned.

"They have got to be brought together figuratively if not actually. They have got to talk, to haggle, through us." She beamed at her badgered spouse. "Through *you!*"

"You make me feel like a legal pander."

"Well, you know what I've always thought about the law."

"Left to yourself you'd like to see this mess decided with matched pistols at ten paces, I suppose?"

"Left to itself I'm afraid that's how it might be decided!"

He gave her an uneasy glance. "What do you mean?"

"Well, from the little I've learned about the character of Mark Bycroft, he suggests the sort of man who might prefer matched pistols to all this legal fenagling and hypocrisy." When he remained silent she went on earnestly: "Dick, you have to put it over. You have to make your lousy old law *work!*"

Dick had gone about his business with the word ringing in his ears, like a threat. He brooded over it in private. What would have happened in the elevator of the Hotel Rotterdam that evening, if Bycroft had had a gun, or even if he'd had his wits about him? Word for word, Dick recalled Symes' recital of that encounter. and light began to break upon the whole tragicomedy. Luck had saved Symes once—would it save him again? Driven into a corner, would Bycroft come out shooting? A state of mind induced by four years of war made the melodramatic idea more than a mere possibility. "You have got to make your lousy old law *work!*" cried Miriam, and she had not needed to add: "If you fail, anything could happen."

To his eternal credit—in his wife's eyes, in the eyes of Stella and of Mark also, Dick made his old law work. Moved—though this was something he never would admit—moved by Miriam's passionate espousal of her friends, moved by a meeting with Mark and by the sudden ignition of sympathy between them, Dick found himself, in the end, exerting all his talent in an ironic and paradoxical defense of his friends. From Regan he extracted information which she in her turn had extracted from her son: "Father likes Mrs. Harmon the way you like Mr. Symes." From Octavia Evans he got little, but sufficient for his purpose: "I know nothing about Mrs. Bycroft's private life, but I guess she's a real smart woman."

"You mean clever?"

"I mean more than clever."

And from Bill Symes he got, at last, the promise that Neddy would eventually be returned to Mark. There remained only the job of convincing Mark himself that in order to win he must first be prepared to lose. "It's a formality, that's all," Dick explained as they sat—he and Miriam, Stella and Mark—at Philippe's, drinking beer. "A formality," Dick repeated. "Doesn't mean much aside from all the legal verbiage. After that you're free, Regan is free. And in a year it will all be forgotten."

"I see," said Mark. His glance rested on Stella. Reading it, Miriam caught her breath. They were seated at the table where Mark had sat the day when she first set eyes on him. The restaurant cat, somewhat larger and thinner, slept on the shelf among the bottles. "I see. A mere formality, then it will all be forgotten." He turned to Dick. "There is one thing, though. I don't want to meet Symes."

"No reason why you should," said Dick heartily. "No reason, actually, why you need to show up at all. Johnson will handle your end of the case. He's a good man."

"I don't want to meet Symes," Mark repeated as if he were talking to himself. "Not now. Maybe some day I shall meet him. In an elevator . . . or perhaps even out in the open. Yes, I'd like to meet him out in the open."

On this autumn afternoon as Miriam sat watching Dick pack his clothes for their visit to Jarley she said: "Well, we did help them, didn't we? It makes me feel good to know that we shall have a share in their happiness."

"How do you feel about Symes' happiness, and Regan's?" he asked drily.

She pondered. "You mean we have helped them get their own way?"

"They've won, haven't they? They've got what *they* wanted."

"I wonder how far it will take them."

He laughed. "You're hoping, aren't you, that they'll get their come-uppance? But why should they? They're human like the rest of us."

"They're human, but they're not like the rest of us." She

hesitated, frowning. "I don't want to moralize—it doesn't do much good in our world anyway, where things are no longer black and white, good or bad, but just a sort of indefinite *gray!* We continue to be human, but people like Symes and Regan . . ."

"Well?" he demanded as she paused.

"They want so much, and they feel so little!"

"And you believe that Mark and Stella are better people because they feel too much?" He laughed rather bitterly. "You believe that *their* marriage is going to work?"

She looked at him, cautiously rearranging her thoughts to meet his. "I'd be willing to bet on Mark and Stella, where I wouldn't bet on Regan and Symes."

"You *are* a moralist!" He shrugged. "I don't know, Miriam. All this excitement has blinded us—blinded me, anyway, to something else. To something quite important, perhaps the most important thing of all: the fact that Stella should have put Alec out of her mind as she seems to have done."

"What makes you think she has put him out of her mind?"

"I can see it. Time has simply dropped away from her. She has lost that look of a wooden image dedicated to grief. She's in love with Mark."

"You dare to call me a moralist—you sentimentalist!"

Dick gave her a shrewd look. "Have you no reservations about them . . . about Mark? He's the one I'd watch, if I were you."

She stayed silent for several minutes, then made a sudden impatient gesture of dismissal. "I believe they are both lucky—luckier, much luckier, than Symes and Regan. I'm not trying to be Pollyanna about it—I'm not even being sentimental, but I believe in those two." She finished with a kind of passion:

"I tell you I *believe* in them!"

"O.K.! Personally, I shall reserve judgment till we've been to Jarley."

Husband and wife were silent for some minutes, then Miriam said slowly: "It's going to be up to Mark. I concede that much . . . everything is going to be up to Mark."

28

THE ISLAND was flat, its southern end grown up to fir trees, black and twisted by the weather. Here and there on the pink granite surface a great rock stood up or lay on its side, giving, from the water, an impression of ruins. The island was a fragment of the mainland, cracked off and stranded in the slate-colored sea. So stranded, it seemed to have developed a character of its own, separate and self-sufficient. On this fine October morning it boasted two inhabitants, hunters who crouched among the ledges with guns across their knees, staring across the water which sparkled under the full weight of the sun.

"Guess they've quit flying for the day," remarked James Anderson, and reached in his breast pocket for cigarettes.

"Looks like it," said Mark. His pipe was out. He tapped the bowl on his heel and filled it with chilled fingers. Sea and shoreline moved before his eyes. He had watched, since daybreak, the shaggy purple islands of cloud form in the sky, crack apart and admit the sun. Hour by hour the color changed, faded; real islands appeared, then the mainland with its scattered windows signalling the light. The ducks had come in well to the decoys strung along the tip of the granite point. There had been white-wings, blacks, a few Old Squaw. Mark had not shot for years but he managed to acquit himself fairly well in the critical eyes of his companion.

"Yeah," said James Anderson, flicking a match into the sea-weed. "They've quit. We might as well, too. Be afternoon by the time we get back and Stella'll be looking for you."

His gaze roved keenly in his impassive face, his great hands lay loosely clasping his gun. Watching him, Mark thought: Some of this granite, some of this salt, has gone into him. Not even the war could wash it out, not even his own blood. He looked away from Anderson to where the sea fingered small stones, and shifted the carcass of a duck which he had killed half an hour before. It lay partly in the water, the incoming tide pushing it towards them.

"Guess I better pick up my game," said Mark, but Anderson moved first, stretching his arms, hitching himself to his feet. "Let me. I'll bring the dory round while you collect the stuff and carry it down."

Mark watched him walk down to the water's edge to retrieve the duck. It was still terrible for him to watch Anderson move, the mechanical legs seemed always so stiff and unresponsive, like the legs of an epileptic. He was half man and half metal, and what was not man was affected by what was, the contra-diction flinging an otherwise superb body into complete inco-herence. At the beginning of their acquaintance, in order not to appear as if he were trying to dodge the subject, Mark had asked him how it felt.

"My legs? About the way any machine feels when you first use it. A new typewriter, say, or a new gun. Don't react like you'd expect. Too slow, or too fast. Then again it's like the feeling at the ends of your fingers, the feeling runs down to the ends and from there the machine takes over. Only with fake legs like these the feeling ends too soon. That's what the medics are after when they tell you, you got to learn how to use mechanical limbs. You got to learn how, and to expect that end of feeling sooner than you used to expect it when you was whole."

"I see," said Mark, and he saw more than he wanted, saw how it might happen that feeling should end sooner than one expected, end before it arrived at the heart, end before it resolved itself in the proportions of the whole. He never heard Anderson complain, but whether this was due to courage or to despair he could not be sure. The man was not much given to speech; he seemed a sort of thinking rock, astonishing Mark by his mere sentience. There was little he didn't know about wind and weather, about the peculiarities of sea and shore, of firearms, and the habits of wild things. He was not a type met in cities or towns, but a creature truly native to one spot, sprung, Mark believed, from the stones and marshes of Jarley. They had sent him to fight in the Pacific, and there, on some forsaken atoll his legs were sheared from under him. But he came back at last to his own sea and his own islands, as the birds he hunted came back to their old breeding ground at the turn of the year.

Mark watched him now as he paused to adjust the mechanism of his legs. Then he stooped, ungainly as a puppet, and picked up the duck. "I'll be a little while getting the dory," he shouted. "You wait round in case something shows up!"

Mark waved assent and watched him struggle off down the shore towards the rocks where they had hauled up their boat. Anderson's wife, Myrtle, had warned his friends not to offer help unless asked for it directly. "It's one of the things the doctors told me. Don't treat him like you think he's going to fall apart

if he lifts a hand, they said. If he wants help he'll ask for it."
And so, thought Mark, everything becomes artificial, including
one's own response. If Anderson were whole and hearty I'd
jump to give him a hand, but because he's crippled I have to
wait till he asks me! How be natural? What was naturalness
under such conditions? He turned to stare at the long stride of
the sea, seeking some consolation in its effortless performance.

The staccato sputter of the dory's outboard motor reached
him, and he rose, stiff from long sitting. Collecting the satchel
of shells, the guns, the lunch bag, he made his way across the
ledges to the water's edge, there to wait for Anderson. Cold air
bathed his face. The sea quivered slate and silver, and he noticed
for the first time the blond stretches of uncut hay on the
mainland.

He thought of Stella in slacks and flannel shirt, brewing
coffee on the kitchen stove. She would be wearing her hair tied
with a ribbon, like a little girl's, and her cheeks would be rough
with color like everything in this bronze and frosty season. He
saw her walking through the rooms which had become his, saw
her arranging late marigolds in a jar for the parlor table, killing
a fly which buzzed against the window, pausing to stare across
the pasture to the sea, waiting for a sight of Anderson's dory
lifting its gray nose above the water.

Mark laid his gear on the seaweed and walked to and fro to
warm himself. Debris from the ocean was scattered everywhere,
objects simplified or complicated by the tide. He found an old
barrel stave inscribed by some marine bug, a square of soft
wood worn to a satin texture, fragments of pop bottles turned
to emerald and amethyst, and he was oddly touched by the

appearance of a straw hat which lay among the pebbles and the seaweed. Removing his own peaked hunting cap he placed the pathetic flotsam on his head, and heard Anderson's sudden laughter as the dory came nosing in over the shallows.

Mark waded out in his rubber boots and placed his gear between the seats, leaving room for the decoys. Then he pushed off with one foot and eased himself into the bow as Anderson took up the oars. "You pick up the decoys," said Anderson. "I'll row."

It was a cold, wet job, reaching into the water to lift the wooden birds, winding the icy cord neatly to avoid a hopeless tangle. The sun beat on their heads, but the sea cut like a razor. "Christ," said Mark as a wave spewed over his knees. "God damn!"

"Yeah," said Anderson, easing the dory alongside another bunch of decoys, "cold, all right. Not like them Pacific waters. No sharks, neither."

"Nor the same kind of gunning, eh?"

He got them in at last, stacked in the bow, and seated himself facing Anderson, who shipped the oars and started up the motor. They circled in the calm sea and headed towards the mainland, and Mark felt the tremor of the motor running the length of the boat. He was sleepy from exposure, but content-ment glowed along the edges of his mind. Anderson was star-ing at him. "You going to keep the hat?"

"It's a bit damp, but it fits."

Anderson smiled. "Queer thing," he began, then stopped. His great hand moved on the tiller and a long, glistening swell flowed beneath their bows.

"What's queer?" asked Mark.

"You in that hat." His blue eyes filled with silvery gleams, like the sea behind him. "I never did see it till this minute. Makes you look like Alec."

Mark took off the hat and examined it. Sea-stained, battered, it still retained identity as a hat. Defiantly, he replaced it on his head. "I've meant to ask you whether you saw any resemblance. It's supposed to be quite marked."

"Can't say I did till now."

The island was falling away, flattening out behind them, and Mark had a feeling of intimacy about it, a kind of nostalgia. That fragment of earth possessed, for him, the half-happy and half-melancholy character of a childhood memory, or of some irrelevant and innocent dream.

"Did you ever shoot on that island, with him?"

"With Alec? Hell, yes. There isn't an island around we didn't shoot offen. We used to camp on Flint when we was kids." And he began to talk about his friend and of the times when they hid among the ledges, shooting ducks, the times they tramped the alder covers on the mainland after woodcock, the times they hunted deer, or went fishing for trout in the spring. In the flat, unaccented idiom of the place Anderson resurrected the dead boy, conjuring him out of the sapphire air and the salt taste of the sea. He spoke without emotion, but in the end he said: "You got the feeling, about him, like he was immortal. Know what I mean? There are guys like that, so full of life, seems they can't die. So full of life, they got more than they need and some of it spills over into your life, giving you an edge over yourself."

"You must miss him."

Anderson made no reply. He was sitting with his back to the wind, and now he bent low over a match, holding it to his cigarette. Twisting round, Mark could pick out the features of the mainland. It rose in vistas of copper and gold, with the occasional pointing finger of pine. In a little while he would see the house, white among the apple trees, the sky rushing up behind it in a solid wall of blue.

Anderson said: "It's good you're going to marry Stella. It'll be good to see lights in the windows again. Maybe you'll have your kid with you, come winter?"

"I expect to."

"Then if I ever get used to these—legs, we can take him rabbiting back of my place, with my boys." He added gravely: "You and Stella'd ought to have a kid too. Then everything'll be as it should be."

The simplicity of it touched Mark. Everything will be as it should be! He gazed at the maimed figure which had survived the charnel house, and which still insisted that things could be as they should be. For Anderson death was the only finality.

It was high noon when they steered into the shallow water off the beach. He cut the engine and let the boat slide above the shingle, and Mark scrambled out, lugging his gun and satchels. "Tell Stella hullo for me," said Anderson as Mark, up to his calves in water, pushed the boat off again. "Myrtle and I'll be coming round to visit one of these days."

"Thanks. That was a swell morning. Take me again when you feel like it, if you can stand my lousy shooting!"

"Nothing the matter with your shooting, only you need a bit of practice. And another thing," he nodded solemnly, "better get that gun lengthened. It's too short for you. You got a longer reach than Alec had. Send it to the makers and have them put a piece on the end of the stock."

"You think it would improve my shooting?"

"It'd help. Well, be seeing you!"

The dory drifted back on the swell and the motor purred once more. She veered, then set off towards the eastward, Anderson crouched in the stern, the sun beating on his red jacket. Mark lingered on the sunny beach, watching the boat till it rounded the point, then he turned and trudged up the shore towards the pasture. Frost still spored the shady places under the trees, but where the sunlight fell the earth gave out a scent like summer. He was glad to stretch his limbs after the long cold of the morning's vigil. The grass made a crisp sound under his boots, and a few late robins fled at his approach. Presently the chimneys of the house appeared above a rise in the ground, then the house itself, and the apple trees casting their shadows on the grass. He and Stella had come to Jarley too late to do much about the garden, but he had cut away the dead wood from the apples and the balm o' Gilead beside the kitchen door, and scythed the grass and uprooted the weeds.

Stella did not come to meet him, and from the look of the empty windows and the silence, he guessed that she was not at home. Consciousness of her absence deepened as he drew near the house; a sense that came from his feeling for her, from his intense concern with her personality. She is not here, whispered a dry leaf sailing earthward from its branch. She is not here, shrilled a cricket in the grass at his feet. She is not here, breathed the house.

Two robins fled into the woods. He set his gun on the granite step and walked down the path to the mail box. There was a *New York Times* in its long brown cover, and letters for him and for Stella. Back in the house again everything smelled of marigolds and brown sugar. She has not been gone long, he decided, and felt that her presence brushed against him lightly, as though she had left this impalpable reminder to console him till her return.

He placed all the stuff on the table beside the windows, and picked up his letters. One was from Regan, and he examined her handwriting on the envelope with a sense of wonder that it should ever have excited him. Turning it in his hand he read the name stamped on the back. Something cold blew through Mark, something ended. "You got to learn . . . and to expect that end of feeling sooner than you used to expect it when you was whole." Anderson's words echoed in his ear, and he shrugged. Regan's letter was brief and concerned entirely with Neddy. The child was very well, he was going to a new school, which he seemed to like. He expected to be with his father later in the year and was looking forward to the visit. In the meantime he sent his love. Appended were three small black crosses in pencil, three kisses from Neddy. The letter ended: "With good wishes, Regan."

Mark tossed the letter on the table and gazed out of the window at the sea. His vision ended on a taut line of horizon, and came back to the table and its clutter of objects. There was a postcard from the Sparrows, announcing their imminent arrival at Jarley, and a letter to him from Octavia Evans. He read it standing in his rubber boots, the salvaged straw hat still on his head. Octavia described her unwilling participation in the divorce proceedings which had set him free. "They asked me," she wrote in her upright, indignant hand, "they asked me if I believed you was in your right mind, Colonel Bycroft, and I told them that in my opinion nobody was ever righter. But when I said it I saw how it might hurt your case, for it did seem to make you more responsible than they held you to be. What else could I say? It was all they got out of me, though they tried hard enough. Even Mr. Sparrow tried, though I knew why *he* was trying, that like me he was on your side in his heart. Yet I could have cried, knowing all the truth I told helped paint you blacker and lost you Neddy. Mr. Sparrow told me it was you who really won, and I pray he's right. He told me Mrs. Harmon has surely forgiven me the mistake I made about her. I could not lift my head for shame, only I know that everything I did, I did for your sake." And she signed herself, "Sincerely, Octavia."

Sincerely, Octavia. Mark could picture her, small and indomitable, standing up in his defense, and the vision was part of the freshness and the health of this autumn day; it was part of his prevision of the future in which she and Neddy would surely have their share.

He wandered through rooms warmed by the sun, and by log fires burning in the big fireplaces. To pass the time till Stella came back, he decided he would chop some kindling, and went into the shed which adjoined the kitchen. The shadow of the balm o' Gilead leaped on the wall, and he thought that in spring, after rain, the scent of its leaves would reach him as he worked. A pair of gloves hung beside the door—white canvas gloves with faded blue cuffs. Mark put them on. At first they felt cold, but his hands warmed them and made them flexible. He wore them as he split the birch logs into kindling, and when he took them off they wore, as usual, the shape of his own hands. He replaced them on their nail and went into the kitchen for a drink of water. Propped against the clock was a note from Stella: "I have gone over to see Myrtle. Come and meet me."

To reach the Andersons house one took a path through the woods. Mark went through the kitchen door and across the rough grass, past the mail box, into the woods, which smelled rank from the night's frost. He liked the green and humid path made by Alec and James Anderson when they were boys, and as he strode under its perpetual twilight he imagined he heard their voices shouting beyond the trees. A log felled by Alec lay moss-grown beside the path, and his initials were scored deep in the bark of another. The demon in Mark stirred anew. His love for Stella was all uncertainty and suspense, built not on the realities which he had been prepared to accept, but upon the dreams in which she dwelt. Must he be content with this?

He heard her coming towards him down the path. It widened where firs were interrupted by a stand of birches, and here the sun shone as if falling from immense distance, gilding fallen leaves and moss in glowing, archaic colors. Stella appeared, bareheaded. She looked like a girl of fifteen, and at sight of her an inarticulate protest rose in Mark's throat. He went to her and took her in his arms. "I missed you," he said.

She laughed. "Where did you get the hat?"

"I found it on Flint Island when I was gunning with James." He took it off and flung it in the bushes. "Kiss me, Stella."

She kissed him, and he held her away, staring at her. "I said kiss *me!*"

"But darling, I did!"

"Me, I said. Me, me!" He caught her against him, kissing her wildly. "Christ, I mean me myself . . ."

They stood in the wavering tide of light and shadow, two separate beings striving to be one, striving to lose their alien identities, their divided past in the passion of an embrace. Then Mark released her, and they walked slowly back down the path to the house.

29

ON THANKSGIVING the first snow of the year began to fall, large leisurely flakes eddying out of the sky in droves, melting when they touched the warm earth. With the approach of winter the land seemed to increase in bulk, the fir trees to grow blacker, the few remaining leaves more brilliant, in defiance of the pitiless season. A storm had roused the sea and the sound of its unrest was borne across the pasture to the house. Mark drove the new tractor plow down the field towards the rock where Dick Sparrow and James Anderson stood watching him. Glancing back he saw with satisfaction the level wake left by the blade, where the soil rolled sleek and shining, as if laced with steel. He shut off the motor and sat blowing on his fingers. "Pretty good, considering the state of the ground," he remarked to Anderson. "Guess I'll lime it heavily come spring."

"She don't need lime," replied Anderson. "It's damn good soil, well rested too. One year Alec planted it to buckwheat, took all the strength out of it, like I warned him it would. But it come back and it's been good ever since." He spat into the furrow. "There's just one kind of fertilizer for this soil, or any other. Kind folks has always used." He named it. The sound of their laughter, and an explosive sputter from the tractor as Mark started it again reached Stella and Miriam where they worked in the kitchen, preparing the evening feast. Stella looked at the turkey which lay on the kitchen table. "Stuffing that thing is like trying to stuff a cathedral!" she complained.

Miriam was stirring cranberry sauce on the stove. "I'm glad you asked the Andersons. Poor Myrtle!"

"Why poor? I think James meant it when he said that this baby was his and Myrtle's contribution to the new era."

"But he has four other contributions! And no job."

"He never had one that amounted to much. A little farming, a little fishing, and the rest hunting, was all the job James ever wanted."

The smell of boiling cranberries mingled with the fragrance of driftwood and birch fires. The house radiated life; glimpsed from the windows, even the empty rooms had an expectant and fraternal air. In the drawer of an ancient dresser in the parlor, a portrait of Alec lay among daguerrotypes of his grand-parents, his school diplomas and his war letters. His work gloves hung on their nail in the shed, and the loose board which he had nailed down in the living room still held firm. But now the fire crackled, sending puffs of sea-smoke into the air, making a draft that moved the crimson curtains at the window overlook-ing the pasture and the sea, and Mark's muddy boots had left their imprint on the floorboards. He came in, followed by Dick and James Anderson, and the wind came with them, bringing a whirl of snow. James clapped his hands and caught them under his armpits for warmth.

"Tractor works good," he declared in his outdoor voice. "Be a help next year if Mark don't bust it trying to plow up ice!"

"I just wanted to see how it worked before making up my mind to buy it."

They went into the kitchen. "This snow would just stay on the ground, we'd get some deer hunting!"

Miriam looked up from her cranberries. "Do you ever think of anything besides hunting, James Anderson?"

He grinned at her boldly. "Sure do!"

"You haven't changed. You never did have but two thoughts in your head."

He laughed. "No, I ain't changed so you'd notice, only for these damned legs. Kind of tend to buckle when I've had a drink."

"They used to buckle in the old days, too," she reminded him. They chaffed each other in the direct fashion of old friends. Heat from the stove united with the aromatic scent of herbs and spice, and Mark looked at Stella, flushed and angelic in her blue apron. She met his eyes. "How did the tractor work out, Mark?"

"First rate."

Dick was washing at the sink, scrubbing his neck with a kitchen towel, and presently Anderson said he had to go home and shave and prepare for the evening's festivities. "You're sure you want the kids?" he asked Stella on his way to the door. "There's a pile of us to feed, Stella!"

"I want you all, every single one including Humphrey!"

"Well, all right. I suppose you might as well get in training, having kids around, you and Alec." He tramped off and they heard the door crash shut after him.

"Delicate as an elephant," remarked Miriam. "But thank the Lord he doesn't act tragic about his legs." She glanced apprehensively at Mark, who was lighting his pipe. He said equably: "I wish James would try and remember my name."

"We'll be needing wood, Mark," said Stella.

"Can't you make her see *you*?"

"Not since we've been living here. It was different in New York. Yes, I think it was really different there. I didn't feel, as I've felt just lately, that I was being made to live a sort of insubstantial existence."

"Listen, Mark. Alec is dead."

"I know that."

"Well then?"

"Stella doesn't know it."

"Oh for God's sake!"

"She doesn't know it, or she won't believe it."

"She went to Italy this spring. She went of her own accord, to find out."

They were silent for a minute, and a curious idea occurred to Dick. He said abruptly: "It's not just that you feel guilty, is it?"

Mark raised his eyes slowly. "Guilty?" He frowned. "Guilty?"

The shed door slammed and Miriam appeared. "Where is that firewood, you two?"

They passed into the kitchen with their burden, and Dick's question remained unanswered.

Through the afternoon and into the evening snow rustled past the windows, and as the air grew colder it shone on the dead leaves of the balm o' Gilead and the apple trees. The Anderson children, piling out of James' ancient car in the golden oblong of light from the open door, cried: "Look't snow!" as if they had never seen snow before. "Look't!" they screamed, prancing like gnomes among the darting flakes. They held their newly washed hands out to catch the stuff, and the youngest tilted his head and opened his mouth to receive it as if it were manna. "Get inside before you dirties yourselves," commanded James Anderson, herding them into the house. He took his wife's arm. "Watch your step, honey. We don't want to lose Humphrey."

"Way you talk," she protested, but laughed as she leaned on his arm. The pair—she big and sleek with child, he with his creaking artificial legs, loomed through the door into the parlor where Mark and Stella greeted them. Dick Sparrow appeared carrying a pitcher of stone-fence, a concoction of rum and hard cider, followed by Miriam bearing a tray of glasses.

James' eyes kindled. "God Almighty, just like old times, isn't it, Myrtle?"

She sank into a chair, the children squirming round her. "Yeah, it's just like old times. Only the kids is older; you'd hardly know it wasn't before the war!" She smiled at her husband. He lifted the glass in his great crimson hand, saluting her, then Stella. Something seemed to struggle for speech within him, but died without utterance. Tilting his glass he drained it in a single prolonged gulp, then set it down. "Rum and cider, by God! Rum and cider!"

Presently Stella led them to the dining room. The children's faces glowed among the dishes and bowls of marigolds. James talked of the snow that was to come, of deer hunting, of the criminal injustice of all game laws, of new automobiles, of atomic power, of farming, fishing, and the business prospects of the community. Dick passed the pitcher of stone fence and

James got speedily and contentedly drunk. He got drunk much faster than Dick or Mark, and they passed up the liquor and demanded black coffee instead. The children watched their father with delight. Liquor released the speech dammed up within him, and they applauded shrilly when he told stories about hunting, and the glorious days when he used to outwit the wardens in woods and byways as familiar to him as the palm of his hand. Towards the end of the meal, when the pitcher at his elbow was almost empty, he suddenly pointed a finger at Mark. "Remember the time on Flint Island when we was shooting eiders—the year the law was on them—and Raikes had us cornered? We had fourteen eider duck hidden away in cracks in them ledges, and not a feather did he ever find! You told him we was after coot, remember? Coot! And our eider decoys riding the water right under his nose!"

Myrtle Anderson shook her head and laughed with embarrassment. "James, you sure are drunk tonight! That wasn't Mark with you the time you killed the eiders. It was Alec."

"Sure it was Alec! I meant Alec."

"All right," said Mark. "All right then. When you mean Alec say Alec, and when you mean me, say Mark!"

The youngest Anderson mercifully spilled his milk across the table cloth, and James' mistake and Mark's flash of temper passed into limbo, which already housed other incidents, larger and lesser, of this evening's festival. Food, heat, liquor all conspired to produce the semblance of a gaiety without which such gatherings would be a mockery, but only the children were really happy, since only they could afford the expense of innocence. For them nothing untoward had happened; the tragedy of their father's wound was not a tragedy to them, because he refused to have it so; when the strong undertow of emotion which moved their elders had communicated itself at last to their infant minds, they responded in the only fashion they understood. "Let's play!" they screamed, and one seized Dick's arm. "Let's dance!" cried another, and offered his little hand to Mark.

"O.K.," said Mark. "Let's dance."

There was a radio, but they preferred an old victrola remembered by the eldest child. Rugs were rolled up and furniture pushed against the walls. Stella found an album of records, and music from another world and another time flowed into the room. Dick offered his arm to Myrtle Anderson and she rose sportingly in the center of her brood, whose shadows repeated themselves a hundred times on walls and ceilings. James Anderson sat beside the fire, the liquor running strong in his veins. His hands trembled. "Gosh," he whispered, watching the revellers. "Gosh!"

Stella slipped from Mark's arms and went to him. "Dance with me, James?"

"I'm no good."

"Yes, you are. Look at Myrtle! Please, James."

He rose, swept her into his arms. "Stella," he muttered. "O my God, Stella!"

"It's all right, James. Everything is all right."

"No, it ain't all right."

"Listen to the music, James!"

Mark went to the victrola and cranked it up again and

changed the record. Every one was dancing except Miriam, who had gone to the kitchen to heat up more coffee. Mark followed her. He took the coffee pot from her and set it back on the stove. "Let's dance, Miriam."

The music reached them across eons, music remembered from some old delirium. He looked down at Miriam's face and saw that it was lifted towards his, soft with expectancy, of longing recklessly revealed. He stopped dancing and held her firmly by the arms. "Get this," he said, "I'm not Alec."

Recognition came back to her eyes. "Yes," she murmured. "I know."

She freed herself and went to the stove. "Try to understand," she said in her normal voice. "Don't let it hurt you when poor James makes a slip like that, at dinner."

"I'm not in the least hurt."

"Nor are you in the least like Alec."

"You sound as if you had just found that out."

She was silent and he went and stood beside her near the stove. "Alec would have kissed you a minute ago, wouldn't he?"

She replied in a bitter whisper: "He's dead. Let him be, let him be!"

Mark put his arms round her and kissed her lips. She murmured: "It isn't that one feels old, or even that one is fooled. One feels only loss, loss!"

The music came grotesquely to an end, a single note foundering amid the wild laughter of the children. Some one cranked up the victrola again. "Not so bad!" shouted James Anderson. "By giminy, not so bad, except the damned things do creak some on those tricky steps of yours, Stella! Let's try the waltz again. It's just about my speed."

Miriam said: "There is something I think you should know. It may have some bearing . . . it may mean something. Stella ran away, in Italy."

"What?"

"She went to visit Alec's grave, but when she got there she couldn't face it."

She picked up the coffee pot, holding one hand near it to test the heat. "She didn't want to see the grave. She didn't want to know." Bravely, Miriam withstood his gaze. "I'm not sure, now, that she does know."

"You mean she knows, but won't believe?"

"What difference does it make? I wouldn't have told you so much, but I can see that there is something wrong between you, very wrong. I don't know what it is . . . but I do know that she shirked . . . that she may still be shirking."

"How could she shirk it? What about the usual letter of confirmation, the details? You were her friend, closer to her than anybody. What did she do, say, when she got that letter?"

Miriam hesitated and he saw the torment in her face. She said at last: "There was a letter. I was with her when she got it, in New York. She burned it."

"What did the letter say?"

"She burned it, I tell you. She burned it without opening it!"

He let her pass then, and followed her back to the parlor. Standing in the door he could see the snow which danced in the gloom beyond the windows, and the shadows of the chil-

dren and of Stella dancing like phantoms on the wall. Miriam
set her coffee pot on the hearth and held out her arms to her
husband.

"Our dance, I believe!" she said gaily, and they joined
Myrtle and James, and Stella and the children to the thin far-
away strains of a tune that Mark had long forgotten.

It was past midnight when he went outdoors to say goodbye
to the Andersons. For some minutes he stood listening to the
noise of the old car as it bore them away through the falling
snow. Returning to the house he stopped abruptly, arrested by
the sight of a lighted window and of Stella framed in it—
laughing, her head thrown back, all mirth and strange wanton
brilliance.

He went in and she ran to meet him. "Mark, where did you
go?"

"I went out to say goodnight to the Andersons." He ached
with hostility and despair.

"God," muttered Dick. "James was certainly drunk. Hope
he gets Myrtle and the kids home safely."

Miriam rose, yawning. "Me for bed. Oh those poor infants!"

Later, when Mark went to Stella's room he found her sitting
up in bed brushing her hair. Snow beat on the windows, a lamp
cast its gleam on her bare arms and loosened hair. She threw
down the brush and greeted him. "Mark, what a lovely
evening!"

He sat on the edge of the bed and looked at her. "Just like
the old days, wasn't it?" he asked, and saw her as Alec must
have seen her often, saw her as all youth and softness and love,
saw her as Alec's bride, Alec's eternity.

"You didn't mind poor James getting tight, did you?" she asked, lightly.

"Why should I mind? I like James."

"I love them both. They're like Jarley itself—they never change."

"No, they never change. Nothing changes, not in Jarley, not in this whole damned country! We go to war, we lose our legs, our lives . . . but in Jarley nothing changes."

She looked at him and it seemed to him that something strange and sly crept across her eyes. "Don't moralize, Mark. The other world is dead, but it was not our fault, was it? This is our world."

He leaned forward. "Stella, why did you go to Italy this spring?"

"What?"

"You heard me. Why did you go to Italy?"

"I told you why."

"Did you find Alec's grave?"

She answered steadily: "Of course. It was what I went for."

"And you found him?"

"Mark . . ."

"Did you?"

"Yes!"

How did he know that she was lying? For he knew, and knew quite without the aid of Miriam's revelation. For a moment he sat gazing at her with cold, appraising eyes. She cried: "Don't hurt me! You hurt me once, you misjudged me—don't do it again. I couldn't stand it. I couldn't!"

"I think you could stand it. I think you could stand anything."

"Mark, my dear love!" Her voice filled with seduction, its lie was part of the deception of the evening, part of the greater lie in which he felt that he had been living, and at which he had connived ever since he came to Jarley. Out of the confusion and horror which beset him there emerged the face of Regan as he had seen it on his first night home from Europe, when she slept with him for her conscience's sake.

Stella was brushing her hair again and in the easy, practiced motions of her hand Mark saw all the motions of liars and sleepwalkers. Words rushed from some unsuspected source in his mind: "Stella, would you go back to Italy with me?"

Her hand dropped on the bedclothes as if some nerve had been cut. "No!"

"Then I must go away."

"You mean you're going to leave me?"

"I mean I shall have to leave you."

"But why?" she cried. "Why, why?" and without waiting for an answer she flung herself into his arms, tearing at him with her nails, twisting and moaning like some half-murdered creature. Mark saw her shadow and his as two convulsed figures on the wall behind the bed, and he remembered the dancing figures he'd seen this evening, he remembered Stella laughing like a child among the other children, her eyes empty of everything except a meaningless vitality. The decision which had been forming in his brain hardened to a resolve. He left her weeping among the bedclothes and went back to his own room.

30

A SLEEPLESS night did nothing to alter his resolve, nor could the bewildered arguments of his friends, and the next day he returned to New York. There, a week later, Stella joined him. All the color and life seemed drained out of her; she said listlessly: "I'll go with you to Italy."

It should have been victory enough for Mark, but by now the decision had become an obsession and he felt powerless to rescind it. He knew himself to be as deeply involved in the outcome as Stella herself, though whatever he or she stood to gain or to lose from such a journey was no longer as clear to him as it had seemed on Thanksgiving night. Doubt served only to make him more dogged, immune to the wan look of Stella's eyes, deaf to the baffled protests of Dick and Miriam, indifferent to the contingencies of the succeeding weeks.

Back in New York, Miriam confided to her husband that she felt, herself, more involved in disaster now than she had ever been during the course of war. Dick said little, but one night when both were in bed he startled her by bursting into a sudden, rather mirthless laugh.

"Dick! What is it?"

"There's been trouble about the passports, and guess who I went to for advice?"

She waited, staring incredulously into the dark.

"Yes," Dick murmured malevolently beside her. "Symes

himself. That guy's hard to beat. No one's going to beat him—
not even Regan!"

"But what about the passports?"

"Oh, Symes will fix it up if any one can. Mark and Stella
don't know, of course. Mark is moving heaven and earth—or
imagines that he is. But if he and Stella get to Italy, it will be
thanks to Symes."

"What did he say when you went to him?"

"He was the perfect man of the world, as usual. Assured me
there was little he wouldn't do for an old friend. Spoke con-
descendingly of Mark . . . of course, he couldn't make any
promises, naturally . . . But I came away with a distinct feeling
that our friends will get to Montescari."

Miriam stirred restlessly.

"What did you say?" Dick asked, after a pause.

"Nothing . . . nothing!"

The air was rough and the big plane staggered through it
like a wounded bird. Mark could see the sky, all gray conten-
tion, and the sea sullen and remote beneath. Beside him Stella
was reading, or pretending to read. She seemed indifferent to
her surroundings, to him, and to the roughness of their passage.
He had given up speculating on her thoughts, for his own were
uncomfortable enough. He longed to talk to her, but when he
ventured a remark she merely nodded without looking up from
her book. With every hour of their journey Mark became more
disquieted by the consequences of his own stubborn will.

The plane seemed to skid, then to spring forward, and he
noticed the swiftly concealed fear of some of the passengers. A

steward, competent and assured, moved down the aisle, distilling confidence. Mark wondered how long the man's professional composure would endure actual disaster, and permitted himself a brief mental vision of the plane falling in flames into the sea, carrying Stella and himself with it. He would take her in his arms, and so wait for the end. The end! He made a slight motion of denial. In spite of all his doubts, he was not prepared for the end. Not yet. Less prepared now, less reconciled than at any time he could remember. Now, in this stormy air above the Italian coast, he thought of the spring and of the months in New York when Regan left him. Time had retreated, broken into blurred and meaningless particles which took their place among the ruins of the past five years. Had those years been real, had they a moral which might relate to himself and Stella? Or was he brooding like a sick man obsessed by absolutes— a symptom of the sickness of the world?

He looked out of the window and saw the purple vistas of Italy veer towards the sky. Something seemed to hit the plane a violent blow, and he took Stella's hand. "Scared?" he murmured.

"No. Are you?"

"Yes." It came from him humbly, and he saw that she guessed his meaning. The steward walked down the aisle, looking more competent than ever. "Belts," he murmured pleasantly. "May be a bit rough, landing."

They adjusted their belts, and Mark took Stella's hand again. "It'll be all right, but it's a hell of a wind to land in anyway."

Her hand remained unresponsive. There seemed so little life

in her that it occurred to him she would be indifferent to disaster, to that shock, physical and imaginative, with which he believed the human mind recognizes finality. He saw that the other passengers were tense, all wore smiles in pitiable contradiction to the alarm in their eyes. Mark thought of the pilot up forward, and envied the disciplined animal his job.

"We're going down," he said to Stella, and clasped her hand closely. As they lost altitude the wind became more violent, resisting, with every trick, the pilot's intention to land. He saw the steward braced against one of the seats, talking brightly with an agitated lady, who gazed up at him with the air of a suppliant.

Stella looked out of the window. "We're going in," she said expressionlessly. "I can see the lights." She turned to Mark. "I think maybe we're going to crash."

He started to say something adoring and humble, something which might last them both through whatever was coming— and perhaps beyond it. Vainly he tried to read her eyes, and saw himself reflected in their depths. A minute later the plane was rushing along the strip, lights streamed past the windows in a single ribbon which stretched, wavered, then separated into single, separate spheres. The sound of the motors had changed, and the steward's smile became authentic. He bent cheerfully over the frightened lady. "Rome, ma'am."

It was raining at Montescari on the evening of their arrival, two days later. It had rained all the way from Rome, a cold mist blurred the windows, parting to reveal fragments of a shattered landscape. Stella said little, but in spite of her indifferent air Mark felt the tension mounting in her. His own fortitude had

become threadbare in the miserable weather and with his growing sense of apprehension. At Montescari there was no Guido
Vitelli to meet them; but the station master's nephew Pietro, a
bright-eyed boy of sixteen, was on hand with Guido's truck.
Mark said: "We might as well go straight to Vitelli's and fix
up about rooms. You look frozen."

But Stella had turned to Pietro, who stood waiting, a suitcase in either hand.

"Take us to the house of Mr. Curtis," she told him in English. "Mr. Alben Curtis, at the American military cemetery."

Bianchi spoke to the boy in rapid Italian. Mark protested:
"We've got ample time, Stella. I'm cold, and so are you. Let's
go to the Vitelli's first."

But she had turned and was following Pietro down the steps
towards the street. They drove through the drizzling mist, and
Mark felt that if he touched her she might break like some
substance fissured through by unseen currents. They came to the
cemetery road and Pietro swerved into it through a chain of
puddles crusted with ice. *"Fa freddo,"* the boy murmured,
shivering. "Cold, cold!"

Fields and hedges were visible, but the mountains had disappeared and the air which blew from them tasted of snow.
Outside the caretaker's cottage Pietro stopped the car and
climbed out. He smiled and waved to indicate that they were
there. Across the road stood the cemetery fence, the flagpole
shone white in the gloom, bare of the flag which had been
taken down against the weather. The nearer graves were white
too, white against the dark earth, but as their numbers retreated
they mingled with the mist and vanished.

"All right," said Mark, "we'll go in . . ." He was suddenly unable to look at Stella, and they walked through the gate to the door of the cottage, which opened at once, for their arrival had been observed from a window. A large, friendly American greeted them and introduced himself as Mr. Curtis, ex-sergeant Alben Curtis of Milwaukee, Wisconsin. He led them to his office and Mark had a vague impression of holly and tinsel, and remembered that here too the Christmas season was approaching. What did they call it in Italian? *Natale* . . .

"You couldn't have chosen a worse time to come," their host remarked genially, as he set a chair for Stella. "Summer's the time, summer or spring."

He had a clean-shaven, healthy face, and was perhaps forty years old. They talked a little about the United States, about New York, about Montescari and its battles. Curtis told them he was going back to Milwaukee in the summer with his Italian wife and their little girl. The room, the whole house might have been in some American suburb, the office of a lawyer or a doctor. The filing cabinets were American, so was the wallpaper, which had come direct from a hardware store in Curtis' native city. The man's quiet tact impressed Mark; he had received them at once not as strangers bent on a painful mission, but as acquaintances—people whom he could understand and who understood him. His glance went frequently to Stella, and it was to her that he turned at last, when they had finished the first ceremonial cigarette and the chill of embarrassment had passed. "Now tell me what I can do for you."

"I've come to see my husband's grave. I have the papers here. . . ."

"That's all right." He lounged to his feet. "I can find it. Harmon, you said. Private Alexander Harmon, number . . ."

They watched him leaf through the card-index files, a big expert man going calmly about his business. Mark wanted to say something to Stella, he longed to bridge the gulf between them, to utter some word that might restore their comradeship, but she remained aloof, utterly different from the woman he had known. Sounds of domesticity reached them from other parts of the house: a woman's voice talking Italian, the shrill voice of a child, and that of Pietro who had come in to warm himself beside Signora Curtis's hospitable fire.

"I have it," said Curtis, at last. "Aisle five, plot fifty-three. That would be west of the gate as you go in . . ."

They rose, and he asked: "Think you can find it all right?"

"Yes, thanks," said Mark. His lips felt dry. He wanted to take Stella's arm, but she moved away, her face expressionless. Curtis accompanied them to the door. "Got that number? Aisle five, plot fifty-three. To your left . . ."

They crossed the road and passed through the main gate into the cemetery. The rain had stopped but the whispering sound of water was everywhere. Mist clung to the trees and moved wraith-like across the pale ranks of crosses, revealing, then obscuring, a name here, and there a sprig of ivy or a wreath of waxen flowers.

"Ground's wet," said Mark. "I'm afraid you'll be soaked."

Stella said nothing, and they walked together up the gravelled path which made a level wake between the graves. Plot fifty-three was some distance from the gate, but they found Alec at last, where he lay among his friends. These had come a long way. No doubt each of them had believed he would return to fulfill his life, or to relinquish it near the scene of his beginning, but now the earth enclosed him, and his silence encompassed everything—the past, the present, the future; it encompassed the living and laid its finger on their lips.

In a little while Stella put her hand on Mark's arm, and they made their way back down the mist-shrouded path, guided by the bright summons of Pietro's voice.

31

IN JARLEY snow had fallen, its glittering coverlet lay stained with blue shadow from shore to woods, stifling all sound except the sound of the sea. Standing in her doorway Stella gazed from the limits of an immobilized world to the living water beyond. Contrast and contradiction met her gaze from the frozen contours of the pasture to the flashing reaches of the sea, from the curious sense of peace in her heart to the vivid suspense in her mind. She had awakened in this mood, sure that there would be a message for her, today, from Mark. Once or twice in her life she had experienced this kind of certainty germinating in the very center of doubt, emerging at last as undeniable as the sun itself.

Now as she stood appraising the scene, she saw the figure of James Anderson detach itself from the line of trees and come plodding towards her on his snowshoes. He tramped into the house, blowing trumpets of steam, his face burnt by the weather. "Tried to get you on the phone, Stella, but the wires is down. Myrtle got to worrying, thinking about you out here alone. Roads all plugged, too. Be dark before the plow gets this far."

He handed her a bundle of newspapers and letters. "I stopped in the post office and picked up your mail. Figured you might want it."

She thanked him and stood for a moment with the peculiar sense of having done this identical thing a moment before

. . . but when? James blew on his cold fingers and kicked a log in the fireplace. He began to tell her about the storm, excited in his deliberate fashion by a vision of a familiar universe stopped in its traces; trees had fallen, highways were blocked, landmarks buried, snowplows moved forth like battleships into the crystalline flood. The sound of James' voice was part of the elements, and Stella answered in monosyllables while she sorted her letters and found one from Mark. He wrote:

"I was going to wait until I heard from you, but then I asked myself why? Why wait? You see, I've clung to the stupid idea that you should be left alone and that I should be left alone in order to make up our minds . . . but yesterday Miriam said to me 'How do you know that Stella is not waiting down there at Jarley, waiting for some signal from you?' And it recurred to me how much of our time is spent in uncertainty and mistrust, in a kind of hypocrisy which we've never learned to recognize, or recognizing it, to acknowledge. I let you go back to Jarley while I stayed in New York, and I suppose both of us were depending on a miracle to bring us together again. The belief in miracles is part of our hypocrisy, like the belief that death is somehow better than life, simply because we're afraid of one and don't know anything about the other. But what is life, Stella?—the real feeling of life? Sometimes I think I can guess —I know there is such a thing, that it is here and now, and not hereafter. I don't want to harp on Alec, except to quote something James Anderson said to me once, that Alec was a man so filled with vitality, it spilled over into other people's lives. James' remark made me feel hopelessly inadequate. Now I wonder, isn't there something more to life besides vitality, or the mere grim will to survive? Perhaps too much vitality can lead a man to die before his time, as it led Alec, just as the mere will to survive keeps the thought of death constantly before us. It occurred to me that day at Montescari—that we don't know what life is, we have never been told, we have never tried to find out. But Stella, it is something I want to know, something I want my children to know. Life, not as an illusion, but as fulfillment. I might as well confess that when I came to love you I found myself jealous of Alec—jealous, and at the same time remorseful. I felt that I had to prove to you as well as to myself, that Alec was dead, finished—more dead, more finished than I was! And I think I can guess, now, why you came with me to Montescari. You came for my sake, not for your own. You had already decided that whatever you and I can make of our discovery is all that matters now. Neddy is with me. Do you want us?"

Stella put down the letter and turned to meet Anderson's gaze.

"Would you send a telegram for me, James? Otherwise, I shall have to wait for the plow before I can get to town."

He towered before her, his eyes mutely questioning, then: "Sure, I'll take it. Myrtle and I, all these weeks we been wondering . . ." Words failed him. He turned to the fireplace and gave the logs a great kick. "You write out the telegram, Stella. I'll see it gets sent."

She wrote her message to Mark, and James folded it carefully and stowed it in his breast pocket. He drew on his mittens and went to the door, from where he growled: "Time comes to meet that train, they'd ought to have the roads cleared all right. I'll be around and pick you up in plenty of time."

"Thanks a lot, James."

She followed him to the door and stood while he laced his snowshoes and started back across the shining expanse towards the woods-path. He had not gone far when he turned and stood for a moment motionless, staring at her. She waited, but whatever he had been moved to say proved too much for him in the end. He gave her a slow smile, waved, and walked on, leaving a wake of blue shadows on the snow. Stella watched him out of sight, then she turned away to prepare the house for Mark.